YUMA COUNTY
LIBRARY DISTRICT
2951 S. 21st Dr. Yuma, AZ 85364
(928) 782-1871
www.yumalibrary.org

THE PRACTICAL NAVIGATOR

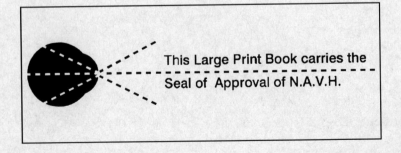

This Large Print Book carries the
Seal of Approval of N.A.V.H.

THE PRACTICAL NAVIGATOR

STEPHEN METCALFE

THORNDIKE PRESS

A part of Gale, Cengage Learning

GALE
CENGAGE Learning®

Farmington Hills, Mich • San Francisco • New York • Waterville, Maine
Meriden, Conn • Mason, Ohio • Chicago

GALE
CENGAGE Learning·

Copyright © 2016 by Stephen Metcalfe.
Thorndike Press, a part of Gale, Cengage Learning.

ALL RIGHTS RESERVED

Thorndike Press® Large Print Reviewers' Choice.
The text of this Large Print edition is unabridged.
Other aspects of the book may vary from the original edition.
Set in 16 pt. Plantin.

LIBRARY OF CONGRESS CATALOGING-IN-PUBLICATION DATA

Names: Metcalfe, Steve, author.
Title: The practical navigator / by Stephen Metcalfe.
Description: Large print edition. | Waterville, Maine : Thorndike Press, 2016.
 |Series: Thorndike Press large print reviewers' choice
Identifiers: LCCN 2016032642| ISBN 9781410494511 (hardcover) | ISBN 1410494519 (hardcover)
Subjects: LCSH: Large type books. | Domestic fiction.
Classification: LCC PS3563.E833 P73 2016b | DDC 813/.54—dc23
LC record available at https://lccn.loc.gov/2016032642

Published in 2016 by arrangement with St. Martin's Press, LLC

Printed in Mexico
1 2 3 4 5 6 7 20 19 18 17 16

To Claudia, Olivia, and Wesley, with love.
I couldn't do it without you.

ACKNOWLEDGMENTS

A sincere thank-you to Linda Chester, Sara Goodman, and the wonderful people at St. Martin's Press.

The American Practical Navigator, first published in 1802 by Nathaniel Bowditch, is an encyclopedia of navigation. It serves as a valuable handbook on oceanography and meteorology, and contains useful tables and a maritime glossary. In 1867 the copyright and plates were bought by the Hydrographic Office of the United States Navy, and as a U.S. Government publication. The text has evolved with the advances in navigation practices since that first issue and continues to serve as a valuable reference for marine navigation in the modern day. It is considered one of America's nautical institutions.

Navigation is the process of charting a course from one place to another.

1

The ocean never sleeps. The ocean is ever restless.

It is early morning, Southern California, a winter swell and the surfers are out. They dive as they paddle out into the white cresting water. They sit, bobbing like ducks on a turbulent pond. A wave rises, arms churn, a quick hop and crouching, two of them move forward, down and across the face. At the bottom, they cut frantically away from each another, one falling, the other moving up the wall of water, only to reverse course at the top and descend again. Up, down. Rise, fall. As the wave tumbles and breaks, the surfer bails out in a haze of spray, man and board jettisoning free. Water crashes on rocky shore. Green sheen on dark sand. Sucking foam.

Michael Hodge hangs deep beneath the water, naked, vertical and still, as if unaffected by the surge. His eyes are open. He is bemused to find himself here. How odd. Water above, water below, opaque and translucent, fading into shadow. How did this happen? How did he get here? He doesn't know. It just is. He looks up to see the flash of a board overhead. He did that once. No more.

It is peaceful here. Michael could close his eyes and drift till he just faded away. And it is with this thought that he realizes — or is it that he remembers? — his head is bleeding, copper tendrils in too clear water, and that he is drowning. He starts for the surface — and goes nowhere. He flails, panicking, rubbery legs kicking, hands clawing. He might as well try to climb through air. Bubbles gush from his open mouth. Michael tries to pull them back, watches them slip through his fingers. Drowning and reaching, drowning and reaching —

— to come awake with a stifled cry, lurching up, twisting at the tangle of sheets.

It takes a moment to realize. It was the dream.

Again.

He forces himself to breathe. He listens to his heart as it slows down. When all is quiet and working properly, he settles back. And hits his head sharply on the headboard. Even in his own bed, a man has to be aware of danger. He is awake now. He tosses the sweat-soggy sheets aside and rises. Michael Hodge still has the broad shoulders and long smooth muscles of a swimmer. A swimmer who is afraid of the water.

In the bathroom, he pees and is reminded that the toilet bowls in the house are in need of cleaning. At the sink, he douses his face with water. His mouth tastes like a birdcage. He squeezes some toothpaste onto his tongue, chews and swallows it. He rinses and spits. He looks at himself in the mirror. Something's increasingly different and it's not becoming.

The kitchen is as he left it. Dinner dishes in the sink. Pots and pans on the stove. A trio of beer bottles on the counter. He's got to do better than this. He notices that the answering machine on the counter is blinking. He vaguely remembers the phone ringing last night in the middle of some inane cable show about zombies. He almost never answers the house line anymore. Anyone worth talking to gets him on the cell. He hits the message button and turns to get juice from the fridge. Penelope Hodge has the remains of an English accent.

"Michael? This is your mother. I do wish you'd answer your phone. Michael, I just wanted to tell you, the tests came back from

15

the doctor's and it's official. I don't have Alzheimer's. Love you, darling."

Michael ponders this. Tests? Alzheimer's? What the — *Beep!*

As he drinks some juice from the carton, the second message plays. "Michael, it's me. Guess what, sweetheart? I don't have Alzheimer's. Oh — and happy birthday, Michael."

Michael doesn't feel happy. Not happy at all. He presses the erase button on the machine and turns to address the dishes in the sink.

Penance.

The bundle under the quilt has been awake for a while. Michael has heard the murmurs, the muted whispers, and the silence as the prospect of facing the day grows closer. Michael enters the bedroom and sits on the edge of the bed. He lightly places his hand on the part of the bundle that is a shoulder.

"Jamie. Time to get up now."

The quilt, bedecked with Minions — small yellow cylinder-shaped creatures — lowers and Jamie looks at him, the blond hair like a haystack, the eyes deep and green.

"I don't have to go to school today." The voice is a soft monotone.

"Yeah, you do. Mrs. McKenzie is going to

be waiting for you. C'mon, big hug."

Jamie rises to his arms, all little-boy smell. He puts his arms around Michael's neck. "Hold me," he whispers. "Hold me tight."

In the kitchen Michael fries eggs, knowing Jamie won't eat them but hoping he might. For a while it was all he ate. Then he stopped eating the yolks. Then he ate the yolks but not the whites. Now he's stopped eating eggs altogether. It's frozen fruit that he likes these days, blueberries, rock-hard strawberries, and wedges of precut mango. Michael's teeth ache at the thought of it. Before eggs and frozen fruit it was oven-heated fish nuggets for breakfast. Soon it will be something else.

Jamie is at the table, playing with a small plastic toy soldier, shaking it, holding it close to his face, intently focused on it.

"Jamie."

Jamie quickly puts the plastic toy into his lap. He spoons some icy fruit into his mouth.

"Sleep well, kiddo?"

"I'm eating." The voice is insistent and just a bit annoyed. One thing at a time, it demands.

"Me too," says Michael. He eats the eggs directly from the pan. One less plate to

17

clean.

They come out of the house and move across a wide, wooden deck that is silver with age. A large pepper tree grows from a hole in the middle of the deck and its rain of pods and slim, dark leaves is incessant. Michael goes through a push broom every six months. The one-story house, once just a summer bungalow, has been added on to and expanded piece by piece over the years. Rumor has it that it was once a retreat owned by the film actors Douglas Fairbanks and Mary Pickford. Michael knows this. He started the rumor. Beyond the deck and across a small stamp of grass is a head-high hedge of privet and juniper that provides some small privacy. Michael is in neat khakis and a faded chambray shirt. Jamie wears cargo shorts and a T-shirt, the labels removed, always. Michael holds Jamie's knapsack. In it is his Power Rangers lunchbox. In that, slices of Gouda cheese and whole wheat bread, green cornichons, each in its own separate plastic bag, again, always. Jamie still holds the plastic soldier. The wooden gate bangs shut behind them and Jamie skips into the small driveway.

"I want Mrs. McKenzie to miss me."

"Climb aboard, little man."

"I want her to *miss* me!"

They get in the pickup, a five-year-old white Ford F-150 that has never seen the inside of the closed garage. HODGE CONSTRUCTION is written in black letters on the side door, a contractor's license number below. Michael starts the truck up and they pull out of the short drive. Many of the adjacent houses on the street fill their small lots completely. Big, strapping bodies put into small clothes. It wasn't always like this. Birdrock used to be a neighborhood of working people — day laborers, teachers, and surfers four to a house sharing rent. But it's a quick jaunt to the beach and if you get high enough up on the hill, ever-growing, nonindigenous trees permitting, you can see south all the way to the Coronado Islands, and so, over the past ten years, people have bought, torn down, refinanced, and rebuilt, Michael working any number of the jobs, first doing the grunt work, digging foundations, sawing boards, and banging nails, then graduating to masonry, tile, and cabinetry work, picking up both Spanish and craft from the illegals, most of whom have forgotten more about carpentry than Michael will ever know. He sometimes wonders where those men are now.

Turning, they drive north on the boulevard. The traffic is slow moving. All the old beach communities have changed: fast-food franchises, chain drugstores, personal work-out centers offering bargain fifty-dollar massages. The mammoth Vons supermarket sells everything from fruit smoothies to birthday cards to organic endive. There's a Brooks Brothers in the village now, presumably shilling preppie clothes to transplanted financial consultants from the East Coast. In Michael's youth, the biggest retailers were surf shops. The most popular restaurant was a waffle shop.

Michael lucks into a parking place just down the street from the elementary school and walks Jamie to the entrance. Jamie lags and Michael waits. There's no rushing him, he'll just go slower. At the open gate, with the playground beyond and the children running and shouting, they stop and Michael kneels. Jamie's head is down and his mouth is a thin line of anxiety. His hand is tight in front of his face, not so much flapping as vibrating.

"Nana will pick me up." It's a question as much as a statement.

"Doesn't Nana always pick you up?"

"She will pick me up."

"And I'll pick you up at Nana's. What else?"

"I won't run to look for you."

"Because?"

"Because even if you're not there, you love me."

"How much?"

"To infinity and beyond."

"You got it."

Michael looks up. Beyond the gate, a tall, middle-aged woman in a long dress is approaching across the playground. Michael hands Jamie his knapsack. "There's Mrs. McKenzie. Go on now." Jamie doesn't move and so Michael nudges him. Nudges gently again. Jamie finally turns and hurries forward through the gate to meet his teacher.

Seeing him advance, Karen McKenzie stops and waits. Once he's in front of her, she looks down her long nose at him with mock formality. "*Mister* Hodge. Are we ready for second grade today?"

Jamie briefly meets her eyes and then his head bows and he studies the ground. There is a small smile on his lips. "Are you having tuna for lunch?"

"Yes, I am. And I am sharing it with *you.*"

A murmur of pleasure. A single word. "Okay." All is now right with the world. Karen McKenzie throws a quick reassuring look to Michael, takes Jamie's hand, and they turn and move across the playground together. Michael fights the urge to call Jamie back. All too often, he feels that he is sending a lamb out into a world of wolves. Thank goodness there are shepherds. On the way back to the truck, his cell phone rings. The day has begun.

2

In the Upper Muirlands, a house is being built. The workers' pickups and old-model cars are parked on the street among the neighborhood's BMWs, Range Rovers, and Lexus Hybrids. For all their money, people who live in this upscale neighborhood never seem to use their driveways or garages. Instead they park on both sides of the already narrow street, turning it into a one-lane road so as to play chicken with one another when they approach from different directions. The winners are invariably soccer moms in SUVs late to pick their children up at school.

Leo, a thickset, red-bearded man of forty, and Luis, an impassive Mexican, roughly the size and strength of an oak tree, are unloading building materials from Leo's pickup. Leo is the construction foreman. Which, to Luis's mind, means Leo stands around most of the time, talks too much, and lets others do most of the work.

"You got how many kids, Luis?"

"Cuatro," grunts Luis. Four.

"By how many wives?"

Luis shrugs. "Two a them I no marry."

"But you pay support."

Another shrug. Luis does. It's like feeding worms to starving, clamoring baby birds. There's never enough.

"Luis —" Leo sounds exasperated. They've only had this conversation a million times before. "You get your high school equivalency, you can get a job with the city. You get a pension, benefits. You're golden. They're hiring beaners, Luis. They gotta, it's their civic duty."

Luis would like to explain to Leo that the city of San Diego is hiring no one, especially beaners. They're too wrapped up in pension overruns, football stadiums, and the endless sexual-harassment suits still being brought against the ugly *judio* mayor who couldn't keep his stupid hands to himself. As a matter of fact, the only interest the city of San Diego has in beaners is in deporting them. But explaining anything would be a useless waste of time. Leo has no use for facts. Luis has noted that a lot of white men doing manual labor are like that. They spend too much time dreaming of the fishing boats

24

they're going to retire to someday down in Baja. In Luis's humble opinion, boats sink and fish stink. Luis would rather drown on dry land close to Petco Park and a good taco shop.

"You gonna talk or you gonna work?"

Work is important to Luis, he likes it and he's good at it. You don't work, you don't get paid. And you don't have to be *un genio* to know that the whole construction biz is precarious, sometimes up, sometimes down, rarely steady. And without the construction trades, Latinos, blacks, and, at the bottom of the food chain, uneducated whites, even well-meaning, *pelirrojo* ones like Leo, are pretty much screwed. Ah, well, there's always yard work. In fact, Luis's sister-in-law's son, Rafael, runs a crew and Luis makes a mental note to call him, just in case there's nothing else immediately available when this construction job is over.

Leo and Luis both turn as Michael's pickup pulls up and parks on the street behind a shiny Porsche. Michael gets out and approaches. Luis likes Michael. He's a good boss, fair and generous and more than willing to get his hands dirty.

"Hey, big chief," says Leo, grinning.

"Where is he?" says Michael, his face grim.

25

"He's checking out his ocean view. Location, location!"

Michael turns and continues on into the building site. Leo glances at Luis, the shit-eating smile still on his face. "This oughta be good," he says. A good excuse not to work, thinks Luis. He reaches for a stack of two-by-fours.

Michael crosses the rough yard. The foundation has already been poured, the first-floor deck is in place, and Bobby, a lean, muscular white kid in jeans and a bandana, and Jose, both his arms sleeved in tattoos, have begun the framing on the first floor's interior walls. Out beyond them on what will be the back deck of the house, a short, balding man in a polo shirt, sports coat, and pleated slacks stands talking on his cell phone. In truth, thinks Michael, Robert Caulfield has just a glimpse of ocean view. Still, not bad for a dermatologist who only practices three days a week. He turns as Michael approaches. He holds up a finger, telling Michael to wait.

"Uh-huh, uh-huh. What's the option date again? Uh-huh. Uh-huh. And for how much?"

Robert Caulfield listens a moment and then rolls his eyes at Michael as if to say, *all I deal with are idiots.* Which is probably right.

26

When not burning precancerous cells with frozen nitrogen, Caulfield makes it known to all who will listen and those who have no other choice that he's made his *real money* investing in privately funded REITs — real estate investment trusts — available to only a select, privileged few.

"No, no. Forget it. I don't care what he says about the upside, tell him it's off. I don't want to hear about it again."

Michael has long since realized that a lot of the guys in high school who couldn't throw balls or get dates now seem to be the ones who drive Porsches, wear expensive clothes, and, in particular, order people around on cell phones.

"Look, I gotta go here. Yeah, yeah, I'll call you from the car. *Okay,* already! Yeah, good-bye."

Caulfield disconnects and immediately shifts from annoyed deal breaker to ebullient glad-hander. "Mikie, my man! How ya doin', buddy? It's really coming along here, huh?"

"Glad you think so," says Michael.

"Are you kidding? It's looking great, you're the best, the best! But hey!" Robert Caulfield clasps Michael on the shoulder, confirming that they're in this together, joined — if not at the hip at least near the upper armpit. "You know what I was think-ing? Instead of the open deck here" — Caulfield gestures vaguely — "what about a glass-enclosed sunroom? We could still do the Jacuzzi. What do you think?"

This is nothing new. Caulfield changes the floor plans on a weekly basis, extended fam-ily room to home theater, master bath to his and her *toilettes;* and Michael usually tries his best to be accommodating. After all, it's not his house. But today it is, at least part of it.

"Leo tells me we're still having a little problem with our cash flow."

Caulfield frowns as if surprised. "Huh? Oh. Yeah, no problem. I'll get a check in the mail, end of the week."

"Leo was supposed to have it today."

Caulfield chuckles. "Mikie, I forgot. You know how it goes."

"As a matter of fact, no, I don't. What I know is I have men doing a job and I pay them for it. You don't pay me, they still get paid but they do the job somewhere else."

Caulfield stares at Michael. His eyes have narrowed. All the false bonhomie has gone out the window.

"Is that a threat?"

"No, that's how it goes."

Caulfield now looks about as friendly as a

shark with gastritis. "I'm not sure I'm satisfied with the work."

"Oh, really?"

"Maybe I should just get myself another contractor."

It's both a threat and a challenge. Other contractors would get in line for the job and both Caulfield and Michael know it. Michael turns and calls back over his shoulder.

"Leo!"

Leo has moved from the pickup truck to the edge of the foundation. His arms are crossed. He's been waiting.

"Yeah, boss?"

"Tell the guys to start tearing down the framing. We're out of here."

"You got it!" Leo turns away, happily calling out in Spanglish. *"Luis! Jose! Consiga the fucking lodoso martillos!"*

Behind his wire-rims, Robert Caulfield's eyes have widened in surprise. "What? Hey, wait, wait — Michael, what are you doing?"

"I'm quitting."

"What?"

"Quitting. As in out of here."

Michael turns quickly away. Just as quickly Caulfield follows, blinking and sputtering. "Wait, what? You can't."

Michael turns back, abruptly enough that Robert Caulfield stumbles so as not to bump into him. "You want another contractor? No problem. But believe me, I take what you haven't paid for with me."

"You can't do that."

"No?" Michael calls out to Bobby who's loving this. "Bobby! Pull those pipes and start loading them onto the truck!"

"Got it, boss!" Bobby drops the nail gun and heads toward the plumbing fixtures. Again, Michael turns and starts walking, and again Robert Caulfield follows. The crease in his golf slacks seems to have evaporated. Amazing what saying no does to a man who's not used to it.

"Michael, please, let's start over here. You gotta know, I want you on this job!"

"Nah, you're just saying that because you're seeing your January move-in date fly out the window. You'll be lucky now if it's *next* January. Good luck explaining it to your wife."

Wham!

Nails shriek and wood splits as what was going to be the framing for an inner kitchen wall goes down, the victim of Luis's twenty-pound sledge-hammer.

"Knock it down, Luis!" Michael calls. "Every bit of it!"

Robert Caulfield looks pale. "Michael, for the love of Christ, how can I prove to you I want you on this job!?"

Breathing an inner sigh of relief, Michael turns to gaze at Robert Caulfield. Too often it's like this. Workers, men barely getting by, are most often open and honest, willing to give you more than you give them if you treat them with honesty and respect. Those hiring are just as often suspicious and manipulative and more than happy to take advantage of you at a moment's notice. Maybe it's not their fault. Maybe they've been screwed one too many times in the past. Still. Is it any wonder Michael feels the occasional need to throw off his clothes and run naked and gibbering down main street, waiting for God knows who to take him away to somewhere safe and sane? The world is that crazy.

3

It's around eleven when Michael arrives at the office to find that his receptionist, accountant, purchasing agent, and secretary, Rosalina Guerrero, is, as usual, at her desk, working.

Michael's office is in a low-set building on a shady side street near a church. He shares the building complex, more like a series of converted trailers than anything else, with a landscape architect and a man who tutors high school students on college aptitude tests. Both the architect and the tutor seem to consider both a contractor and each other beneath them and so all seldom speak to one another.

Rosalina, called Rose, is a dark-skinned, amber-eyed, overweight woman in her mid-thirties who will suffer fools but always makes sure they know she disapproves of them. Rose, who has never married, and much to the alarm of her Mexican mother, whom she lives with and cares for, has no children, can be sarcastic in both Spanish and English, is effortlessly organized and coldly efficient, and Michael, who is neither, would be lost without her. Beyond that, she has forgone paychecks without telling him on more than one occasion.

"Morning, Rose."

Rose doesn't so much as glance up from her computer screen. "It's after ten, Michael, it's no longer morning. I'm already on chapter four." When not working on her computer, Rose reads. Thick, serious-looking books are almost always on the desk alongside her time sheets and she averages one every two days. Michael lightly waves the check in front of her. She looks at it, then takes it. She studies it a moment and, deciding not to be unimpressed, raises a heavy, unplucked eyebrow. "And this is?"

"Back payment plus an advance."

"Do I want to know how you pried it loose?"

"No, you don't."

"I'll take it down to the bank and deposit it before that *poca cagada* changes his mind."

"Poca cagada?" asks Michael.

"Little turd."

Michael smiles. "I learn something from

you every day, Rose." It's a statement of fact as well as a compliment and Rose nods, accepting it as both. Michael turns toward his adjacent office. The door is open. His desk is not nearly so well ordered as Rose's.

"Oh, Michael, a doctor —" Rose checks the message pad up on her desk. She hesitates, wanting to get the pronunciation right. "Akrepede's office called. She reminds you to stop in around noon today for your . . ." Rose looks up at him, her tawny eyes curious. "Annual?"

Michael tries to hide his surprise.

"Nothing wrong, is there?" asks Rose. Just a bit too casual.

"No, not at all," says Michael. "Just a checkup."

"Good. You need one," says Rose, her curiosity and her computer with its resources and search engine ever present. "She's *una loquera.*"

"What's that?"

"A shrink."

4

The clock on the waiting room wall reads quarter after twelve. Michael sits alone, thinking he should have known better. Doctors — even *loqueras* — always run late. The room is the first floor of a narrow, old two-story wooden cottage built into the hill, several blocks above Coast Avenue. It is comfortable and tastefully decorated with what to Michael's mind look like real antiques. There is Middle Eastern art on the walls and on the sideboard. There are back issues of magazines neatly arranged on the heavy wooden chest that serves as a coffee table — *Psychology Today, Spirituality & Health, Yoga Journal.* It makes Michael ponder if there aren't any other people who, like him, read *Sports Illustrated* and have the quiet desire to steal the couch. He looks up as the door to an inner office opens. A timid-looking middle-aged woman comes out. The woman following her is dressed in a fashionable skirt and jacket, her thick black hair pulled up and back off her face. The middle-aged woman has obviously been crying and now the dark-haired woman, at least a decade younger, folds her into a maternal embrace. They hold each other quietly and tenderly in the way, Michael thinks, that women sharing an emotional connection often do. The middle-aged woman forces a grateful, trembling smile and turns away. She doesn't look at Michael as she passes. The outer door closes behind her. The woman in the doorway regards Michael for a moment, her carefully made-up eyes as dark as her hair.

"I'm sorry to keep you waiting, Michael, please come in." There is just the trace of an accent. Michael rises. The woman waits to let him pass and then follows closely behind him into the inner sanctum. She smells of sandalwood and jasmine.

Entering, Michael takes in the bookcases filled with psychology and self-help tomes, the diplomas on the wall. He has never understood why doctors, even simple Ph.D.s, feel a need to showcase all their books and diplomas. People wouldn't come to them if they didn't think they were smart. A rectangular writing table substitutes as a desk. Two overstuffed chairs face each other across the small, bright room. A handwoven rug is on the floor between them. The dark-haired woman closes the door behind her. She moves past Michael toward the single picture window. Beyond rooftops and an apartment building there is just a sliver of the sea. Putting down the file, she draws the curtains. She turns back, taking off her jacket.

"Get undressed, pleased."

Taken aback, Michael is silent. The dark-haired woman glances at him. She frowns slightly. "Your clothes, please. Take them off."

"Here?" says Michael. As if the small, comfortable office might have eyes.

The dark-haired woman gives him a cool, authoritative look. "Is there a problem?"

"No. No problem." Nonplussed, Michael starts to unbutton his shirt.

"Wait." The woman reaches back behind her head, pulls a pin and shakes. Her dark hair falls in a thick tumble, framing her face, turning it from severe to sensual. She kicks out of her high heels and, suddenly inches shorter, moves toward him. "I'll do it." Crossing, the woman reaches out with both hands and slowly and carefully unfastens the top button of Michael's shirt. She glances at him, softly biting her full lower lip, and then her fingers drop to the second button, then the third. Parting his shirt, she leans forward. Michael gasps as her lips brush first one nipple, then another. In a bizarre, out-of-body moment, he flashes back to a skinny kid in high school, Fred Galloway, who had such a big dick, guys would joke that he probably passed out when he got a hard-on due to loss of blood to the brain. It seems possible. Even with standard-issue equipment, Michael is feeling decidedly dizzy.

"I thought you were a shrink."

It's a silly joke but the woman giggles, sending exquisite tingles through his sternum and into his spine. Raising her head, she presses close and kisses Michael on the lips. "Happy birthday, Michael," she whispers.

"And many more," Michael says. He takes Fari Akrepede, his unexpected lover of the last six months, gently to the floor.

The cottage is off the street, the entrance to the office in the back, and Michael and Fari come down the brick steps to the sidewalk and walk toward Michael's truck together. It's free parking here, a short stroll to the village proper, and each parking place is filled. Michael was lucky to find a space.

"Does this mean we're no longer on for Saturday night?"

Fari's dark hair is once more pulled up and back. Her makeup is perfect again. She might have spent the last thirty minutes giving dictation. Michael, who can feel the raw spots on his knees and elbows from making love on the coarsely woven carpet, feels disheveled in comparison.

"If you're not fully recovered, we can always go to a movie," says Fari. She seems prim now, almost formal.

Michael is not nearly so disciplined. His pleasure with her company is in his voice and on his sleeve. "I'll manage," he says. His hand grazes hers but does not clasp. She doesn't like or tolerate public displays of affection.

"Something is on your mind," Fari says. He glances at her. How she should know this, be right about it, is beyond him. Perhaps it's training. Professional clairvoyance.

"My mother might have Alzheimer's," Michael says.

"Oh, Michael."

"No, it's okay. With her, Alzheimer's might be an improvement."

"That's not funny."

"I know. But it does mean I may have to

start looking for a new babysitter."

They're at the truck now. They stop. She turns to face him. "We'll cross that bridge when we come to it," she says firmly. She is big on crossing bridges. She is big on taking baby steps. Michael assumes it's a Psych 301 thing.

"Among others," he says, teasing her. He turns and moves to the driver's side of the truck. He's left it unlocked. In the back of his mind is the hope that someone will steal it. In the back of his mind is the hope for a lot of things, most of them unformed and unspoken. He opens the door and turns back to Fari.

"Thanks for the birthday present."

"You're very welcome."

"I can hardly wait to give you yours."

"Mmm." She glances up and down the sidewalk, suddenly nervous. He is much less reticent in public than she is. Careful, she seems to say.

"Did I mention you have the most gorgeous ass in the entire world?"

"Surely you exaggerate."

"I could lick it like an ice cream cone. And suck on your beautiful, big tits for dessert."

He's made her blush red. It's the color of her nipples, the color of her sex when he goes down on her. Pleased and feeling

40

vindicated, Michael gets into the truck. He starts it up and backs out of his spot. Another car is already waiting for it. Michael smiles, waves, and blows a kiss as he drives away.

5

It's dusk when Michael leaves the office, having returned to transform the blueprints for a deck into a sunroom and to sign the checks Rose has waiting for him. He drives south down the boulevard. North of Bird-rock, he turns up the hill and then turns yet again, up and into a cul-de-sac of neat, well-tended older houses. Toward the top of the hill, he stops and gets out in front of a house where an English garden has gone mad. Behind a picket fence and a trellis gate wrapped in climbing roses — BEWARE OF DOG, says the small sign — flowers of various colors and blooms grow indiscriminately and everywhere. Shrubberies sweep over herb-planted beds and one could lie down and disappear in the dense shin-high bunches of fescue and grass that constitute the lawn. The overall effect is both bizarre and wonderful at the same time. Michael opens the gate and, closing it behind him, proceeds along a crumbling stone path toward the rear of the house.

Unlike the front of the house, the backyard is a tree-shaded fairy garden, the ground an abstract checkerboard of aging flagstone and green pennyroyal. There are hanging topiary, ferns, and everywhere, on the fence and ground, the tea table and its chairs, potted plants.

"Almost done, Nana!" Jamie calls. Naked as a cupid, he is happily watering a large flowerpot full of bare dirt.

"Yes, Jamie, lovely, and when you finish, there's a pot for you to water over here, my dove."

Penelope Hodge is at a gardening bench, repotting orchids. She is an eccentric woman, knows it and enjoys it. A fat, old golden retriever, the dog to beware of, lies panting on the potting discards, moss, bark, and perlite attached to her shaggy coat. Penelope frowns with disapproval. "Abigail, do move. You drag all that into bed with us at night and it's most unpleasant."

The dog's ears perk up as Michael comes around the side of the house. It rises stiffly and moves toward him, its whole body wagging.

"Well, look who's finally here," says Penelope.

"Hi, Dad!" calls Jamie.

"Looks like you lost your clothes there, little man," says Michael as he bends to pet the dog. Jamie is still watering the pot and now has it to overflowing.

"They got messy so we took them off you're late," says Penelope. His mother, Michael knows, never says hello, rarely says good-bye, and always runs her sentences together, segueing from the innocuous to what's really on her mind without so much as missing a beat.

"How would you know, you don't keep track of time."

"No, but my stomach does and I'm hungry."

The dog now has her nose sunk firmly into Michael's crotch and, as he scratches her ears, croons with ecstasy.

"I didn't know you were making dinner tonight."

Penelope Hodge pushes a strand of gray hair that isn't there out of her face. She wears her hair short like an aging pixie. Pixies don't cook and, unless forced to, neither do the English.

"Don't be boring, Michael. However, I did splurge for lamb chops and if you're

44

nice I'll let you grill them for us."

"I'll think about it," says Michael, knowing it's a done deal.

"Hey, Dad!"

Michael turns. An arc of gold just catches a ray of evening light. Jamie, grinning back over his shoulder, has gone from watering a flowerpot to peeing in one.

"Help me water!"

Jamie giggles. The sound, Michael thinks, is as sweet as the backyard's wind chimes.

If the front yard of Penelope Hodge's house is an English garden gone amok, then the inside is the same motif carried forward as interior design. Upholstered chairs and couches, frayed silk-covered duvets, wooden side tables and antique lamps, all having nothing to do with one another, and all softened by age, use, needle, thread, and furniture polish, have been thrown together to somehow create something wonderful. The bookcases are triumphs of disorder, and on the walls, the picture frames are more interesting and certainly more valuable than the prints and paintings they hold within.

Jamie, still naked but with a quilt around him, is sitting on the floor with the dog, watching a Raffi tape on the TV. Just because he likes it, he is holding a silver-framed photo of a much younger Penelope in a wedding dress. She stands posed with a handsome if distant-looking naval officer in dress uniform. Jamie's been told the good parts of the story a hundred times. His grandparents met on the island of Crete. She was a thirty-six-year-old schoolteacher on a group tour and Thomas Hodge, five years her senior, was a surface warfare officer on furlough from a ship docked in Athens. In three days of ouzo, grilled fish, and stuffed grape leaves, they fell in splendid infatuation with each other and were married a year later in a typically English town in the Cotswolds, the landlocked, rolling green countryside from which Thomas Hodge couldn't get away fast enough. Their honeymoon was a weekend in Virginia Beach, and the Monday following, Thomas left for six months of sea duty and Penelope went home to Devonshire. Michael was born five months later, at eight-plus pounds either one of the largest premature babies in medical history or, more likely, the reason that two essential loners had decided to marry in the first place.

Penelope likes to say that her husband spent half their married life at sea and the other half wishing he was. "A misanthrope,

46

Michael. Absolutely lost when he wasn't out on his ships with all his instruments, telling people where to go."

When Michael was fifteen, his father, now stuck behind a desk at the naval base down on Coronado, went swimming in the ocean late one afternoon. An expert swimmer, Thomas Hodge did this several times a week. Only this time, he didn't come back. All that was found on the beach was a towel and his old Rolex with the leather strap.

"Well, of course he's in Thailand, darling. Sipping a cool drink, laughing about it with us."

But both she and Michael knew Thomas Hodge didn't like Thailand any more than he liked San Diego. The only place he was ever truly happy was on a boat.

"Jamie, dinner's getting cold," Michael calls from the adjacent dining room. Jamie doesn't answer. It's as if he doesn't even hear. Michael turns back. Penelope is at the heavy dining room table. It is formally set with linen napkins, china, and silver. After her husband's death, life insurance, pension, and a small nest egg bought the house in Upper Hermosa and Penelope found a job working in a village bookstore that was as energetically eclectic as she was. As always, she sits upright, fork in the left hand

47

with the tines pointing down, knife in the right. Her bite of lamb chop comes to her, never she to it.

"Let him be. He had a good half pound of cheddar when he got home from school."

"All that cheese isn't good for him," says Michael, sitting down.

"You did just fine on it."

Michael sits. He takes a sip of red wine, six bucks a bottle at Trader Joe's, not bad. He hesitates, then, as casually as possible broaches the unbroachable.

"So what's this about Alzheimer's?"

Penelope glances up at him. "I mentioned that, did I?"

"Yeah, you did. You left a message. *Twice.*"

The word sits a moment. Penelope touches her napkin to her mouth, returns it to her lap. "Yes, well, I was feeling just a little forgetful and so I went to see Dr. Haggarty. He said not to worry, that the human mind is like a computer and as we get older the hard drive gets filled up. Consequently, every time we learn something new, we forget something old to make space for it."

"I didn't know you were so computer literate," says Michael, beginning to eat.

"Mmm." Penelope carefully swallows. "That's the problem, isn't it. I learn about things I have no interest in and to make room for them I forget where I put my keys, this lamb's delicious."

"You're changing the subject."

"It's boring. Let's talk about you. How's work?"

"It's all right." The lamb *is* good.

"Liar," says Penelope. "But at least we're working."

"We?"

"Did I say we? I meant you."

"Mom, do you have Alzheimer's?"

"We'll see, won't we. I did remember your birthday cake."

The cake proves to be a chocolate scone complete with lit candle, and because Jamie for some unknown reason can't bear "Happy Birthday," they sing "Feliz Navidad" to it. Michael makes a wish, the same wish he's made for the last several years, and blows it out.

It takes forever to get Jamie dressed and out the door. It has to be addressed in the right order and there are traps and snares to overcome. Underwear that has been misplaced must be found. A foot must go in and out of a pant leg a certain number of times. Heads do *not* fit through sleeves. Socks go on the right foot and then the left and it can only be determined if it is the *correct* sock assigned to the correct foot once it is *on* the foot. After innumerable stops and starts and sputters and squawks, they stand in the light on the front stoop beginning what Michael thinks of as the curtain scene.

"Thanks, Mom. Good night."

"Thank *you,* darling. Shall we do it again tomorrow?"

"Well, not *tomorrow.*"

"I want to," says Jamie.

"Later this week then, darling."

"I want to," says Jamie.

"We'll figure it out," says Michael with just a touch of exasperation. "Oh, and don't worry about picking him up at school Thursday."

"Don't be silly," Penelope says, frowning. "I enjoy picking him up."

"Tisha called yesterday," says Michael. "She wants to." Tisha. Short for Patricia. The *other* grandmother.

"I want Nana to pick me up," says Jamie, suddenly staring straight ahead.

"Thursday it's Tisha's turn. She's family too."

"I hate Tisha."

"No you don't," says Michael.

"I do!" Jamie turns and runs for the front gate.

"Jamie!"

Too late. Jamie pushes open the gate, gets in the pickup, and slams the door behind him. Michael can hear the door locks click into place.

"I don't blame him," says Penelope. "If it wasn't against the law, that woman would have devoured her own children at birth."

"She thinks a lot of you too."

Penelope's tone is dismissive. "I could care less what she thinks. As long as you do. Think of me, that is."

Michael smiles. "I do." Kissing his mother's cheek, he turns and moves down the brick walk toward the gate. As he comes out to the truck, Jamie unlocks the door and rolls down the window. He leans out. "I love you, Nana!" he calls.

Penelope has been waiting for it. "And I, you, Jamie, my dove! Sleep well, my sweet! And may flights of angels sing thee to thy rest!"

Michael remembering that she used to say the same thing to him at bedtime when he was a boy, and until he was forced to study Shakespeare in high school, he assumed, because it wasn't at all beyond her, that Penelope had made it up herself.

6

" 'Then something began to hurt Mowgli inside him' " — Michael reads out loud — " 'as he had never been hurt before and he caught his breath and sobbed and the tears ran down his face.' "

It's not Shakespeare. It's *The Jungle Book* by Rudyard Kipling. It's Jamie's favorite and though Michael constantly suggests other books — *Tom Sawyer, Twenty Thousand Leagues, Lemony Snicket* — Jamie insists it be read every night.

" 'What is it? What is it?' " he said. " 'I do not wish to leave the jungle and I do not know what this is? Am I dying, Baghera?' "

" 'No, Little Brother. Those are only tears such as men use.' "

Lately Michael wonders if Jamie isn't too old to be read to, too old for Michael to be curled up next to him on the narrow bed.

" 'So Mowgli sat and cried as though his heart would break and he had never cried in all his life before.' "

Jamie hasn't cried since he was a baby. The falls and bruises that would bring any other child to tears have always left him seemingly puzzled, as if they were something unfathomable that needed to be figured out.

" 'Now,' " he said, " 'I will go to men. But first I must say farewell to my mother.' "

Both of them know that as Mowgli says good-bye, he will cry on her coat. "I loved thee more than ever I loved my cubs," she will say.

" 'The dawn was beginning to break when Mowgli went down the hillside alone, to meet those mysterious things called men.' " Michael closes the book. "Bedtime, bub." He quickly rises.

"Where's my mom?" Jamie is looking straight ahead.

Michael is aware of the sudden tension in his stomach. A tug. A flutter.

"You know the answer to that, Jamie."

"She's working."

"Yes."

"She's traveling."

"Yes."

"She's out in the world of men," says Jamie, "and she is busy but she loves me."

Thank you, Mr. Kipling.

"You got it."

53

"I want to sleep."

He quickly rolls away. Michael turns off the light. He bends to kiss Jamie.

" 'Night, little man."

Jamie doesn't answer. The light in the bathroom is on and Michael moves around the bed and goes in to turn it off. There are clippings taped on the tile above the counter. Michael doesn't have to look at them to know they're there. One is an old cover from *Surfing* magazine. A younger Michael cuts across the face of a wave. *Michael Hodge at Pipeline.* On it, Jamie has scrawled a word in clumsy Magic Marker.

DAD.

Next to the cover is an old print ad from a magazine. The woman in the photo, a blond young mother holding a baby, is beautiful, confident, and serene in the way that mothers can only be in the minds of advertisers.

MOM.

Out in the world of men.

Navigation is the blending of both science and art. The science of navigation can be taught, but the art of navigation must be developed from experience.

7

Making an abrupt left turn from the right lane, Anita Beacham cuts off a Mercedes SUV and pulls her Toyota Prius into the parking place, nose in to the curb. The woman in the Mercedes, children in the backseat behind her, gives an angry bleat on the horn. Another. Anita ignores her and the woman finally drives on. Every man and woman for him or herself. Anita's been cruising up and down this goddamn, silly street for the last twenty minutes, waiting to park somewhere, anywhere, close but not too close, to the entrance of the elementary school.

It might already be too late.

And now, sitting here, her heart beating *far* too fast, she realizes this isn't going to work at all. The Prius might be good on gas but it is lousy with blind spots. With the rearview mirror showing her nothing and the cars tight on either side of her, she can't see the school or the children being dropped off. She could get out of the car and stand but she's not willing to expose herself. Not yet. Perhaps not ever.

She turns in her seat. Craning her neck, she looks out the rear window. Between the slowly passing cars, she can see the sidewalk on the opposite side of the street. Maybe she'll see them pass. Even a glimpse would do for the time being. Maybe that's all she wants or needs. Maybe.

Ten minutes later, the sidewalks having cleared and the street traffic settled, and having seen nothing and no one she remotely cares about, Anita starts the car up, backs out of the stolen parking place, and leaves.

The old coffee shop with its wooden porch and tile-topped tables, its chess sets and young, tattooed waitstaff, is thankfully still there on Girard, and Anita orders a Keith Richards. It is three shots of strong espresso mixed with white hot chocolate and Anita's been contemplating one for over a month now. She sits at a small corner table outside. The resident sparrows, all half tame, flap and swoop, stopping fearlessly for muffin crumbs. Across the porch several men check her out. They're professional coffee drinkers pretending to be intellectuals and they'll spend half the day here going for cheap refills. Anita is used to men's glances but these both annoy and depress her. It took her forever to decide what to wear this morning. She wanted to be casual but presentable. Attractive but asexual. Flowing skirt or tailored slacks? Sneakers and jeans? It probably doesn't matter. Attractive is easy, asexual is hard no matter what she wears.

There is a newspaper on the adjacent table, and rising, Anita reaches for it. Her bag falls from the table and she fumbles, trying to catch it. She succeeds only in opening it. Coins and pills scatter and fall through the cracks of the porch as the bag hits the floor.

"Shit," Anita murmurs.

She bends to pick things up. Some of the pills are small white pentagons, slow-release Alprazolam for anxiety, and Anita, who's had two already this morning, wonders if she should go for a third. No, discipline is important in this, her new life. She pushes them down into the crack between the two boards and picks up the change.

As Anita rises and sits back she sees that a woman carrying coffee-to-go is approaching at what can only be called a fast flutter. The woman wears designer sunglasses, a low-cut sleeveless top, and the skintight yoga pants that even women who don't do yoga seem to wear everywhere these days.

"Anita? Anita, is it you?"

The woman's thrilled, breathless trill carries out over the entire porch, drawing stares, and Anita tries not to cringe.

"Oh, my gosh, it is! An*ee*-ta! Well, it's *me*! Bitsy! Bitsy Grant!" The woman seems dumbfounded that Anita doesn't recognize her. Anita rises slightly, trying to force a smile. The woman might as well be from another galaxy. With a name like Bitsy, maybe she is.

"Oh, my goodness — yeah, right — hi!"

The woman's head jerks forward like one of the circling birds and her lips brush Anita's cheek. Anita has no choice but to respond in kind. Kiss-kiss.

Who the fuck is Bitsy Grant?

"Oh, look at *youuu*!" the woman warbles. "You look so *greeaatttt*!" The stranger who calls herself Bitsy Grant places a large Louis Vuitton purse on the tabletop. A thousand bucks for a leather bag festooned with ugly letters. She sits down across the table from Anita and settles back, making herself comfortable as if she and her container of coffee have nothing better to do now than stay awhile. She pushes her sunglasses to

60

the top of her head, exposing perfectly made-up eyes. "Now, let's see," she says, as if beginning a list. "Are you still doing your little acting thing? Oh, but then you were always so talented. That senior musical? What was that again?" The woman's voice is like a flute running scales.

"I . . . don't remember." Oh, my God, where is this coming from? It was *Little Mary Sunshine* and it was an embarrassing disaster. Canadian Mounties and damsels in distress. Insufferable lyrics filled with double entendres. The highlight of her theater career.

Bitsy Grant squeezes her shoulders forward like an excited cheerleader. There is a little gold cross dangling in the middle of her exposed cleavage. The cross disappears. Bitsy Grant's smile turns her eyes to slits and wrinkles her already perky nose. "Oh, isn't it horrible how everything's changed around here? Jimmy says it's nothing but horrible retirees from the Midwest and Phoenix."

Bitsy Grant might as well be a bumblebee flying from flower to flower speaking gibberish.

"Jimmy?" asks Anita.

"Jimmy. Little Jimmy Damon? His father owned all those car dealerships?"

61

Oh, God. It's starting to come back. *Bitsy fucking Grant.*

"Oh. Right, yeah. Jimmy. You were . . . going out with him."

"Honey, I *married* him." Like it was a steep hill to climb. Bitsy Grant holds out a manicured hand. A diamond the size of a bird's egg and a jewel-encrusted wedding band are on her ring finger. She takes a sip of her coffee. She squeezes her boobs together again and beams. "Oh, but we are all just going to have to get together. They still do the nicest seafood buffet at the country club."

Anita would rather go to hell than to the country club. "Yeah. We'll do that. Well, listen, it's been really nice seeing you, Bits."

It's an invitation to leave but Bitsy Grant is going nowhere. Her face grows solemn. There is serious business to discuss, only females of the species and old friends invited. "*So.* Does Michael know you're back?"

"No," says Anita, suddenly dreading what's to come.

"Well, *that* should be interesting. I think he still has that little contracting business. I don't know *how* he's getting by in this economy. Oh, but that little boy of yours, *so* cute."

Bitsy Grant. Always so innocent and smiling, eyes like ice daggers. Anita remembers now. Bitsy Grant was a jealous, self-serving, backstabbing snake in high school.

"So, what exactly *have* you been doing, Neetsie?" Bitsy Grant sips her coffee and wrinkles her nose expectantly. "Hmmm?"

The "Neetsie" is what does it.

"Blowing Little Jimmy at the car dealership, now get out of my face!"

The porch goes silent. People look up to stare. Bitsy Grant blinks as if slapped.

"I said, beat it, you bitch!"

Bitsy's eyes turn from shocked to cold and calm. Her mouth purses in a tight, superior little smile. The mask gone, she is easily recognizable now. "So nice to see you too." Rising, she picks up her bag and, looking neither right nor left, walks across the porch and down the steps toward the sidewalk. Her voice trickles back.

"Such a loser."

Anita feels the eyes on her. Hears the amused whispers. There's a white pentagon next to her foot. She leans out of the chair and, bending down, picks it up. She puts it in her mouth and quickly washes it down with Keith Richards. Maybe she'll have another. Of both.

8

"Michael Hodge? I'm here to see Mr. Nash?"

If Michael's herringbone sports jacket is out of season, his tie never had one. And confidence doesn't announce its arrival with question marks.

The modern reception area has floor-to-ceiling views of San Diego harbor. The scripted logo on the opaque wall behind the receptionist's desk — THE NASH GROUP — suggests success and money. So does the blond receptionist. Miss California with computer skills.

"Do you have an appointment?" She's polite but skeptical.

"No, I don't," says Michael. "But I think he'll see me. I'm a friend of the family."

It's worth a try. And it works.

"Michael!"

John Nash is a lean, vital man in his sixties. Like Robert Caulfield, he wears the casual but expensive uniform of the California businessman — expensive loafers, tailored slacks, and golf shirt. The more exclusive the golf club, the higher on the pecking order a man stands, and John Nash has the small crossed-golf-clubs logo of Pine Valley on his breast. He rises and comes out from behind his desk, smiling warmly, as Michael, led by the receptionist, enters. Like the reception area, his office has a view of the harbor but also looks down on the Nash-built marina shopping center.

"Hello, John. Thanks for seeing me." They shake hands. John's is strong and overly firm. It always has been. As if he's proving a point.

"Are you kidding? I'm delighted. But you shoulda called first, we'da had lunch or something. Come on, come on, sit down. You want some coffee, something to drink? Get us some coffee and sparkling water, Denise."

The young woman nods. She turns to Michael, smiling. "Cream and sugar, sir?"

Sir. Depending on who one knows, in five minutes, even a man in an ill-fitting sports coat can come up in the world.

"Just cream."

With a swirl of blond hair, the young woman exits. John Nash gestures toward the couch and some upholstered chairs.

"C'mon. I only have a couple of minutes here, so sit."

Michael sits and sinks awkwardly back into the plush cushions. It feels like a defensive position.

"How're Jack and Doug doing?"

John Nash grins, happy to talk family. "Aw, Christ, they're great — great! Jack's in Richmond. Runs the East Coast office. Married, two kids. Dougie's in Sun Valley, in charge of one of our condo projects up there. Having fun is what he's doing. You should give'm both a call. They'd love to hear from you. I'll have Denise give you their numbers before you leave."

Michael nods. Jack, who was his age, was always the student. Fun but straight-arrow serious. Football player, scratch golfer, Duke University. Never a doubt he'd work for his father. Doug, the younger of the two, sold drugs, partied, and finally flunked out of Arizona State, which was like failing at fucking off. Why bother trying when your father will always find you a job?

"What about you, still surfing?"

"No, not for a while now."

"Jesus, Michael, I thought you went pro."

"Being one and calling yourself one aren't quite the same thing, John."

"Good," says John Nash. "Well, that's good. You were smart enough to realize that."

Easy to figure out, Michael thinks, when you're sitting on a beach without enough money for a meal let alone a plane ticket home.

"So. What can I do for you, Michael?"

What can't you do? Where does a man begin?

More than once of late, Michael feels as if he has never made a proactive decision in his life. Things occurred, events took place, and he responded as best he could, hoping he was making the right move. What was that movie with Tom Hanks? A brainless innocent symbolized by a feather being blown by the wind, turning one shit pile after another into gold, never aware of what was happening to him until after it happened. That's me, thinks Michael. Only not so innocent and certainly not so lucky.

"John, I'm not sure you know that I've spent the last several years as a general contractor. Mostly single-family homes and remodels, but we've done good work, have a good local reputation. The thing is —"

What is the thing? Is there a thing?

"We've sort of reached our limit — *I* have — and what'd I'd like to do now is step it

67

up to the next level."

"What level is that, Michael?"

"I understand you bought the Delaney house down in the Barber Tract."

"Sure did," says John Nash with a satisfied smile. "Beautiful property."

Charles Delaney was a movie actor. The "property" is an unheard-of three quarters of an acre of land right on Marine Beach. Michael can't begin to imagine what it cost.

"I've heard you're going to tear down the existing house and rebuild."

"That's the plan."

"I'd like to bid on the job."

John Nash has grown serious. "Aw, Jesus, I don't know, Michael. This is a little more than a remodel."

"I've built houses, John."

"I'm sure you have but not like this. I'm looking at plans for fifteen to twenty thousand square feet. Underground garage with elevator, implanted girders, seawall. I can already tell you the building restrictions are gonna be a bitch to deal with."

Restrictions. Developers hate restrictions. Especially those who are trying to tear down a historically designated house in a community-regulated coastal zone. Michael reaches into his binder and removes neatly folded printouts.

"I know that. In fact, I've pulled the overlays on the property and I can already tell you what it's subject to. And I think I can help with the permit reviews. I have relationships with people on the town council and the coastal commission. I can tell you, John, they'd all like to see a local contractor."

And now John Nash looks amused. "I wouldn't be in business very long if I worried about *town councils,* Michael."

Michael used to surf and play golf with Jack and occasionally with Doug. Skipped school when the waves were too choice to resist. Ate dinner at their house, stayed over. More than once he was taken by the family to Hawaii. "Enjoy it," said Penelope, "but don't get used to it. And never count on those people for anything."

"John, all I'm asking for is the opportunity to show you the work I've done and what I'm capable of. At the end of the day, you'll make your own decisions."

John Nash shakes his head. "I'd like to help you, Michael, but really, it'd be a waste of your time. You're certainly entitled to make a bid but . . ."

Word on the street is that John Nash was caught sleeping with a bridesmaid at his own daughter's wedding. His wife, her story similar to that of Job, divorced him for it. That's why the new house. Fifteen thousand feet for a single, sixty-five-year-old man currently dating a twenty-three-year-old Asian model. Good luck.

John Nash rises. "So listen, you give Jack and Dougie a call, okay."

"I will," says Michael, rising with him.

"And hey, if the right thing rears its head . . ." John Nash points a finger at Michael as if it's a promise, something that might actually happen.

"Thanks for seeing me, John."

"Anytime, Michael. You're family."

Family. John Nash banished his younger son to Idaho through subordinates. His older son lives in Richmond, Virginia, because it's a full continent away from his father.

What was I thinking?

Michael turns for the door. He passes the blonde as he exits. She holds a cup of coffee in one hand, a small bottle of Perrier in the other. She seems surprised that Michael is leaving. Even more so when he pulls off his tie and hands it to her on the way out.

He is going north on Interstate 5 when his cell phone rings.

9

"He's on his way, right?"

"Last I heard."

Leo sits in Michael's outer office fiddling impatiently, both annoyed and relieved that Rose Guerrero is ignoring him. Women have always made Leo nervous and Rose is a lot of woman.

" 'Cause we gotta go over these plans." He holds up the carefully rolled engineering paper for emphasis.

"That's the tenth time you told me that," says Rose, not looking at him, her nose in some book.

"Yeah? Well, that's 'cause we do." It occurs to Leo he'd better set Rose straight on a few things. " 'Cause if you think I'm sitting here waiting 'cause I don't have better things to do, you're wrong."

"I'm not thinking of you at all, Leo."

Leo finds himself *doubly* annoyed and yes, relieved, that Rose is not thinking of him at all. He would like to leave it at that and keep his big mouth shut but that's not why he's here. I am courage, hear me roar.

"So when are we getting together, Rose."

"Leo." Rose is looking at him now, looking at him with her crazy, golden eyes. Camel eyes, she calls them, eyes, she says, that can put the *mal de ojo* — the evil eye — on those who deserve it, which is hopefully not him. "How many times I gotta tell you, you're not my type."

"Yeah, you keep sayin' that but what you don't do is tell me what that is."

"Not you."

Ouch. She might as well be talking about stamps at the post office. "Not me? Why not me? How long we known each other, Rose? How long, huh?"

"Too long. That's why this is so stupid on your part."

Stupid. Probably so. The truth is Leo had known about Rose forever and never thought twice about her. And then one day a year ago, her mother took a fall and, not wanting to wait for the bus, Rose needed a ride home. Michael wasn't available and so Leo stepped to the plate, driving immediately to the office to pick her up. Halfway to East San Diego it struck Leo that the woman sitting next to him, though certainly plump, was voluptuous, exotic, and in all ways attractive. That this happened to be the first woman to sit anywhere near Leo in several years only occurred to him later. He was a man dying of thirst discovering he was near potable water and by the time he dropped Rose off at her apartment in City Heights, Leo was infatuated.

"Uh-huh. So what is your type, Rose, huh? Antonio Banderas?"

"It's none of your business what it is. You want a date, go online where they can't see you."

Again, ouch. Leo has had no luck with online dating. His ideal companion boiled down to a woman who liked to cook, eat, and help clean up after, sex appreciated but optional. Much to his surprise, he got no matches. As for social media like Facebook, his friends seemed limited to people who post photos of their dogs and their children.

"Yeah, well, you shouldn't judge a book by its cover."

Even though she has an actual book in her hands, it's as if Rose doesn't hear him. The problem with the world is that women ignore heavy guys in work boots. Even women who are carrying a couple of pounds themselves. Even women whose lips, full and juicy as they may be, move slightly when they read.

"I'm not askin' again, Rose."

"Good," says Rose, closing her book and putting it aside. It's an intimidatingly thick book with a plain, dark hard cover. Rose's books all come from the library. Leo can only assume they're incomprehensible.

" 'Cause the truth is, if you want to know the truth, the truth is I'm seeing somebody already."

Where has *this* come from? But at least he now has Rose's attention.

"Seeing someone," says Rose. It's Rose who now, if it's possible, looks uncertain.

Leo shrugs. "Why wouldn't I be?"

"Give me a name, what's her name."

"Linda." It's his mother's name but it's the best he can do on short notice.

"Linda," says Rose. She crosses her arms under her breasts. Her bosom pushes up and out as if to confront Leo. "This Linda, is she cute?"

"Yeah," says Leo. "Very."

"Blonde or brunette?"

"Dark hair."

"Sexy?"

" 'Course she is," says Leo. "Built." He can see Linda in his mind's eye. She suddenly looks a lot like Rose.

"Then what's she doing with you?"

Cackling evilly, Rose uncrosses her arms, deflates her bosom, and turns to her computer. Leo rises. He puts the rolls of paper on the desk.

"Give these to Mike when he comes in."

With quiet dignity Leo turns and walks out the door. It's not until he is getting in his truck that he realizes what he's done. He wonders if Rose will unroll the sheets of engineering paper, wonders if she'll see that they are blank. If she does, Leo hopes that she will realize that they are love letters and will stare at the pages for a long time.

10

In front of his mother's house, Michael's truck pulls to a fast stop. He gets out and hurries through the open gate. Penelope is waiting for him.

"There was no need to rush," she says, "he's feeling fine now."

"Think he was faking it?"

"You did. What difference does it make? He's home."

They enter the house. In the living room, Jamie sits in front of the TV, naked, watching *Teletubbies,* as always seemingly transfixed by the bright colors, unchanging faces, and repetitive nonverbal dialogue of the sack-like creatures.

"Give us a second," Michael says to his mother.

"Be sweet."

"I'm always sweet."

"No, not always."

Jamie looks up as Michael crosses the living room, turns off the TV, and sits down on the couch, saying nothing. Jamie looks away.

"Hi, Dad."

"How you feeling, little man?"

"Good."

"Not so good at school though, huh?"

"My stomach was sick."

"Bad enough you had to go to the nurse?"

"Yes."

"But it's okay now."

"Yes."

"Good. Because I know if your stomach still felt sick, you'd tell me. And if it wasn't sick to begin with, you'd tell me that too. Because you and I always tell one another the truth, don't we."

"Yes."

"Good."

Michael waits, watching the tender quiet in his son's face. He feels what's coming before knowing what it is.

"I want Tisha to miss me."

Oh, shit, thinks Michael. How could he have been so stupid. Not to listen. *Really* listen. He knows better. Or should. Still, there are lessons that must be taught. There is a future to prepare for. Isn't there?

"You can't just come home when you don't like things, Jamie."

77

"I'll get in a car," says Jamie. "I'll drive away. I'll drive!"

"Even worse. Where would you go?"

"Away."

"I would be very unhappy without you. So would Nana."

"I hate Tisha," says Jamie, staring at the floor, his mouth trembling. "I hate that house."

"Come here," Michael says.

Jamie stands and moves to him. When Michael puts an arm around him and pulls him close, Jamie buries his face into Michael's shoulder. He's too big to be held like this but at the moment, Michael doesn't care. Out in the world anything could happen to his son. Here he's safe.

"You don't ever have to go to Tisha's again."

The future will take care of itself.

11

Sitting at her mother's kitchen table, Anita finds herself flashing on a Hollywood party where a famous movie moment was explained to her by a drunken wannabe film director. Pinned into a corner, a woman crouches as if trying to hide. The camera's point of view hovers. Behind her, the corner joint of the walls has been purposely rebuilt, stretched up and out of normal proportion. The resulting skewed perspective traps and overwhelms the woman. There is nowhere to go. The director then cuts to a close-up of the woman's face to capture an expression not so much of terror as of speechless guilt.

"He's not comfortable coming over here."

Anita can hear their voices as they approach through the dining room and into the pantry.

"Nonsense. He was here at Christmas with all the grandchildren. He had a wonderful time."

"That's because I was with him."

"And you didn't stay long, did you. Whose fault was that?"

Anita wants to rise from her chair, wants to turn for the back stairs, wants to run, but just like in the movie, the ceiling above her head is a weight pressing her down, squashing her.

"It's nobody's fault. This isn't about fault. It's about Jamie. Routines are important to him."

"Well, I think that's silly. How's he going to get to know any of us, if he doesn't make the attempt?"

She should have left when her mother got off the phone. She should have run then.

"That was Michael," Tisha Beacham had said.

"What?"

"Jamie went home early from school today."

"What are you *talking* about?"

"I was supposed to pick him up and bring him over here." Matter-of-fact about it, as if talking about the weather.

"Without *telling* me?"

"Well, he's not coming now, is he."

"Thank God!"

"Michael is."

"Mother — !"

She should have run then, run like crazy, because the first meeting wasn't supposed to happen like this, it wasn't supposed to *be* like this, wasn't supposed to —

As if jabbed by a bolt of electricity, Anita half rises out of her chair as they enter the kitchen. Her mother, Tisha, is a tall, slim woman in her sixties, still more beautiful than she has any right to be. Her hair, never dyed, is ash blond and her skin is flawless. She rarely wears makeup, not needing it. Her expression, as always, is severe.

The better to bully you with, my dear.

Michael, Anita sees, is still Michael. A bit more flesh on his strong, lanky frame. A real haircut. A button-down shirt and shoes with actual laces. But still him.

It's still him.

Michael stops in his tracks at the sight of her, too stunned to even speak.

"Hello, Michael," Anita murmurs. A million charming things she'd planned to say and hello is the best she can do. Hardly audible at that, sounding as if she's swallowed her own tongue.

Oh, and Michael — Michael, according to her mother, one of the seven archangels in heaven and the leader of heaven's armies . . .

Thanks, Mom, I'll remember that!

81

. . . Michael is looking at her as if he'd mistakenly been told she'd died.

I did.

"Well," says Tisha Beacham, as if it's all just a pleasantly anticipated get-together of old friends. "Shall I make us some coffee or tea?"

Us.

Michael's jaw tightens. His expression turns from one of uncertainty to ugly contempt. "Don't bother." And just like that he's out of the kitchen and gone, somehow taking the horrible weight in the room with him.

Anita, finally able to move, rises fully from the chair and pushes past her mother. "I told you," she hisses. She hurries after him.

Michael comes out of the house into the open courtyard. The Beacham house is off Scenic Drive on a fenced and secluded half acre of land. The neighborhood is old and exclusive and, when the Spanish-style house was built some eighty-five years ago, virulently anti-Semitic. The cars in the driveway are not new. Old money doesn't like ostentation. Michael made note of the Christian fish symbol on the bumper of the Escalade when coming in. This last Christmas, Tisha had insisted on taking Jamie to church

82

services. Some assembly of born-agains out in Lemon Grove. Just another thing the poor kid had hated.

"Michael, please!"

Anita has come out the front door behind him.

"Michael!"

He can't help himself. He turns back. Even to his own ears, his voice sounds ugly. "He was just going to come over after school? Have some milk and cookies and hey, guess who this is? Was that it?"

"I didn't know. She didn't tell me until after you called."

"Like I believe that."

"I'm not a liar, Michael. I tell the truth till it hurts."

He knows this. To her own detriment, she always has.

"I'm not sure I'm even ready to see him. The thought of it scares me to death."

"It should," says Michael. "And you can forget about coming anywhere near him."

"She's watching," Anita says quietly. Michael follows her gaze. Tisha Beacham is at an upstairs window, looking down over the courtyard at them. Without expression, she turns away. And then Michael's hand is on Anita's shoulder and he's aiming her, pushing her toward the truck.

"Get in."

"Are we going somewhere?"

"Just *get* — in the *truck.*"

She does. Gratefully.

Stepping to a window in the guest bedroom, Tisha Beacham watches as the pickup starts with a roar and then pulls out of the court-yard and moves down the drive and through the open gate into the street. Her head is pounding and her throat feels swollen. She hopes she isn't coming down with some-thing. There's a lot going around these days.

They drive in silence, not looking at each other. The narrow winding road that takes them out of the Upper Muirlands was originally built for mules not cars and the tires of the truck squeal as they come around a curve. The truck veers into the opposing lane and then back again. A car is approaching. There is some space on the shoulder and etiquette would dictate that Michael pull to the side and let the oncom-ing car pass. He will have none of it. He hits both the horn and the gas. The truck surges forward. Horn blaring back, the car is forced to swerve hard into a driveway.

"If you're going to kill me," says Anita, "please don't do it with a truck."

Ignoring her, Michael runs the red light onto Nautilus.

"So how you been?" Anita says. *Casually.* Michael answers her with a derisive snort. His lips are clenched. He seems to be chewing on his inner cheek. As good a reason as any to answer the question herself. "Why, just fine, Anita, thanks. How have *you* been? Oh, just peachy as well, thank you. Just swell." She hesitates. "Actually I'm a mess," she says softly.

"*Still?*" Michael, biting the word.

He turns the wheel hard. With a squeal of tires, the truck veers to the side of the road and comes to an abrupt halt. Michael slams the truck into park. He's breathing fast and hard, sucking air as if from the mask in a falling airplane.

"Hit me if it'll make you feel better." She watches Michael shake his head. "Then tell me about Jamie." She waits as he puts the palms of his hands to his eyes. He inhales, then exhales deeply. He lowers his hands. His face still looks brittle but there is a semblance of composure now.

"What do you want to know?"

"My mother says he's not quite right."

"Your mother's the one who's not quite right." Michael stares straight ahead, not looking at her. "He has Asperger's," he says quietly.

It's a word that Anita has heard before but doesn't quite recognize. "I don't know what that —"

"It's autism."

She feels her body clench. She's read about this in newspapers. Children who don't speak, can't function, won't survive alone.

Rain Man.

"He's autistic?"

"Did I say that?" Michael says sharply. Inhale again — exhale again. Control is a good thing. "He's wired different, that's all. He learns different. He has a hard time with people he doesn't know or trust. He doesn't like to play with other kids. When he doesn't want to do something, he screams his head off for help."

"Sounds pretty normal to me," says Anita, already convinced it's not.

"He's a great kid," says Michael, and in doing so, puts Anita's fears momentarily to rest. "If you'd ever been in touch, you'd know that."

She looks away. "I'd have made things worse."

"You're so sure of that."

"It's what I tell myself."

"You don't want to know what I tell my-self."

"I can guess." And she can. Derelict mom. Prodigal wife returned.

"I *do* want to see him, Michael."

"I'm not sure how we're going to handle that."

"No rush."

He looks at her. For the very first time, really *looks* at her. His eyes are question marks and she realizes, despite his anger, he is concerned for her. Not what she expected or even knew she wanted.

"I'm tired, Michael. I need to be home for a while. I won't bother you, I promise. I'll wait for you to tell me what to do."

Michael nods. A moment passes and he puts the truck in gear. He does a U-turn across the lane and heads back up the hill.

"Can I call you?" she says.

Neither of them have spoken on the ride back to the house and now, as she's about to get out of the truck, Anita feels she has to.

"Your mother has my cell."

"All right." She hesitates. She has to say it. "It's good to see you, Michael. I've missed you." He stares straight ahead, not saying a word.

What did you expect?

She opens the door and is halfway out when she hears his voice.

"Anita."

She turns back. Michael is still looking straight ahead. Anywhere but at her.

"You find what you were looking for?"

"Not even close," says Anita, trying and failing to make it a joke. Michael nods. Elsewhere. A place where you don't really care about answers.

Anita closes the door of the truck. She stands, watching him drive away, taking her time before turning and going in the house. She has to decide if she'll give her mother an argument or the silent treatment. Arguing feels better but silence is the more effective means of punishment. Decisions, decisions. One should be as certain about anything as her mother is about everything.

12

"Well, I think it's insane," says Penelope Hodge.

It's been hamburgers tonight. Over-cooked, bloodless, gray hamburgers, which is how Penelope likes them, and after a hell of a lousy day, Michael isn't sure he has the patience to deal with his mother anymore. Time to just finish washing the dishes and get out of here.

"You'd be mad to let her see him."

Penelope hates doing dishes and invariably finds another chore far enough away from the sink to keep her hands dry but not so far she can't continue her end of what she feels to be a meaningful conversation. Her preferred task this evening seems to be refolding already folded dishtowels and replacing them in a different drawer.

"You want to keep your voice down?" says Michael.

"He's not listening."

Jamie is in the living room, having returned to his usual place on the floor in front of the TV. This evening it's been *Bob the Builder* — a bobble-headed construction worker and his anthropomorphic equipment. Even with their inane chatter, Michael wishes he had heavy equipment that did construction work all by themselves.

"Don't kid yourself. He's always listening."

After he drops Anita off at the Beacham house, Michael goes to Bev Mo, buys a six-pack and takes it down to the parking lot overlooking Tourmaline Beach. Alcohol is prohibited on San Diego beaches but the hell with it, let someone try and fine him. Michael pulls into a vacant spot, gets out, and six-pack in hand, walks down to the rail. He cracks a beer and drains half of it in one swallow. He closes his eyes and lets it settle. Why can't things ever be easy? Just when you think you might be heading in the right direction you find out there isn't one. You're back to the starting line, back to square one. He drinks again, sipping now. Tourmaline is a beach break, popular with young beginners and longboarders. This is where Michael first caught waves on his own, where, as a boy, he hung out all summer long. The bathrooms were especially gross, and because they were, Michael has never felt like he's at the shore if the public bathrooms and showers aren't contagious.

As he watches the surfers catch the last waves of the afternoon, he's aware of a spindly figure approaching. The man, bearded and with long, tangled sun-streaked hair, is barefoot, wears ragged jeans and a faded Quicksilver T-shirt. The man stops. He eyes the beer hungrily.

"Hey, got an extra, bra?"

The man looks familiar. Almost but not quite. Michael knows the type. A self-styled surf guru. An aging man-child who probably lives in his car and spends his days on the sand, smoking dope and discussing the wave conditions, past and present, with anyone who will take the time to listen. Michael lives now in an alternate universe. He pulls a beer from the plastic ring and flips it to the burned-out man who snatches it out of the air and grins. "Tight, bra." Foam bubbles and spills as he pops it and sucks it in happily. He looks toward the water. "Dunzo out there, huh, dude?" Dunzo. Meaning the best ever. The guy would be funny if he wasn't serious.

"Yeah, pretty good." In truth it's weak. Without even thinking about it, Michael knows the knee-high waves are coming in fifteen-second intervals, a northwest wind is working against a southwest swell. Crossed-up lines with some workable corners and a choppy surface.

The surf rat stares at Michael a moment. His brow furrows as if he's struggling to remember something. Where he lives. What day of the week it is. He gestures with the beer.

"Yo, you Michael Hodge?"

Michael answers before he thinks to lie. "Yeah."

The bum breaks into a huge, happy grin. "Dude! Aw, man, whoa, it is a complete and total honor, dude." He thrusts his sunburned hand out at Michael. Michael has no choice but to take it. The bum's fingers are dry and scaly. He pumps Michael's hand up and down with enthusiasm.

"I was on the beach when you took the ASP event up at Trestles. You were so totally, bitchin' badass, man?"

"Thanks," says Michael, retrieving his hand.

"Michael freakin' Hodge!" The bum shakes his head as if he can't believe it. As if the name is as good as the cold beer. And then he looks lost again, as if he's suddenly not sure it really happened. "Hey, when was that, man, what year?"

"Oh four," says Michael.

"Yeah!" The rat grins, both happy and relieved. "And bra, you were milfy. You were the boss!"

"I was lucky," says Michael. "Garcia couldn't catch a decent ride in the final heat and handed it to me."

"Yeah, but thems the breaks!" says the rat as if he remembers. "You put out or shit or lock the doors on Fort Pitt. And I was there!"

"I'm glad you were."

The bum gulps some beer. He nods toward the water. "Hey, you should be out there with us. Showin' the newbies how it's done."

Us.

"You know what's wrong with surfing?" says Michael. He doesn't wait for an answer. "The waves take you in the wrong direction."

The bum frowns, then chuckles uncertainly. "Too heavy for me, man. I just like to get fucked up."

"Be my guest." Michael hands him the rest of the six-pack and turns back toward the truck. As he's tossing his unfinished beer into a trash can, he can hear the bum calling out to someone on the beach.

"Hey, dude, hey! Know who that is? That is Michael Hodge, man! He used to tear it up! He used to *be* somebody."

Somebody.

Used to be.

"She's his mother," Michael says to Penelope, trying to control his impatience. He puts the last plate into the drying rack and pulls the stopper in the sink. Time to get out of here now.

"No, I'm sorry. She forfeited that title when she ran out on him. What would make any rational person do such a thing, Michael, explain that to me, please."

Drying his hands, Michael sighs. "Okay, you never liked her."

"Wrong," says Penelope. "I adored Anita. From the moment you first brought her home, my heart went out to her. But I will not forgive her for hurting you. And I will not forgive you if you let her do it again."

Before Michael can answer, Jamie appears in the doorway.

"I'm ready to go now."

"Yeah. Me too."

One never attempts to win an argument with Penelope Hodge, one just leaves her to put away her own dishes.

Memories follow him home. He lets them. It gives perspective.

"I think you better take a look at something."

It's two years earlier. Jamie has just turned five. It's quitting time and Michael and the crew have been pouring cement for eight hours and are exhausted. Leo has been acting strangely all day. At least strange for Leo. Quiet. Subdued. And now he hands Michael the slip of paper.

"What is it?"

"I'm not gonna say a word, just take a look." Leo turns away to his truck. Michael looks at the slip of paper. It's a Web address.

That night, at home, a night similar to this one, with Jamie in bed and with a drink in hand, Michael goes into the small spare bedroom that is his semblance of an office, turns on the ancient computer, and taps in the link. He already knows, from the name of the Web site, what it's going to be. Michael isn't an avid fan of pornography but, unless it's crude and abusive, he doesn't have a problem with it. Leo, he suspects, is a connoisseur.

The clip begins and it's the usual fake

moanings and groanings, nothing different from anything Michael has ever seen before. Several couples are in a brightly lit, badly decorated living room as if there's safety in numbers. The men are nothing more than their appendages. The girls are far too young and pretty to be pretending they like this. The video camera pans to the woman on the couch. She is on hands and knees. There is a scarlet ribbon around her neck. There is a faceless man behind her. She turns to look over her shoulder and in doing so faces the camera. Even in the long, dark wig and heavy makeup, Michael recognizes her. The sounds she makes are foreign to him. The look on her face is one he's never seen before. By the end of the evening, Michael has located the movie online and purchased it. It arrives a week later. The woman in the wig is in several scenes. Since then, not often, but usually after a couple of drinks late at night, Michael has thrown it in the DVD player. He does it so as not to romanticize the good times. He does it to make himself remember what she's capable of. He does it because it makes him angry and he has found that anger is a good insulation for the heart. Tonight is one of those nights. He keeps the sound low. He keeps the remote in his hand. As always, it's like passing a car wreck and seeing the body of someone you love.

Oh, Anita.

The good navigator thinks strategically, operationally, and tactically. He gathers information from a variety of sources and evaluates this information to determine his ship's position. He anticipates dangerous situations well before they arise, and always stays "ahead of the vessel."

13

"I don't think we're giving him everything he needs."

It is three o'clock, pickup time, and Michael has taken on the task himself today. Pickup is harder than drop-off. Most of the kids are running, screaming, and playing together after school, letting off steam. Jamie is, as always, by himself. He was hopping up and down when Michael entered the playground today, erratic and without objective, lost in his own world, shaking his hand in front of his face.

The village idiot.

Michael doesn't know the name of the father he overheard say it one day, thinking he was being funny. He knows that it was all he could do not to hit the man.

"I don't mean you," says Mrs. McKenzie. "I mean the school. When you keep him on task, he does well, but when you don't . . ." She doesn't finish the sentence. She doesn't need to.

"What about the extra teacher?" asks Michael. "A part-time aide was supposed to be part of his IEP."

"The money's not there."

"It's supposed to be."

"That's something you'll have to take up with the school board," says Mrs. McKenzie. Both of them knowing that the district is broke. They're laying off teachers. Transferring others. Cramming forty kids into a single classroom. The special-ed classes are even worse. Most of them nothing more than babysitting for troubled, hyperactive kids, half of them Spanish-speaking with little or no English. The mentally impaired children sit alone at separate tables, playing with Legos.

"I'm not sure you know this, but they've started a study program at UCSD for children with developmental disorders," Mrs. McKenzie says.

Study programs. From what Michael has seen, people put more money into studying disabled kids than they do into helping them. "What, are they looking for guinea pigs?"

Karen McKenzie ignores the bitterness in his voice. She likes Michael. She likes that he faces facts, doesn't pretend or insist there isn't a problem as a lot of parents do.

"It's just a phase. He'll grow out of it."

No, she all too often wants to say. He won't. Your child needs help.

"As a matter of fact, there's a waiting list. But I know some of the people conducting the study and I think I can arrange it." Michael nods, already coming around to the idea as she knew he would.

"Yeah . . . okay, that'd be great."

"We're all doing the best we can, Michael."

"I know you are," says Michael.

Both of them again thinking the same thing. What do you do when the best doesn't seem to be nearly enough?

14

Rats, rats, lousy, stinkin' rats!

Come quitting time, workers flee a building site like rodents from a sinking ship, thinks Leo, annoyed that today he's somehow been left to load his own tools onto his pickup truck, doubly annoyed because he usually manages his time better than this, making sure the job falls to someone else. Seniority and a bad back have their perks. But small annoyances are quickly forgotten as the Toyota Prius pulls to the curb in front of him and the driver gets out and smiles. It's that smile that turns your bones to jelly, the smile that he remembers so well.

"Well, look what the cat's drug by," says Leo.

"You still imbibe?" Anita asks, holding up a large thermos.

"Does the pope shit in the woods?" says Leo. "Ding-a-ling-a-ling! The drinking lamp is lit."

Five minutes later, they're sitting, legs dangling off what will be a rich man's back deck, Leo realizing that the slice of view might not show the ocean but that there is a breathtaking horizon. Anita has made her special tequila gimlets, Silver Patrón with Rose's lime juice, shaken with ice and strained into an honest-to-God real martini glass. No paper or plastic cup ever made good enough for Anita. Filling one to the brim, she hands it to him.

"Salud."

"What about you?"

"Not drinking these days."

"Oh. 'Cause I don't need to."

"Leo. Enjoy."

Leo sips and moans softly with pleasure. The drink is cold, smooth, and delicious. It is Leo's opinion that societies and religions that forbid drinking breed angry, aggressive men. What's worse, terrorists or alcoholics? It's probably a trade-off but Leo opts for the alcoholics as occasionally they can be amusing.

"So how you been?" asks Leo.

Off the cuff.

Anita shrugs and sips from a bottle of sparkling water. "Not great but no big deal. You?"

"Ah, you know. The good, the bad, the

ugly. Mostly pretty good though."

"You look good."

"Since when you like bearded fat guys?" says Leo.

Anita smiles. "I was talking about your soul, Leo." She refills his glass from the thermos, as Leo wonders when was the last time he felt this simple and content.

"How's Michael?"

Contentment vanishes to be replaced by caution. Leo sips, sucks the taste of lime off his tongue. How *is* Michael? For someone he's known for almost a third of his life and considers his closest friend, Leo realizes he isn't sure.

The kid comes wandering onto a building site one day, he's maybe nineteen or twenty, looking for work, anything. Usually Leo would tell him to beat it but the kid is strong looking and Leo has a no-show that day.

"You do drugs?" Leo asks.

"A little pot on occasion."

"You drink?"

"Little beer on occasion."

"What do you do more than on occasion?" Leo says.

"Surf."

"I don't like surfers. A ripple in the water, they don't show up."

"I surf at dawn and sunset."

Leo likes the kid. "You got a sense of humor?"

"Guy's walking his dog," says the kid. "He goes into a bar. The bartender sees him — hey, no dogs! It's a seeing-eye dog, the guy says, I'm blind. Since when is a Chihuahua a seeing-eye dog, says the bartender. Damn, says the guy, they gave me a Chihuahua?"

"Unload those bricks," says Leo, laughing. "Eight bucks an hour, we'll see if you last the day."

Michael did. He came back the next day. And the next. And the week after. Smart. Curious. Willing to do anything asked of him if you showed him how.

"I need to take the next couple of days off."

It had been three months.

"Why?" says Leo.

"There's a surf contest in Redondo Beach."

"Is there money?"

"Yeah."

"See you next Monday."

Michael had come back the following Monday with a huge grin and two hundred dollars and to celebrate bought a case of imported beer for the crew.

"You must be good," says Leo.

"Just okay," says Michael.

The next contest is local and on a cold, gray day, the temperature in the high fifties. Leo, who is allergic to bathing suits on the best of days, goes to watch. It blows him away. One moment a guy is like a floating head out in the water, the next he is up on his tiny board, screaming down the face of a wave, pirouetting at the bottom, cutting up, then down, back and forth, in constant motion, sometimes skating across the top of the wave, balanced on its cascading edge, one surfer actually going *under* the curl, then shooting out the side, some of them, including Michael, going up the face and taking off, turning an impossible 180 degrees in midair, Leo wondering if the board is attached to them or they to it, coming down, carving at the bottom, going back up to do it again, on and on. And they were tireless. Coming in, they'd immediately turn and, with hungry strokes, paddle out again through the heavy water as if it were a race to see how many rides they could get before they died of exhaustion.

"I have a sponsor."

It was a year later, Michael now up to fourteen an hour, and hearing the news, Leo felt like a proud older brother.

"What, you mean you don't want to do

drywall the rest of your life?"

That night they went out and got happily incoherent on curb shooters, Baileys floated in a shot glass of Bacardi 151. Michael introducing him to Anita who arrived around the second round, the two of them obviously crazy about each other.

"What'd you do," Leo said the next day, "to get a honey like that?"

"Lucky, I guess."

But as time passes, Leo wonders. Anita, moody to say the least. When around, usually attentive, smart-funny, and smiling, but then growing quiet and distant, then suddenly gone for days at a time, Michael miserable, knowing he shouldn't go to that place but beside himself with worry.

"It's a piece of crap."

Leo, shaking his head when Michael somehow got the mortgage on the bungalow.

"Yeah, but it's my piece of crap."

Leo had shrugged. "So we'll make it better."

Michael and Anita, now world travelers, Hawaii, Australia, South Africa, Fiji. Michael making modest bank, living the dream, but smart enough to be aware that it wouldn't last forever, that the time would come when he'd want a place to return to, not knowing that it'd be sooner than later, that like a ship running aground on a hidden reef, he would never see the rocks that shattered his knee and cracked his skull and put him in a coma for three days. Never dreaming that within two years it would all be over. A surfer who had lost his balance. A swimmer who, having been pulled from the ocean unconscious and half drowned, was now afraid of the water. Call it post-traumatic near death syndrome.

Leo was working on a site the day the pickup truck pulled up and Michael got out. He approached, limping.

"You do drugs?" Leo said.

"Any I can get."

"You drink?"

"Like a fish."

"You got a sense of humor?"

"A guy gets hit by a rock."

"And?"

"That's it."

"Unload those bricks," said Leo. "We'll see if you last a day."

Two and a half years later, Michael knowing more about contracting than Leo ever had. The following year, breaking away to start his own company, taking Leo with him, slow at first but then the projects getting bigger and better. And then in 2012 the local housing market nose-diving again, all of them scrambling ever since, sometimes up, sometimes down, never at rest.

"How is he?" says Leo. "Okay, I think."

This is a lie. Truth be known, Leo worries about Michael. A good guy who's been thrown too much with no breaks in between.

Including you.

"Work is good?"

"We're getting by," says Leo.

"And Jamie?" Anita not looking at him.

"You want the facts or you want my opinion?"

"Since when have I ever cared about facts, Leo?"

Never, thinks Leo.

That's the problem.

"I wouldn't trade Jamie for whatever a normal kid is if you asked me to," says Leo. He feels annoyed at the questions now. Time to ask his own questions. "What are you doin', Anita, huh? Not a word for I don't know how long and now you're back outta nowhere? I mean, you know I love you, and I appreciate the drink, but Jesus Christ."

It takes a moment for Anita to answer. "I want to matter again, Leo. Simple as that."

"He's not going to take you back, you know."

"You're sure?"

No, Leo is not sure. He is not sure what Michael will or will not do, and whatever it turns out to be, is not sure if it would be a good thing or a bad thing. When you get right down to it, Leo is not sure of much. Only that he cares about these people.

"He's seeing somebody."

If this is news to Anita, she doesn't let on. "What's she like?"

Leo shrugs. "I didn't say I'd met her, I just know he's seeing someone."

"How serious can it be if he hasn't introduced her to you?"

Leo laughs. "You kiddin'? She'd run for the hills she knows he has guys like me for friends."

"And exes like me."

They laugh together. They grow quiet together. Leo can see she's now in a different place, a different time, who's to say? Michael telling him once that Anita's silences often preceded bouts of depression. "What does *she* have to be depressed about?" Leo had asked.

"Neeta? You okay?"

"I won't fuck things up for him again, Leo. I promise."

The red-gold globe that is the sun is touching the horizon. In moments it will start to spread and melt like butter. Leo has been told that the sun itself is already below the horizon, that a sunset is merely refracted light, subject to air particles and altitude, that in its own way, it's a mirage and that a mirage can be shaped by the mind.

"Hey, you ever seen a green flash?"

"Only in a glass," says Anita, pouring the last of the gimlet into Leo's drink.

"Australian Aborigines," says Leo, "consider it good luck. Success, good fortune, that kinda stuff."

"I never knew that," says Anita.

" 'Course not, I'm making it the hell up."

They belly-laugh sweet. Making Anita laugh is like being kissed, thinks Leo. He toasts the horizon. Tequila touched with lime. "Come on, green flash."

"Oh, *yeah.*"

15

Fari appears at the front door wearing faded Levi's jeans, a man's white button-down cotton shirt, and a tweed jacket not dissimilar to the one Michael owns but that on her seems tailored and stylish. It's a look that he likes, one she doesn't mind wearing for him, and besides, she is of the opinion that with expensive shoes and a good leather belt, one can get away with anything. They take her car, one of the smaller BMW sedans, fire-engine red with a manual transmission. Michael drives, enjoying the stick shift and the handling.

They meet for the first time when Fari hits him while parallel parking. The car is new to her and she is trying to reverse into a space, backing in, coming out, backing in again, trying to no avail to get close to the curb. Exasperated, she gives up, puts it in first, glances in the side-view mirror, and inadvertently popping the clutch, lurches forward into the street. She sees the man in front of her just in time to frantically hit the brakes, but still, he is knocked back off his feet onto the pavement. She shrieks as the car shudders once and stalls. And then she is out the door, sure she's killed or maimed him, that she will go to jail or be sued, that a moment ago everything was one way and now it's irrevocably another. She kneels, her hands fluttering over him. He is alive, thank God, his eyes are open. She tells him not to move, that it's all her fault, she wasn't looking, that she has insurance, is he all right, is he all right?

"I'm so sorry, I'm sorry, are you *all right*?!"

"What?" he says.

It is only then that she realizes she is babbling in Farsi, that under duress, English, her second language, has flown the coop.

"It's okay," the man says. "No harm done, I'm fine, really." He starts to rise.

"No, you shouldn't," she says. "You shouldn't move."

"Why not?" the man says.

"You might be hurt," she says.

"I'm not," the man insists. "You were hardly moving."

"I was trying to park," Fari says. It sounds feeble and terribly incompetent. People are stopping to look. It's all horrible. "I didn't see you."

"I know that, it's okay," the man says as if talking to a child. "Now if you let me get up, I'll get in my truck and you can have my space."

"No," Fari says, sitting back. "I'm finished."

A week later they run into each other in the produce section of the local supermarket. He is pushing a cart. She carries a basket.

"Hey, how you doing?" he says, as if pleased to see her. She is disquieted but tries to be polite.

"I should be asking you that question."

"Black-and-blue," Michael says, his hand brushing his rear end. "I should sue." Her heart skips a beat. "Hey," he says. "Akrapeedie. What is that?"

What? How is it possible he knows her name? And then she remembers. Her business card. She gave it to him. Wrote her home number down on the back and, though he protested, the name of her insurance company as well.

"Akrepede," she says, pronouncing it correctly for him. "It's Iranian." His name is Michael, she now remembers. Michael Hodge.

"Really? Cool." He seems genuinely delighted. Why he should be, she has no idea. "But your accent, it sounds sort of English."

"I studied there. In London."

"Psychology."

"Yes." She's feeling more and more out of her comfort zone. She doesn't like or trust things that happen by chance. Planning and knowing what to expect is important to her. "It was nice to see you." She starts to turn away.

"Hey, there's a Starbucks up front, you want to grab a quick cup of coffee?"

For the first time she realizes he's not wearing a wedding ring. And that he's attractive and very masculine. And they are comparable in age and that he's been flirting with her.

"Or a smoothie. There's a smoothie place," he says.

She wonders if he makes a habit of picking up strange women in supermarkets. She is suddenly concerned that she is coming across as the kind of woman who could be. Smoothie suddenly has sexual connotations.

"Or you could hit me with your car again," he says.

She feels herself almost smile. And immediately feels vulnerable. "Thank you but I really have to go."

"No problem. Next time." He doesn't seem let down. "Good to see you. Happy shopping."

She finds herself mildly disappointed when he turns away.

She's getting into her car when she sees him across the parking lot, transferring his groceries from the cart to the rear of a pickup truck. On sudden impulse, she closes the door of the little Bimmer. She tells herself that it's merely courtesy as she crosses the lot toward him, moving between the parked cars. Nothing more than a friendly gesture. He looks up as she approaches. Again, he seems pleased to see her. Good.

"Hey. What's up?"

"Um . . . actually I think I do have time for some coffee . . . if you're still available."

He glances at his watch. She notices now that it is an old Rolex, one with a leather strap. Similar to the one her father wears.

"Afraid I'm sort of committed to getting home now."

She feels embarrassed. She shouldn't have done this.

"But how about some other time," Michael says.

"Oh. All right. Yes." She's trying to sound

as casual about it as he does and is sure she's failing. Eight years as a practicing therapist, advising and providing support for emotionally dysfunctional people. How can it be that she is as mortified by the rituals of dating as any teenager? But of course, this isn't going to be any kind of date. She's being polite, that's all.

"How about this weekend?"

"I'll have to check my schedule," she says, knowing she has nothing going on. "Let me give you my home number."

"You already did."

He calls and they arrange to go to dinner. She dresses carefully, changing outfits several times. She likes clothes and knows she has a tendency to overdress. He doesn't seem the formal type. She settles on dark slim pants and a cashmere blazer, what to her is a casual look. A good thing because he arrives wearing jeans, flip-flops, and a garish Hawaiian shirt. She has never been in a pickup truck before.

Michael takes her to a place she's never heard of and wishes she'd known about, a French bistro, only moderately expensive and very authentic. He is a contractor, a builder of houses, he says. A laborer, she thinks. He once surfed professionally, he says. She hadn't known one could do such a thing. She tries not to be taken aback when he tells her he's never been to college. He seems bright enough. He tells her he grew up locally, that he is divorced, and that he has a son who lives with him. He asks about her family. She tells him they are still in Iran, that her father is — *was* — a professor of political science and her mother, a published poet. If he's curious as to why she isn't with them, he doesn't inquire. Instead, he asks what brought her to California. She tells him that Southern California has one of the largest Iranian populations outside of Iran, that in fact Los Angeles is known as "Tehrangeles" because, like the capital of Iran, it is a mountain-ringed, traffic-plagued, smog-filled bowl. That's the long answer. The short answer is she received her doctorate in psychology at UCLA and did her clinical training in Orange County.

When he orders a second glass of wine, she hesitates but then joins him. The waiter leaves the bottle.

She decides to be honest up front and tells him that she is married and that her husband, like her family, is back in Iran. Must be tough, he says, long distance. She shrugs. She quickly changes the subject.

Her sole amandine is delicious. Michael shares the *pommes frites* that come with his steak au poivre. Afterward she asks for a cappuccino. Michael orders coffee. They split a piece of flourless chocolate cake. The wine bottle is empty. "I could go for one more glass," he says. They end up splitting another bottle. Much to her annoyance he has paid the entire bill when she returns from the ladies' room.

One moment he is opening the passenger door of his truck so she can get in, the next they are up against the cab, glued together as if they haven't had enough food for dinner. It is the wine, she vaguely thinks as he touches her belly, her breasts, blame it on the wine. With his hand resting on her thigh, she feels as if she's on the verge of orgasm all the way home. They fuck in the entryway, barely over the threshold, not even taking the time to get their clothes off, Michael's pants around his ankles, she still in one leg of her designer slacks. She comes, crying out, before he does. A whore, she thinks, a whore. Somehow they make it to the bedroom before beginning again.

Tonight Michael takes her to a movie. He, of course, likes action movies. Superheroes and sci-fi. Raging, giant Tinkertoys in 3-D.

121

The more flying bullets the better. But he knows that she finds them all the same, sometimes tolerable but rarely thrilling, that she likes the independent and foreign films, the ones where the characters actually talk to one another. And so they trade off. Tonight it's her turn.

This one is about a family, made by a famous Iranian director living in exile. All Michael knows is that it is subtitled and serious, not bad enough to want to leave but not good enough yet to ignore the popcorn. "Is that really what they're saying?" he asks. On-screen, a man with burning eyes is whispering intensely and at length to a homely woman in a burka. The subtitles seem to only cover a third of the conversation.

"Shush," says Fari.

"You have a large bottom and are in need of a shave."

"*Sshh!*" Fari hisses again. But she smiles despite herself. She would never tell him but she likes his sense of humor. She likes the fact that he isn't afraid to be silly, that he will make himself the butt of his own jokes. Laughter is medicine for the soul, she tells patients. She is suddenly impatient for the movie to be over. When they get back to her house, they will make love. For it is lovemaking now. She is finally able to *look* at Michael. In the beginning, embarrassed for him to see her face, she would want to be taken from behind. Now she likes to be on top, looking down at him. Fuck me, Michael, she whispers to him in Farsi, safe because he doesn't understand. I love your cock. I love your finger in my ass. A whore, she thinks. A whore. But at least one who cooks.

"What are you looking at?" Fari asks, knowing he is looking at her, trying not to be pleased that he is. They are in the kitchen. A mix of ground lamb and vegetables fills a frying pan. She pushes at it with a fork, making sure it doesn't burn. It will be served over rice. She feels relaxed and content. Sated. Smetimes she forgets herself.

"You," says Michael. "You're something."

He is sitting at the kitchen table, watching her. Has been for a while now. Fari wears a green velvet dressing gown, beautiful against her dark skin. Michael is shirtless. She never thought she would find a man's body so attractive. He sips his wine. It's a white Sancerre that she's introduced him to, telling him it was first cultivated by the Romans in the first century AD. Amazing the things

123

she knows.

"The movie was good."

"You seemed bored."

"Only at first. It picked up halfway through."

"Next time we'll go see something you want."

She fills two plates and brings them to the table. It is already set. She sits. They begin to eat.

"Is it really like that? Like in the movie?"

"We had a house similar to that one. Relatives would come over. My parents liked to entertain and had many friends. People in this country don't realize that those that are different from them can also be happy."

"Heard from'm lately?"

Meaning her family. He asks this often and is always surprised that she hasn't. There is something naïve about it. Something American. As if the definition of family is constant contact. Fari shakes her head. "They call my sister, not me." Her sister is in London, married to an English-Iranian businessman whose family got out with the fall of the shah. Michael knows this.

"So what about your husband?"

It seems to come out of nowhere. It is something they almost never talk about and now they are.

"What about him?"

"Heard from *him*?"

"Why would I?"

"He's your husband."

"Michael, let's just eat, shall we?"

"No, really, I'd like to know."

Fari hesitates. The truth or not the truth. Why not both? "He is unsettled by what I've become."

"What have you become?"

"Michael, really, this isn't the time or place."

But he's not to be dissuaded. "No, look, I'm serious. If he's, what — so *unsettled* — why would he wait for you? Why wouldn't he just move on? Why don't you?"

Fari looks at Michael. His face so heartfelt and earnest. He should know better than this. Or should he? She has never told him that it was an arranged marriage. She was called home from London. It was strongly suggested that Reza Shahpour, the son of a prominent cleric, would make a good husband for her. He was a man, it was implied, looking for the respectable label of marriage, but not the responsibilities. Nothing would change. Her life would go on. Still, she remembers looking at her father through tears of disappointment. The man who had sent her out into the world, the man who

125

insisted on the importance of education, was now sentencing her to something else. Only later, well after she'd gone through with the marriage and then quickly fled, did she consider the pressure he was under, struggling to hold on to his job at the university, his livelihood, his very identity.

"I do not move on because he is my husband" is what she says to Michael. "And he doesn't, because I am his wife. Nothing can change that."

"Yeah," says Michael. "Funny how that works."

"Meaning what?" She feels annoyed now, angry that he's ruining the evening.

"Meaning mine's come home."

The kitchen suddenly seems very small to her. "You told me you were divorced, Michael." He is no longer looking at her. She wishes he would.

"We are. Just not on paper yet."

"I don't understand."

"We were together for nine years. We got married just before Jamie was born. I came home one day, she'd dropped him off at my mother's. Left a note saying she needed some time to get things straight in her head. That was almost seven years ago."

Fari feels oddly offended that a wife and mother could do such a thing. Ridiculous and unprofessional. She has spent years studying that people are capable of anything. "Never in touch?"

"A couple of those phone calls late at night. You answer, no one says anything. You hear breathing on the other end. I'm pretty sure it was her."

He seems so matter-of-fact about it.

You're dissembling, Michael. How do you really feel?

"So both of us are married," Fari says. As if needing to confirm it to herself.

"Mmm," says Michael. "Convenient, isn't it."

He feels tense and agitated on the ride home. What should have been an opportunity for communication turned into one long lapsed conversation.

"I'm sure you have a busy day tomorrow."

"I can stay longer if you'd like."

"No. You should probably get going."

He has never once spent the entire night in her bed. Has never been invited, has never asked to.

"Next week then."

"If you find a sitter."

We'll cross that bridge when we come to it.

Well, they haven't. And given the opportunity tonight, they didn't. Maybe because there is no bridge to cross. Maybe there never was and never will be. They're different people. Different backgrounds, different tastes, different expectations. She leans toward the formal, he toward casual. On more than one occasion he has felt stupid in her presence, has wondered if she wasn't quietly analyzing him, judging him and finding him lacking. She doesn't seem to realize that he's traveled the world, has surfed on eight continents, knows beaches and airports intimately . . . and yes, okay, knows next to nothing of other countries and other cultures. Which, hey, makes him a standard, run-of-the-mill American.

Which should be good enough.

Other than in their lovemaking, she holds herself at a distance. Keeps secrets. But then so does he.

Since her, there has only been you.

Michael is on the verge of turning and going back when he is aware of the siren behind him. He looks in the rearview mirror and sees the flashing lights. He pulls to the side of the deserted boulevard and the fire truck flies past, heading south. The sound of the siren fades. The lights diminish in the distance. And in that moment, Michael *knows*. He pushes the pedal to the floor. Within a quarter of a mile, the fire truck is in his sights again. He slows just slightly, praying it won't turn, and of course it does.

Left.

His mother's neighborhood.

16

The house is burning.

Michael drives up the hill as far as he can and then abandons the truck and sprints the rest of the way. It's worse than he could have ever imagined. Flames have burst through the windows and are eating their way upward into the shake roof. The inside of the house is an inferno. Neighbors stand in clustered groups, stunned and watching as the firemen leap out of the truck and into action. "Back!" one shouts. "Back! We need everyone back!" He turns, looking hardly older than a teenager, as Michael pushes his way through the spectators.

"This is my mother's house," Michael shouts. "My mother and my son are in there!"

The fireman turns and shouts toward the burning house, to whom Michael isn't even sure.

"This guy says we have two people! Two

people are in there!"

Present tense. Not were. *Are.*

The fireman turns back to Michael. "Sir," he says, as if reading Michael's mind. "Stay here. The only way to help us is to let us do our jobs." He waits a moment to see that Michael understands and then moves quickly away to join his fellow firefighters. Men are already on a heavy hose. Where the fog of water hits flame, steam hisses and billows. The cone of water moves and the flames crackle up again. They might as well be spitting on it.

"Jamie!" Michael screams. "Jamie!"

No. Got to go in, I've got to —

He jerks away from the sudden touch on his arm. He turns, vaguely recognizes the face. An older man, from down the hill, yes, that's it.

"Over there," the man says. He turns, pointing.

Across the street, surrounded by neighbors, a dazed-looking Penelope is sitting on the ground with a blanket around her. The dog Abigail lies panting at her side. Jamie is behind her, walking back and forth, head turned away, hands agitated and flapping. Penelope weakly raises an arm.

"Michael —"

He runs to them. Not fast enough. His

legs aren't moving right. He stumbles crossing the asphalt, barely regains his balance. And then he's there, at last, falling to the grass, to hug her, rising to pull Jamie to him, trembling.

"It's okay," he mumbles. "It's okay, I'm here."

Across the street, the firemen spray water and foam to no avail. Inside the house something crashes as it gives way and the flames leap toward the sky.

"Mowgli," says Jamie. "Mowgli lit the fire. And everything burned."

Four distinct phases define the navigation process. The navigator must choose methods appropriate to each situation. Each method has advantages and disadvantages. None is effective in all situations.

I. Inland Waterway Phase: Piloting in narrow canals, channels, rivers, and estuaries.

17

"Well, this can be fixed."

Leo has always prided himself on his subtle sense of sarcasm. The house is burned nearly to the foundations, hardly even a shell, and he and Michael stand in the midst of it, staring at the collapsed roof and the remnants of walls, at gray ash, at shards of half-melted pipe and cable, at seared and peeling plaster, and at the blackened brick of the still-standing chimney. The melted bones of what was Penelope's old Chrysler sits on the darkened slab of what was a garage floor. Michael kicks at a piece of charred wood that once was a kitchen chair. The sweet, wet smell of smoke and burned rubber and insulation is everywhere.

"Any idea how it started?" asks Leo.

"She put water on for tea," says Michael.

"Tea is flammable?"

"She forgot about it."

The loss of her house has overnight made Penelope an old woman. After two nights in the hospital for observation, Michael, along with Jamie, brings her home. She gets out of the pickup slowly and with difficulty. Michael is carrying some shopping bags of clothes donated by sympathetic neighbors. It's as if there's been a death in the family except people have been dropping off dresses, shoes, shirts, and slacks as opposed to casseroles and pies.

When they enter the bungalow, Penelope looks around, uncertain and confused, as if she's never been here before. She brightens as the dog, Abigail, hurries in from the living room, its entire body wagging in relief and delight. "Oh, *there* you are," murmurs Penelope, putting her hands tenderly under the dog's muzzle. "Are you my beauty?"

"Abbie missed you, Nana," says Jamie.

"Yes, but she was in very good hands with you, my darling." Penelope gives Jamie a quick hug. "My hero." She has told Michael more than once that it was Jamie who woke her, coming to her on the couch, pushing and prodding and insisting. It was Jamie who got them from the burning house.

"Come on," says Michael. "We'll put your stuff in the bedroom."

They enter the small guest room that is

most often used as a jack-of-all-trades work space, Michael immediately realizing that in his haste to get her home and settled, he hasn't even thought to clean. There is a pile of wrinkled clothes on the unmade bed, an ironing board, a barbell and dumbbells, seldom if ever used, off to the side, and cardboard file boxes in the corner. The desk with its old computer and bulky CRT monitor is covered with dust. Michael's not sure the last time he ran a vacuum in here.

"We're gonna get it all fixed up for you."

"Of course we will. This is going to be quite divine." Penelope looks around and then, as if her body has become too heavy for her, sits down on the bare mattress. The dog jumps up next to her and settles in and she absently strokes its head.

"I'll get rid of the, uh . . ." Michael gestures vaguely at the weights.

"Please," says Penelope. "I doubt I'll be using them."

"Luis, I have to ask you two questions."

As Michael and Leo examine the foundation, Luis surveys the scorched earth of what was the backyard. Jamie, whom Michael has brought along, is right beside him. For some unknown reason, Jamie has always adored Luis, and Luis, though he'd never admit it, enjoys the boy's company. With Jaimito, you never know what you'll get next, and whatever it is, it's never boring.

"What questions?" says Luis, his voice deep as a bellows. The kid is *always* asking him questions.

"Does your penis have a hat?"

Saludo. What the fuck? Luis looks down at the little *chico* who is staring up at him, very serious, waiting for the answer. Luis is reminded of the time he was doing some work at Michael's house and Jamie, naked as *un duende,* after following him around all day, asked to accompany him to the dump. Luis had shrugged. What did he care? It was only when pulling into the Miramar Landfill with its circling trucks and the smell of unburied garbage in his nose that Luis realized the situation he'd put himself in. A very large Mexican with a moustache and Aztec tattoos, riding in a battered pickup with a bare-ass, five-year-old *rubio* next to him in the front seat? Never mind his Tijuana plates, if pulled over he was prison fodder, no questions asked. Luis turned the hell around and got the naked rug rat home fast. And now the boy is asking him about the *prepucio* on his *pene.* His own children wouldn't do such a thing. His own children ignore him completely. Maybe that's why he likes this one.

"Siguiente pregunta," says Luis. "Next question."

"What's your favorite ice cream?" says Jamie.

Good. This one he can answer. *"Almendra,"* says Luis. "Almond. Now, no more questions."

It's a shame about the house. But it's good that the old woman has her son to take her in. From what Luis can tell, most white people don't have the support system of extended families, no uncles or cousins or nieces, no multiple brothers and sisters, no *bisabuelos* to turn to for guidance and to commiserate with. Luis has never understood why people would only have one kid. You have six or seven there's a chance at least one of them is going to turn out okay and that's the one that will take care of you in your old age. This is not to say relatives can't be a pain in the ass. His second cousin, Ramon, is a *pendejo,* selling his dope and, when not in jail, sitting on his ass in the living room, letting his mother wait on him. And according to his crazy sister Connie, Luis's niece Jennifera sees dead people. Still. There are bonds in blood. You look into a face, you see something of your own.

■ ■ ■ ■

"So where's she stand on insurance?" asks Leo, kicking at what might be the remains of the dining room table. In Leo's experience, *no one* has enough home insurance. They go for the minimum, thinking catastrophes will only happen to other property owners, never to them. This is why Leo rents.

"She doesn't have any," says Michael.

Leo grimaces. Old people are the worst. They assume they'll be dead before any kind of disaster hits. "I thought you gave her money."

"She spent it on bulbs."

Lightbulbs?

"Flowers, Leo."

"Oh. Any insurance on them?"

"No, I think we're pretty much screwed here."

Something catches Michael's eye. He picks it up. The silver frame has been blackened and twisted by the heat. The glass is broken. Half the photo is gone. The bride — Penelope — has been burned away. All that's left is the singed but still smiling uniformed groom — his father.

"I want it."

Michael turns. Jamie has quietly approached. His eyes are on the broken silver frame and smudged black-and-white image within.

"Not much here, little man."

"It's what's left."

Out of the mouths of babes. Michael hands Jamie the frame and photo.

"Hold on to it. We'll get it all cleaned up for you."

"We need new pictures."

"We'll take some."

Michael's heart suddenly feels lighter. Things were lost but, given time, things can be replaced. People can't. His mother and son are still here to take bad photos of. As are others. He hasn't called her yet but he will. They'll cross the bridge.

Like his son, he wants this.

18

"Bebe! Everett! No running!"

Anita, in an old, too-small bikini scavenged from a bureau drawer, is sunning by the pool when her younger sister arrives. Beth comes across the dark slate pavement stones of the upper terrace, preceded by two children in swimsuits and followed well behind by a skinny, scowling older boy who wears a T-shirt and baggy jams that fall below his knees. The two children come in a noisy rush down the steps and run straight into the water — boom — splash.

"Dammit!" says Beth. "Did I or did I not say —"

"Ah! Momma, it's cold!"

"Too bad! Jonathan, watch your brother and sister!"

"Mom!" the older boy whines.

"And you can change your attitude or lose computer privileges for the weekend."

"It's not fair!" The boy throws himself into

a lounge chair. "I don't even want to *be* here."

"Well, you are, so deal with it."

Beth drops towels and bags and plops down onto the recliner next to Anita. Leaning back and closing her eyes, she moans as if exhausted. "God, I love my life," she says.

"Hi to you as well." In the pool, the kids are seemingly trying to drown each other. "Which is which here?"

Beth points. "Bebe. Everett."

"Can they swim?"

"Christ, I hope so. I have no intention of going in after them."

Anita smiles. Her sister is funny. Sarcastic, sharp, and self-deprecating, almost always making you laugh as she tells you the truth. Hers was the vocal equivalent of not blinking an eyelash when Anita called her on the phone.

"I'm home for a while."

"Good. 'Cause it really *sucks* around here."

Beth takes off her wide-brimmed straw hat and shakes out her hair. Unlike Anita, she is fair skinned with the freckles and strawberry-blond hair of their father. She slips out of the light jacket she's wearing and settles back. Never entirely comfortable with her body, she wears a one-piece bathing suit.

"Sunscreen?" asks Anita.

"No, I think I'll get a nice burn today."

There's a cooler next to the lounge chair and Anita grabs a bottle of Corona beer, opens it, and hands it to her sister. Beth takes it. Anita is pleased to see that Beth's nails, though short, are neatly filed. When her sister was a little girl they were usually bitten to the bloody quick.

"You look terrific by the way."

"I look like Jabba the Hutt with three kids."

"How's Bob?"

"Still working for Dad down at the bank. We're in debt up to our assholes."

"I see Mom's still on the Jesus kick."

"You haven't had to live with it."

"The health food thing is new."

"Mom gives botulism a good name." Beth sits up in her lounge chair. "Jonathan, you're not watching!"

"Yes I am!"

"No you're not. You're staring at your aunt's tits."

"Mom!" Outraged, the boy turns away, his face turning crimson. "You're such an asshole!"

"Takes one to know one." Beth settles back in the lounge chair. "You believe he talks like that to his mother?"

"Where do they get it from?" says Anita, feigning dismay.

"Not from his father," says Beth, her voice saying she wishes he did. UCLA Bob. Bruin Bob. Bland, boring, dependable Robert Black whom Beth met in Westwood sophomore year and whom everybody likes. Her sister, Anita knows, secretly covets leather-clad rock stars and tattooed, muscled bikers and has serious fantasies about engaging one of each in a torrid threesome.

"Speaking not of which," says Anita, drinking some bottled water, "when did you get the boob job?" It's true. The bathing suit, though modest, emphasizes her sister's newly ample chest.

"Just keeping up with the Kardashians." Beth sounds just a touch defensive. "There's nothing wrong with it."

"Didn't say there was," says Anita.

"You always had great boobs," says Beth. "You still do."

"Yours weren't so bad."

"Now they're better." Eyes closed, Beth puts her head back, happy now. Anita reaches out and takes her sister's hand in her own. "Love you, Bethie," she says.

"Missed you, Neets," Beth replies.

"Family dinner, huh?"

"Gee, maybe Dad will make martinis."

19

"I don't like this!!!"

Sitting at the head of the long dining room table, with a squat cocktail glass of ice and Tanqueray at his fingertips, Neal Beacham takes inventory of his family and, once again, finds it wanting. His granddaughter, called Bebe of all the goddamn things, is squalling as his daughter Beth, who has the mothering skills of an egg-laying reptile, cuts her food. His younger grandson, Everett, is making train noises — "Choo-choo-choo-choo!" — while his older grandson, Jonathan, sulks and pushes food around his plate. His wife's dog, the latest in a long line of pathetic rescue mutts, has its head between the two younger children, hungry for scraps, while Beth's boob of a husband, Bob, whom Neal is forced to suffer at work every day, wolfs his food and stares longingly across the table at his son Neal Beacham Jr.'s latest girlfriend, a voluptuous, blue-streaked blond Barbie doll, who, for some goddamn reason, is eating with chopsticks. Neal Jr., who at the age of thirty-what is it again? still tends *bar* for a living, and as all know, lives in a *condo* provided for him by his parents, is talking popular culture of all the goddamn things, with his mother, seemingly forgetting that Tisha is about as interested in popular culture as she is in sex, which — at least with Neal Beacham — is not at all. And then there's Anita. With all his wife's cold, tensile strength but none of her propriety. Back home, arriving with no word of warning, from who knows where. Anita, who keeps looking at him, studying him, as if with her unsettling gaze she can read his mind and, in doing so, finds what's written there wanting. His wife is constantly telling Neal Beacham that drinking makes him angry and volatile. His wife is full of it. It's not drinking that pisses him off, it's the people he's forced to drink with.

"Well, I thought it was a very *original* movie," says Neal Jr. Anita, serving herself from a bowl of sauced vegetables held by the longtime Mexican housekeeper, Maria, feels that if there's one thing the family all agrees on it's that her brother, a pleasant-looking hybrid of his parents with Tisha's blond hair and Neal's broad features, has never had an original idea in his life.

"I know what it is," says Tisha. "And it's trash."

"How can you say that when you haven't seen it?"

"I don't need to see it. It's nothing but violence and nudity. That's all there is these days."

"Can *I* see it?" says Jonathan, his first words all evening.

"You can shut up," says Beth.

"Honey," says Bruin Bob, as if pained. "Don't tell the boy to shut up."

"Oh, shut up," says Beth, scowling and reaching for the red wine.

"Well, Kayden and I saw it," says Neal Jr. "We liked it, didn't we, Kay?"

"It had a certain grounded energy to it." The girl, Kayden, has a gentle, sonorous voice that belies her dyed hair and hourglass figure. "These vegetables are delicious, by the way."

"Thank you," says Tisha. "So few people appreciate vegetables in this house."

"So few people appreciate *anything* in this house," says Beth.

"Beth," intones Tisha Beacham, frowning in disapproval.

149

"Kidding, Mom," says Beth, trying to smile but wincing. And drinking. Glug-glug.

"What the hell did you say your name was?" Neal Beacham, his food still untouched, is now eyeballing Kayden from his end of the table. Kayden, a mascara-eyed raccoon caught in yard lights, blinks uncertainly at Neal Jr.

"Kayden," says Neal Jr., his mouth full and his brain in neutral. "Dad, this is Kayden."

"Why the hell isn't she eating with proper utensils like everybody else?"

"Kay likes to use chopsticks, Dad, and a lot of places don't have chopsticks, so she brings her own."

"Use not knives at table lest you be reminded of the slaughterhouse," adds Kayden, as if quoting a pleasant proverb.

"On that note, pass the steak," says Beth.

"I think it's damn rude," says Neal Beacham.

"Neal," says Tisha Beacham, "I think *you're* the one being rude."

"We all know what *you* think," growls Neal Beacham, draining his glass.

"Kayden," says Bruin Bob, the subject of the new dinner guest now broached, "you look familiar. Have we met before?"

"I don't think so," Kayden says brightly.

"But it certainly is possible."

"Kay's a dancer," says Neal Jr., spearing another potato from the bowl. "She's done Vegas, Miami, Atlanta, Dallas."

"Ballet?" asks Tisha Beacham, the only adult at the table not to recognize a stripper when they see one.

"Modern," says Kayden, the only adult at the table who takes the question seriously.

"Gee, why don't you give us a show after dinner, *Kay,*" says Beth. "Maybe Bob will remember where you met."

"C'mon, Beth," murmurs Bob.

"I don't understand," says Kayden, suddenly alarmed.

"Don't worry, we're being silly," says Anita, feeling sorry for her. She is reminded of some mind-numbing, highly acclaimed play she saw some years ago where a dysfunctional Oklahoma family carved up the curtains, the carpets, and one another. Amateurs, all of them.

"Oh, for the love of Jeez — what the hell is this?" At the end of the table, Maria has brought the serving bowl to Neal Beacham and he is staring down into the dish as if it's toxic sludge.

"Ratatouille," says Tisha. "If you don't like it, don't ruin it for everybody else."

"Get it away," says Neal Beacham. "Get it away!"

"Gracias, Maria," Anita calls as the woman, serving now done, retreats gratefully to the kitchen to wash dishes.

"I swear," says Tisha Beacham, trying to make it sound amusing, "your father's been so grumpy ever since Dr. Brady told him he needed to lower his cholesterol."

"When was that, Mom," says Beth. "Thirty years ago?"

"Beth, you're not funny," says Tisha.

"I'm kidding, Mom," says Beth. "Don't you know kidding when you hear *kidding*?"

"Don't grit your teeth at me, Beth."

"They're my teeth and I'll grit if I want to. Do you have a *problem* with that?"

"Say, how's the golf game, Daddy-Neal?" says Bruin Bob, trying to divert his wife.

"Jesus Christ, do not call me that," snarls Neal Beacham.

"People at this table," says Tisha, her voice like ice, "will stop taking the Lord's name in vain."

"Hah!" says Neal Beacham, rising and moving to the sideboard, where gin and olives await. "Don't bother talking to me if you're going to talk to me like that."

"Neets," says Neal Jr., still oblivious to anything but his food. "You hear your mother-in-law's house burned down?"

Anita blinks, trying to hide her dismay. "No. When?"

"Sometime the end of last week. It was in the paper."

"What started it?"

"She did," says Neal Jr. "I hear she's losing it." He whistles the theme from *The Twilight Zone* as he waves a finger near his ear — cuckoo-cuckoo.

"That's not nice, Neal," says Tisha.

Neal Jr. frowns at the reprimand. "Why? You never liked her. You didn't say two words to her at Neet's wedding."

"So? She hardly said two words to me at mine," says Beth.

"Beth, I am *warning* you —"

"I am *kidding*!" Beth's voice rises shrilly. "For Christ's sake, Mother, do you know what *kidding* is —"

"And you will not take the Lord's name in —"

"Oh, for the love of — the dog, the dog, the goddamn —" At the head of the table, Neal Beacham is waving, his head turned away in disgust. Midway down the table, Bebe has offered her dinner plate to her canine dinner companion. Food spills to the floor as the dog frantically gobbles.

"Bambi!" yells Beth. "You little shit!" Half

153

rising from her chair, she swipes at the dog. She succeeds only in toppling her full wineglass off the table into her daughter's lap. Bebe drops her plate to the floor and begins to howl.

"Beth, that was *not* Bambi's fault," says Tisha, glaring at her husband's back.

"Oh, really? Then *you* clean it up!" says Beth.

"Beth, it's okay," says Bruin Bob. "Calm down."

"Shut up, Bob! If you can't stand up for me, keep your big mouth shut!"

"I hate dinner here!" screeches Jonathan, his second utterance all evening. "I *hate* it!"

"You little —" Spinning, Beth slaps him across the face.

"Beth!" says Bruin Bob, half rising. "We don't hit!"

"Shutup! Shutup-shutup-shutup!" shrieks Beth, and throwing her napkin at her husband, she turns and runs sobbing toward the kitchen.

"Momma!" cries Bebe, as if abandoned.

"Ahhh!" screams Everett, not to be outdone.

"I have had enough of this idiocy," says Neal Beacham, and glass in hand, he exits toward the living rom.

"Where *has* Maria disappeared to?" says

154

Tisha Beacham, eyeing the table stain and her husband's retreating back with disapproval.

"Are you people always like this?" murmurs Kayden, staring quietly down at her plate.

"Actually this has been one of the better evenings," says Bruin Bob, instantly regreting it.

"So how long you around for, Neets?" says Neal Jr., blithely contemplating leftovers.

"I might be staying," says Anita. "For good."

Silence hits the table like a shrouded rock. Sensing something momentous, even the kids stop their whimpering.

"Well . . ." says Tisha. "Isn't this good news."

"Yeah, but . . . what are you going to do?" says Neal Jr., as if doubtful his sister can do anything.

"I'm not sure yet."

"If you're looking for a job, I know the club is hiring," says Kayden, trying to be helpful.

All find it more than a bit rude that Anita is laughing uncontrollably as she puts down her napkin, rises from her chair, and leaves the room.

20

"How was your day?" asks Penelope, carefully drying a plate.

Michael's not sure if it's dementia kicking in but this seems to be how every conversation begins of late, often more than several times in the course of an evening. It's enough to make him lament the lack of a working dishwasher, not because he's averse to washing dishes by hand but because Penelope, since moving in, now feels it's her duty to dry them. She has him trapped.

Through the doorway, he can see Jamie and Abigail on the living room floor watching *Toy Story* together. It's as if they've taken their space in Penelope's house and transferred it here. The dog is adapting to its new home better than its owner.

"I already told you, my day was fine, Mom. How was your day?"

"Inconvenient," says Penelope, not looking up from the plate in her hands.

This is another thing that's newly disconcerting. His mother has always had the ability to carry on a conversation singlehandedly and at length. Single-word answers and doleful silences now hang uncomfortably in the air. Michael brought home packets of flower seeds today. Impatiens and alyssum and sweet peas. She smiled once and then ignored them.

The doorbell rings, surprising them both.

"Hi," she says.

Anita wears jeans, a sweatshirt, and worn leather Rainbow sandals. Her blond hair is pulled back and she has her arms wrapped around herself as if she's cold. She looks pale and nervous in the light of the deck.

"Sorry to drop by like this but I had to get out of the house. Y'know, one of *those* evenings." She tries to smile. "You've been there."

He has. Still, he says nothing. He waits.

"Michael, I was wondering if I could . . ." She glances past him, as if trying to look inside. "You know . . ."

Like this? Michael wonders.

Like this?

"I just want to see him. I won't stay long."

Why not like this?

Michael steps back and Anita enters. She

looks around as if recognizing old dust motes in the air. She glances toward the kitchen. Penelope peers back at her, an alarmed look on her face.

"Hi, Pen. Sorry to hear about your house."

Penelope nods and quickly retreats. Anita winces slightly. "Mmm. I'd say the cat's got her tongue but she's a dog person."

"He's in the living room," says Michael, ignoring the subject of his mother. He gestures toward the entryway. Anita steps forward and cranes her head around the door frame to look. She stops when she sees him across the room. The slender shoulders. The tumble of fair hair. The eyes that are hers.

"Hold it." Her mouth is suddenly dry. "He's so big," Anita whispers.

"He's almost eight," says Michael.

She nods. No need to tell him that the knowledge and the reality are two different things.

"Okay."

Michael goes first, Anita behind him. On the TV, Buzz Lightyear is at the top of a stairwell, ready to either fly or fall. Michael picks up the remote and turns off the TV.

Jamie starts to protest. "Dad —"

"Jamie. Someone's here to see you."

Anita steps forward. "Hello, Jamie," she

says. She tries desperately to smile. Jamie stares at her as if puzzled. And then recognition — or is it realization? — hits his face.

"No," Jamie says. "No!" He jumps up and runs from the room.

"Well," says Anita. "That went well." Suddenly not sure what she expected. Hugs? Kisses? Why *not* run? She does.

Michael reaches down and picks something up off the floor. "He likes these toys." He hands it to her. She takes it. It's a green plastic soldier.

"Jamie? May I come in?"

He is sitting on the floor, rocking forward and back, forward and back. He doesn't look up at her.

"No, you may not."

"Please?" says Anita. He rocks silently. "Just for a second?" she says. She takes a sample step in. "See, I found this little guy out in the living room. But he won't tell me his name. And I was hoping maybe you could."

Jamie looks up. Anita holds the plastic soldier out to him. "Parachute man," Jamie says.

"Oh . . . of course he is. This is a parachute, isn't it."

"You can't have him."

Sitting down on the floor well across from him, Anita reaches out and hands Jamie the toy figure. "No, of course not, he's yours."

Jamie quickly takes it. Holding it close to his face, he shakes it. A soft, high-pitched, not unpleasant mutter vibrates in his throat. Anita looks around the room. The patterned wallpaper is still the same. What was a crib is a bed now. Little-boy clothes on the floor. More of the toy figurines. Anita reaches for one.

"Who's this guy here?" It's certainly not a soldier. The figure has blue skin, three-fingered hands, yellow eyes set in a demonic face, and a long tail.

"Nightcrawler," says Jamie, reaching for the figure. "He has spiky skin."

"I can see that. Scary." Inching closer, she hands it to him.

"He's good," says Jamie. "He helps people."

"It's nice to help people."

Again looking around, Anita sees that here is an old stuffed bear on the floor, almost beneath the bed. She waits a moment, composing herself, then reaches for it.

"And this . . . ?"

Just outside the door, Michael stands in the hallway, listening. Penelope comes down the hall to join him. "Bear-Bear," they hear

Jamie say. "He rides a motorcycle, see?"

As Jamie offers the toy bike to her, Anita takes it with one hand, and lightly touches Jamie's hand with the other.

"I do. Thank you."

She carefully fits the stuffed bear onto the bike. She moves bike and bear through the air in front of them, a ringmaster moving a trained bear across a high wire.

"You know who Bear-Bear used to belong to?" Anita's voice is wistful. "He belonged to a little girl." She has Jamie's attention now. His green eyes are on her. "I think that little girl would be very glad you have him now."

"Was she you?" asks Jamie.

"Yes," says Anita. "I gave Bear-Bear to your dad to help out while I was away." Even if she didn't, it seems true to her now. "I wanted to know you both were in really good hands."

Penelope gently touches Michael's shoulder. When he looks at her, she nods. And then she turns away and retreats quietly down the hall to her room.

"You may come in now."

Anita opens the bedroom door and peeks in. For the last ten minutes she has been outside, waiting as she told him she would,

161

listening with an almost painful pleasure to the sound of a running faucet and the buzz of an electric toothbrush, thrilling to the sound of a carefully repeated gargle and spit. She has noted that Jamie murmurs to himself as he dresses for bed. Drawers open and close, accompanied by out-of-context phrases and nonsensical words, by sounds, musical notes, mutters, and hums. Her heart has leaped twice as he said what sounded like "mother."

Jamie is in bed when she enters, lying on his back, the blanket drawn to his chin, green eyes open, solemn and unblinking. She can't get over him.

"All set?"

"Yes."

"Good night, sleep tight, don't let the bedbugs bite."

"Yes."

"Do you know the rest?"

"No."

"And if they do, then take your shoe and knock'm till they're black-and-blue." She's hoping for a smile but doesn't get one. "May I kiss you good night, Jamie?"

"No, you may not," he says. Not hurtful. Just a fact.

"Next time then."

He rolls away, not looking at her. She

wants desperately to reach out and stroke his head, but doesn't. Something about autistic kids not liking to be touched. She turns out the light. She turns away. She's at the door when he speaks.

"Good night, Mom," he says.

"Good night, Jamie."

21

She finds him in the garage.

Michael, with rebreather on his face, has mounted a polystyrene blank on a V-shaped horse and, with a paper trace, has begun the rough shaping of a surfboard with a jigsaw. Particles and dust fill the air.

She's watched him do this many times. Watched him shape a board, cut it, sand it, fiberglass it, all in the course of a single night, and then have it out in the water the next afternoon. He stopped after the injury. Turned his steady hand to other things. Or maybe not so steady anymore. Anita flinches as the saw jerks and the foam crumbles in its teeth. Michael curses under his breath. He looks up and sees her. He turns off the saw and takes off the rebreather.

"He asleep?"

"I waited till he was," says Anita. "Think it went okay?"

"Hard to say."

"Will you let me know?"

"Yeah."

Yeah. Such a short, simple word. A word a bus driver might use to tell you that you've paid your fare and now can take a seat. Anita glances toward the rack of blanks, the tools on the counter. "I thought you didn't do this anymore."

"I don't. But I've been thinking about doing one for Jamie. Only they might be too old."

"What about that one?" She points. It's the old wood blank. Cabinet-grade, chambered balsa. Fragile and easily broken but when properly shaped, sanded, and glassed, one of a kind. She remembers when Michael brought it home as collateral on a loan to a down-on-his-luck board shaper, a loan never collected.

"That one, huh?"

"That one."

"You've only just given me about forty hours of work, you know."

"You better get started then."

Michael puts the saw and breather aside. "Want some tea?"

"Since when do you drink tea," says Anita.

"I always drank tea."

"Not at night."

"So now I drink tea at night."

"Sleepy Time?" Her voice is teasing him. "Little pudgy bear in a nightcap?"

"Chamomile."

"I'd love some," says Anita.

She sits at the kitchen table watching as he brings the water to a boil.

"Milk? Honey?"

"You don't remember?"

A shrug. "Things change."

"Still both."

He turns to the refrigerator. The cups and saucers he's brought out are of the fine china, the setting for eight given to them by her mother at their hastily arranged wedding. The last thing they wanted or needed but Anita finds herself pleased to see them now.

"I send you checks, you never cash them."

"I would if I needed to," Michael says.

"I wish you would."

He says nothing. She'd like to tell him that it hurts that he has never let her contribute even from a distance, that it feels as if he's punishing her. But she knows she doesn't have a leg to stand on. "You seeing anyone?" she says instead, pleased that already knowing the answer, she can still sound so chipper.

"I don't think that's any of your business."

"Just making conversation."

He looks at her a moment, then fills the cups with boiling water. The smell of chamomile fills the kitchen.

Conversation.

He wonders why he isn't raging at her. He should be. Has every right to be. Yet somehow seeing Anita with Jamie tonight has flushed the anger right out of him. Fari has told him that men have a tendency to compartmentalize thoughts and emotions in order to deal with immediate needs. He's not sure this is a bad thing if the immediate needs are those of his son.

"I guess I am. A doctor."

"You?"

"Moving *up* in the world." Hmm, maybe he *is* still angry.

"How'd you meet?" says Anita, ignoring the jab.

"She ran me over with her car."

"Ooh, love at first sight. Is it serious?"

"It could be." He is saying more than he wants to now, more than he should but he can't seem not to. "There's some baggage."

"Yours or hers?"

"No comment." Michael sips his tea. He usually takes it without milk or sweetener but in making it for her, has added both to his own. He finds it warm and delicious.

167

"How about you?"

"What, do I have baggage?" Anita laughs. "They fine me when I get on airplanes."

"Yeah, I can see how they would." His voice is flat and humorless. No doubt about it. He *is* angry. "Do they ask for autographs first?"

He sees the moment she realizes that he knows. The color drains from her face. She's like a creature that no longer breathes air.

"You saw it?"

Michael nods. "That's some heavy baggage."

Anita sips her tea, hesitates, tries to laugh again. And then she's out of the chair, bolting around the center island, and at the sink, depositing the milky tea and what dinner she's had into the drain. He listens to the mewing sounds, waits patiently till she's finished.

"I hope you plan on washing the sink."

"Go fuck yourself," Anita says softly.

"Fine. Then leave so I can clean up the mess. Again."

Anita turns and sinks to the floor, her back against the sink cabinet. She wipes her eyes, pulls down on the skin of her face as if trying to take the flesh off the bone. He fights the urge to go to her.

"It was such a bad time, Michael. Bad

place, bad crowd." Anita stares down at the floor. "I don't know. Maybe I thought it'd be empowering. What a laugh. Probably I was just trying to punish myself. I mean, what else is new? The offer was there and I just . . . *did it.*"

Feeling nothing, thinks Michael, has never felt so good.

"I was so disgusted with myself afterward. I don't think I got out of bed for a week. But then I figured nobody'd ever see it. Only these days everybody sees everything."

Michael moves to the sink and pours the remains of his tea down the drain. Without thinking, he turns and slides down the cabinet to sit next to her on the floor. It's only when she rests her head on his shoulder that he realizes what he's done.

Mistake.

But it's not. Not really. "We do things, sometimes we don't know why we do them, we just do them," Michael says.

"You don't."

"You'd be surprised."

"No. You're good, Michael. You only do good things. You're not capable of bad things."

"I'm glad you think so."

"I do. So remind me of something good now."

It takes him a moment to think of it but he does. "Fiji. Tavarua. Perfect three-foot swells."

Anita smiles tightly. "Cloudbreak," she says, naming their favorite spot. "Namotu Left. Wilkes and Desperations. You out on the water. Me watching from the beach. It was so beautiful. You were."

"We were."

"Why did it ever have to end?"

"It didn't. But it had to change. And you couldn't."

"I wanted to. I tried."

"I know."

"I warned you. You know I did."

"You did. Still, I just didn't see it coming."

"So who's the asshole then?"

"Me, definitely."

Both of them smiling ruefully. Anita wiping her eyes, putting her hand on Michael's shoulder for support, rising to her feet. She is almost out of the kitchen when she stops and turns back.

"So what are we going to do, Michael?" she asks.

"About what?" he says, standing.

"Everything."

And then, as always wanting or needing or perhaps just afraid of the last word if it belongs to someone else, she's gone.

We will be together.
He is twenty years old when he sees her for the first time. He is twenty, almost old enough to legally drink, still living at home but certainly no longer a kid. He has worked various part-time jobs since high school, washed cars, bused tables, sold sandals and wet suits in a surf shop, all the while working diligently at his real job — riding a polyurethane board covered with fiberglass cloth and epoxy resin down the face of a barreling wave, a wave created by reef, rock, shoal, or headland and shaped by weather patterns, wind, and current. For the last two months he's begun putting in forty-hour weeks on construction so as to finance surf trips to No-Cal, Hawaii, and Tahiti. He has recently begun competing in ASP sanction events. He hasn't placed yet but he knows it's just a matter of time.

Meaning he is twenty years old and he knows where he is going.

He has smoked dope and found that inhaling smoke and holding your breath underwater don't mix. He has dropped both acid — fun the first time, a horror show the second — and ecstasy, which gave him a sense of euphoria that quickly devolved into

171

nausea, sweating, and muscle cramps. He has snorted cocaine, which allowed him to drink far too much and stay up far too late and left him with such a debilitating hangover, he was dry heaving in the water between sets the next day. He has come to the conclusion that his drug of choice is cold beer. He has had actual, ongoing sex with four different women. He takes relationships seriously. He is selective and doesn't care for random hookups. He is currently seeing Lisa O'Malley, an attractive, perhaps overly outgoing junior at the University of San Diego, who will fuck him at the drop of a hat.

Meaning he is twenty years old and has been around the block.

He considers himself sensible like his father. He looks before he leaps. He believes letting go should be learned before learning to get. He doesn't believe in love at first sight. He isn't sure if he believes in fidelity. He has the whole world ahead of him and for the time being he plans on traveling it solo.

Meaning he is twenty and he knows the score.

And then he sees her across the yard and he realizes he knows nothing.

We will be together.

It is not desire. It is not love, not yet. It is a simple fact, both exhilarating and, in its inevitability, frightening at the same time. It suggests his fate is not his own and that any plans he has ever made are precarious and subject to change.

We will be together.

He doesn't question it. It never occurs to him that it might be a warning as much as a benediction. It never crosses his mind that you can be bound to someone by their absence as much as by their presence. After all, he is just twenty. Practically but not quite a drinking adult.

II. Harbor Phase: Navigating to a harbor entrance through bays and sounds, and negotiating harbor approach channels.

22

Father, in glorifying Christ and sending us your Spirit, you open the way to eternal life. May our sharing in this gift increase our love and make our faith grow stronger.

Tisha Beacham has been told more than once in the fifteen years since being born again that if she prays hard and often enough, God will *return the phone call.* It won't necessarily be a long conversation — God, after all, is busy — but rather an acknowledgment of her dedication and faith, a few tender words confirming she is on the right track, sort of like that movie about baseball she enjoyed — *build it and he will come.* It bothers Tisha Beacham that she seems to keep getting a busy signal.

Strengthen within our hearts the faith you have given us; let not temptation ever quench the fire that your love has kindled within us.

There are people at the church here out in Santee who, Tisha is sure, don't pray nearly as long or hard or as cogently as she does, and yet they — the prayer warriors, they proudly call themselves — report that God talks to them all the time. God, in fact, is a chatterbox, full of wisdom and good cheer. And even when God doesn't pick up the phone the prayer warriors still find great solace in the act of prayer. They report that their senses become more acute, that smells are richer, colors more vibrant, that their thoughts are vibrant and clear. Prayer, they say, gives them confidence and peace.

It's not fair.

Lord God Almighty, keep us faithful to your law in thought, word, and deed. Be our helper, now and always, free us from sin.

Perhaps the problem, Tisha thinks, is that she doesn't like asking anyone, even God, for wisdom and advice about anything.

No. More likely the problem is that even here in church, surrounded by the conservative faithful and all their religious fervor, her mind still has a tendency to wander as she prays. Anita. What *is* she going to do with Anita. Given every advantage and opportunity and such a mess. And Anita's child, the little boy, this autistic thing. The subject not the boy. The boy is sweet. And obviously he would have mental and emotional problems what with Anita running off on him like that. Thank goodness for Michael who is steady and dependable. Still, the boy shouldn't be coddled. Children need a firm hand. Look at her daughter Beth's children. Rude, tantrum-throwing, hyperactive animals. And God forbid her son, Neal Jr., should ever have children. Neal couldn't raise string beans in a hothouse. All the young people these days. Spoiling their offspring. Enabling them. Wanting to be their friends. The women especially. With their nannies and sitters. Even with housekeepers, not keeping proper houses. No excuses. None of them ever having to deal with what *she* did.

Lord, sustain faith within us and make us ever loyal to Christ. Let your church be the sign of salvation for all the nations of the world.

I had to protect them from *him.* The temper, the drinking, the constant demands, the *entitlement.* No wonder they're damaged goods. You should have known better. But how? It was time. No. It was a way out. And Neal Beacham was handsome. Ambitious. A USC boy. Father approved. Neal reminded him of Robert. Of course he did. Her brother, Robert Warren Scribner, who slipped into her bed when she was fifteen and kept at it until he toddled off to Stanford. The relief she felt when he was drafted

179

and subsequently killed in Vietnam a year later was palpable. Good riddance. But her mother, a borderline hysteric under the best of circumstances, effectively lost it. She's checked out, we need you at home, Patricia. She needs someone to look after her. What about you, Father? No. Ridiculous question. Fine then. Go drink and whore yourself to death. *I'm* in charge. *I* will run this house. *I* will pay the bills and arrange the dinner parties. *I* will tend to your insane wife.

Increase in us, Lord, the faith you have given us and bring to a harvest worthy of heaven the praise we offer you at the beginning of this new day.

Mother, you tried to warn me about Neal. Common, you said. Which, coming from a crackpot like you, only made him more attractive. Again, not fair. By the time you realize there are fissures in the façade it's too late. You're married to a self-centered shit who thinks he actually earned everything your family gave him.

God our Father, you conquer the darkness of ignorance by the light of your Word. Strengthen within our hearts the faith you have given us; let not temptation ever quench the fire that your love has kindled within us.

Oh, God, if you are listening, please give me your light. I am not filled with fire so

180

much as I am anger. Still. Anger at my brother for what he did to me. Anger at Mother and Father. At Neal. At you. Is that why you've cursed me? Cursed my Anita? Cursed my family? No, no. Stop that, stop it. Ridiculous. You are not a God of curses. You are a God of forgiveness.

Lord God Almighty, keep us faithful to your law in thought, word, and deed. Be our helper, now and always, free us from —

Tell me that you are. Tell me you're here to save me. You will, won't you? Save me? Of course you will. It's what you do. You who sacrificed your only son.

Almighty God, every good thing comes from you. Fill our hearts with love for you, increase our —

Oh, I'm full of it today. These simple, stupid people, with their fat-faced offspring, mumbling to themselves with their eyes closed. They look like they live in trailer parks and eat doughnuts for dinner. And you should get off your high horse. This is why God won't talk to you. Such ego. You were lucky, that's all. Privileged. Never had to worry a day in your life. Though if you'd had to do it on your own, you'd have done very well. One smart cookie. Smarter than Robert. Smarter than Father. Smarter than your husband who would just love to get his hands on the rest of your money. And you've never been afraid of work. And it's work keeping a home and a family, raising children the right way.

God of power and mercy, may we live the faith we profess and trust your promise of eternal —

And you've failed at it. Admit it. Each of your children is a disaster. They're a reflection of you, not God. They are flesh made from the damage done to you and you know it. Oh, I pray to you, dear God, our Father, who conquers the darkness of ignorance by the light of your Word, strengthen within my heart the faith you have given me. Let it temper the rage. Let it soften this all-consuming bitterness. Answer me. Talk to me just once — *once* — and in return, I will suck you off and spit the cum in your ruthless, unforgiving face. I ask this through your Son, our Lord Jesus Christ, who lives and reigns with you and the Holy Spirit, one God, forever and ever.

Her fellow parishioners have noted that Tisha Beacham often weeps as she prays. She's a beautiful, generous woman, Mrs. Beacham. She'll sometimes put as much as one hundred dollars in the donation plate. God must surely answer her prayers.

182

23

If there is parking anywhere on the twelve-hundred-acre campus of the University of California at San Diego, Michael has yet to find it. There are parking lots, yes. There are metered parking spaces. There are a number of parking garages. There are parking enforcement officers everywhere, buzzing around in their little carts, stopping so often to write tickets, they could be working on commission. What there doesn't seem to be in the nearly forty minutes that he searches, unfolded map in his lap, is any kind of legal, available, suitable space that isn't already taken, claimed, or occupied.

He finally gives up and crosses the boulevard to park in the shopping center a quarter of a mile away. As he reenters and walks across the campus, passing students and what he assumes by their briefcases, beards, and bad haircuts are faculty, he wonders what he missed out on, not going to college. Certainly a degree. What that might have been in, Michael has no idea. His mother was in love with words, Thomas Hodge with math and science, and their opposing passions seemed to cancel each other out in Michael. A decent student until his father died, he drifted through high school, uninterested in anything but wave conditions. A social life? If a social life was parties thrown in holy spots of hedonism worldwide, Michael more than tipped the bartender. Time to think? To grow up? Maybe but probably not. From what Michael has seen most people don't grow up until they have to. Ironic that now, in his thirties, Michael finds himself interested in everything. Science, business, global politics. He's bought an iPad so he can read newspapers and periodicals online and he follows up on things that intrigue him. He is addicted to TED talks. Ideas worth spreading. Suicidal crickets, zombie roaches, and other parasite tales. Are we designed to be sexual omnivores?

Too cool for school.

Youth is definitely wasted on the young. Even so, Michael has to admit that the students he's passing as he makes his way toward the building that houses the Department of Neuroscience appear very mature and serious-minded indeed. But then Neuroscience is part of the School of Medicine and the majority of these doctors-in-training are Indian and Asian.

The children are sitting on a carpeted floor and are in a circle. The youngest, a girl, appears to be about five, the oldest, a boy, around twelve. There are toys. There are stuffed animals and figures. Standing at the one-way mirror of the observation room, Michael recognizes some of them from Jamie's collection. A plush, light blue Sulley from *Monsters, Inc.* Any number of cuddly Uglydolls. Jack Skellington from *The Nightmare Before Christmas.* Michael suddenly wonders if it's autistic kids or kids in general who gravitate to the cutely grotesque.

"Okay, okay!"

Calling for attention, the lone adult in the room, a plain-faced, deep-breasted young woman, pops her eyes open wide and smiles hugely.

"Tell me, tell me! What is my face saying? Austin!"

A boy, perhaps eight, is delighted to know the answer. His hands, drawn into little fists, shake in front of him with excitement.

"Happy!"

"Yes!" the young woman says, smiling

normally now. "Gimme five!" She holds out an open hand and the boy, Austin, lurches forward to slap at it — and misses.

"No! Again!"

The boy is successful this time and he hugs himself with pleasure. "Way to go! Who can make a happy face for Austin? Happy faces, show me!"

As Michael watches, the kids make happy faces, bug-eyed grins and joker smiles, complete with sound effects, gurgles and beeps, giggles and barks.

"Those are the happiest faces!"

Jamie didn't smile until he was three. Jamie, when pleased and happy, can look as if he has no explanation or definition for feelings of delight.

The therapist curls her mouth down. She feigns melodramatic tears. "And now what's my face saying? Bridget?"

"Sad face!" says the blond little girl.

"Yes! And how do we make a sad face?"

How indeed? The children weep piteously. They cry and moan.

"Oooh, those are so sad!" says the young woman. As if sad is a good thing. As if sad is the most wonderful thing in the world.

When unhappy or in pain, when bumped, cut, or bruised, Jamie stares silently into space, unmoving. Unless he runs and hides.

"Michael Hodge?"

Michael turns with a start. Watching the children, wishing he could take this patient, young earth mother home with him to care for his son, he wasn't even aware of the man entering the observation booth behind him.

"Yes?"

"I'm Walter Seskin."

The man Michael is supposed to see. Thirty minutes ago. "Hi, yeah. I'm late, sorry, the parking —"

"Sucks. Always give yourself extra time."

In his mid-forties, the man is short and stocky and wears rumpled khakis and a long-sleeved cotton shirt with ink-stained cuffs. The New Balance running shoes on his feet look like they see pavement. He peers past Michael into the room, where the children and the young woman are still engaged in happy lamentation.

"Pretty neat, huh? We're working on social communication, teaching them body language, facial expressions. It's like introducing them to a foreign language."

"Is that what it is?" To Michael's eye, it's now a competition as to which child can feign the most melodramatic death.

"Oh, yeah. Things most people take for granted. Plus they're having a hell of a lot of fun." Without waiting for a reply, Seskin abruptly turns from the window. "Come on."

Michael takes a last look into the room.

"Who can give me . . . an *angry* face?" says the young woman to her brood of stricken children.

Michael can. Jamie can too. Angry is easy. Angry is open wide and scream.

"Are you a medical doctor?" asks Michael.

Seskin's small office is as comfortably untidy as the man himself, filled with books, papers, pamphlets, and toys.

"Yeah, yeah, pediatrics and neuropsychiatry, I'm a very big deal. C'mon, sit down, sit down." Seskin moves behind his cluttered desk, drops into a chair, and begins sifting through the piles of papers in front of him. "You want something to drink? Coffee, some water? There's a machine just down the hall."

"I'm fine."

"Good. Me too. C'mon, c'mon, *sit.*" Seskin gestures at the single chair, the one with the stack of books in it.

Michael pointedly pushes the books — boom, thud — onto the floor and sits. "But you're a teacher too?"

"Please. Academician. Mere teachers get half as many vacation days. Mostly I do research." Somehow finding the specific sheet of paper he wants in the mess, Seskin grabs a pen and begins scribbling. "Your son, what's his name?"

"Jamie."

"Nice. How old?"

"Seven going on eight."

"What's he like?"

"He has Asperger's."

"Nah, that's just a label. Tell me about *him.*" The pen doesn't seem to be working properly and Walter Seskin begins searching through the mess or another one. "Let's see. He's bright but maybe a little quiet. Kindergarten teachers said he wasn't interacting with the other kids, there might be some ADD, some nonverbal learning disorder, they recommended an evaluation. You went, had some tests done. The tests suggested Asperger's or high-functioning autism. Right so far?"

Michael wishes this man would make eye contact. It's like talking to Jamie, except Seskin talks as if he's running a race. "It was nursery school."

"Uh-huh. They tell you what it meant? Asperger's? Autism? The whole big shebang?"

"They didn't tell me shit."

"They don't. So you, obviously not an

189

unintelligent guy, did a little research, maybe went online, got yourself some information, figured it meant retard and freaked out completely."

"He's not retarded." Michael would now like to hit this man, this babbling *village idiot.*

"I didn't say he was. Though retardation can sometimes be associated with autism. You ought to see some of the head bangers we get in here."

"He's not that either."

"Oh. Well, he sounds pretty normal then."

"He is."

Straightening in his chair, Walter Seskin tosses the pen he's just found aside and looks at Michael, his gaze now about as inattentive as a laser beam.

"Then why are you here, Michael?"

It's a sucker punch. This man has hit him first and Michael didn't see it coming. The anger and resentment at this place and these people, this situation, abruptly drains out of him.

"I just want him to be happy."

Lame.

"Good," says Walter Seskin. "Me too."

There's a framed photo on the desk. Seskin turns it around so Michael can see it. The boy is in his teens. Has the slack expression and loose features of someone deep on the spectrum. The resemblance is obvious. "This is my son, David. Now *he* is a head banger. And guess what? I love him to pieces. And what *I* want is that he understand me when I tell him that."

"I'm sorry," says Michael.

"Why? What have *you* done wrong? Did you ask for your son to be on the autism spectrum? Did I ask for mine? No. We didn't expect it, we can't change it. We can only work with it. We can try to make it better. Unless you want to give up and hope for the best."

"I don't. I'm being an idiot," says Michael.

"No. You've been treading water," says Walter Seskin. "It's time to start swimming."

A swimming analogy, thinks Michael. For a man who has nightmares of drowning.

Why not?

24

For some reason there is a rug on the wall. It is a small rug, not more than a carpet really, nicely framed, its patterns somewhat Arabic looking. However.

It's on the wall.

Anita isn't sure about the pieces of pottery on the sideboard either. They're vaguely Chinese looking, seem to be unglazed jars of some kind. And the painted glass lamps. What's with them? All that's needed is some good dope and a water pipe and it would be "come wiz me to ze Kasbah" time.

Anita laughs to herself.

"Ah, Golden Girl," Michael would say to her, doing his best Pepé Le Pew French, "You are ze corned beef to me, I am ze cabbage to you. Le pant. Le heave. Intimacy iz difficult at zis range."

Crap.

What is she thinking? She can't do this. She was out of her mind to even consider it. Which is the point, isn't it. She's out of her mind. As Anita starts to rise from the couch, the door to the inner hall opens and a dark-haired woman steps out, stopping her in her tracks.

"You must be Anita Beacham."

The woman, dressed in a two-button Armani jacket, a knee-length skirt, and platform pumps, dark hair pulled back from her face, is far too young and striking to be anything so professional as a psychologist.

"Hi. That's me, yes."

Who knew you had to dress up to go get your brain shrink-wrapped?

"I'm sorry to keep you waiting."

"You haven't. No. I was early. I'm an early bird. Early bird gets the worm. Though why anyone would be crazy enough to want a worm, I don't know. Is it all right to say 'crazy' here?"

Stop babbling.

Legally Blonde notwithstanding, Anita has always felt that dark, serious women like this one — Spanish courtesans, Argentinean novelists, executive producers, and overachieving Sabras — make blond highlights seem like the most frivolous thing in the world.

"Actually I was just going to the ladies' room."

"It's out and down the hall. But you'll need the key." The woman starts to move toward the writing table.

"No. No, it's all right. I can wait."

"You're sure?"

"Oh, yeah," says Anita, sure of nothing. "I'll keep a cork in it." She holds out the clipboard. "I filled out the paperwork." The dark-haired woman takes it from her. Anita is trying to place her age and decides the woman is not much older than she is.

"I like your stuff," Anita says.

"What stuff is that?"

"You know, the rug?" Anita points at the wall.

Which I really hate.

"It's a textile. An embroidered panel. From Lebanon."

"And these?" Anita points at the jugs.

"Pharmacy jars. In the fourteenth century they were designed to hold ointments and salves. These are reproductions."

"They're exceptional."

Exceptional, shit. But then, you've been brainwashed by your mother who shops the furniture department at Sotheby's.

Neither of them move.

"I thought you'd be older," says Anita Beacham.

"Please come in," says the woman, this

194

Dr. Akrepe-da-something, stepping back and out of the way.

"Couch or chair," Fari asks the woman, this woman who looks like a Victoria's Secret model, photos of which her brother kept hidden in the bureau under his clothes. Glowing, fair-haired beauties who made Fari feel about as attractive as dark mud.

"Sorry?"

"Would you like to sit or lie back?"

"I'll sit."

"I will too." Fari smiles slightly, trying to put the woman at her ease now. She can see that Anita is trembling and pale with nerves.

"May I ask how you found me?"

"Internet search. Yelp. Four stars under *A.*"

"Really."

"Really-really. Is this a problem?"

"No. It's just that most of my patients come to me as referrals or because I've been recommended."

"Good enough for me."

The blond woman beams. One of *those*. Wisecracks and jokes to hide their discomfort. Fari gives another practiced smile in return. "I should tell you up front I'm not inexpensive. And there's a good chance your health plan won't cover your visits. They should, but too often they don't."

"I don't have one."

"Oh."

"But money's not a problem."

That could be the problem right there, Fari thinks. "Have you ever been in therapy before?"

"*God,* no."

Attitude also a potential problem. "Well. I like to think of a first session as two people getting to know one another. I'll ask some questions. Answer them as best you can. And if you have specific things you'd like to share, I'm interested in that as well. And if at any time you're uncomfortable with my questions or don't feel safe, you should say so. It could be I'm not the therapist for you and it's fine to say that too."

"No. You're good," says Anita Beacham. "I trust you." As if already sure of it.

They stare at each other.

"Where would you like to begin?" Fari asks.

"Well, we could talk about you or we could talk about me. But if it's you, you pay me."

The woman is smart and funny. Fari likes her. Pushing the feeling aside, she settles back, poised, professional, and ready. "Why don't we talk about you."

25

She is seventeen.

She is seventeen and she can't remember a time when she's ever been happy.

She is seventeen going on seventy, her mother tells her, meaning she is exacting and intractable beyond words and has never acted like a little girl. Meaning she is a chip off the old block.

She is seventeen, and in the spring of junior year she has refused to return to the prestigious local private school, where, as the headmaster who insists on being called *Doctor* Schechter constantly tells the students, "Good grades are groovy." That Dr. Schechter, who wears a pen pocket protector, wouldn't know groovy if his balls were stuck in his zipper is beside the point.

She hates the local public school only slightly less than the private one only because the teachers are too overwhelmed and distracted to pay much attention to homework assignments. She hates homework. She hates class. She hates sitting. She hates listening. Her mind is an open gate and her thoughts are wild horses that keep running out to the open prairie.

She suffers from migraines and her father tells her that they are caused by inherited abnormalities in the brain. This is just another reason not to like him. When he's around, her father is constantly on her, telling her she's lazy, she's selfish, that she had better get to work if she plans on getting anywhere in life. She has no idea where anywhere is, doesn't care, and from what she can tell, her father's idea of working hard is telling others what to do.

Boys pay attention. Like her mother, she is beautiful, and like her mother, she knows it and no longer thinks about it. She has noted, however, that a lot of attractive people end up on television and movie screens where the lives they're depicting seem vaguely exciting. It's something to consider. The money is irrelevant. She's known for a long time that there is a family trust, established by her maternal grandfather, and administered by her mother. A prudent amount is to be given on a monthly basis when she and her siblings hit twenty-one and a very significant lump sum is to be dumped in their laps when they are forty.

She joins the school's drama club. Though occasionally embarrassing with its well-earned nerd club–misfit status, it is a diversion. It's fun to pretend to be other people. It's reassuring to know the outcome of a scene or play. She finds memorizing lines easy. It bothers her that she can neither laugh nor cry on cue.

The boys in the drama club mostly pay attention to one another which is a relief. Outside the club it's another matter. Boys clamor and bay. She decides to lose her virginity to Dougie Nash, who is the son of a friend of her father's and is handsome and popular though perpetually stoned. She finds sex not quite the big deal she was led to believe it would be. The act itself is enjoyable enough but the aftermath less so. Dougie Nash wants to talk and she finds talk, especially the listening part, exhausting. She breaks up with Dougie after two weeks, wounding him, as he puts it, "brutally, man." However, they decide to remain friends and as friends they continue to have casual sex on occasion, the difference being they don't have to talk afterward because there's nothing to talk about.

She wonders if she's a lesbian and at a party she allows Amanda Tannenbaum, who *is* a lesbian, albeit a cute one, to kiss her in the kitchen pantry. It's not uninteresting and they adjourn outside to a parked car. Other than the hardware and plumbing, it's not all that different from Dougie Nash. You lose yourself for a brief moment and then it's over. Snap back to reality, here comes gravity. What's different is that Amanda Tannenbaum shadows and then stalks her for weeks before fading miserably into the sunset. Women are more unwavering than men, says her mother. She's talking about local politics, but it obviously applies to relationships as well and it's something to remember.

She has begun to realize she isn't like other people. It's not just the ever-present feeling that something's wrong. It's that she doesn't seem to feel or act the same way. She feels detached. She feels she's constantly *pretending* to be normal. She wonders what it would be like to live in another person's head. Would there be a different view, different emotions, a different interpretation of the five senses? Maybe other people aren't flesh-and-blood human beings at all. Maybe they're oddly programmed robots. Or maybe's *she's* the robot and she doesn't know it.

She applies to college only because she

200

can't think of anything better to do. Her grades are pedestrian but her SATs and ACTs are surprisingly strong. She has choices. And in the end her father has connections. Chapman University is an hour up the road in Irvine. It has a good drama program. Maybe she'll learn something. Maybe it will all get better if she gets away from home.

It doesn't.

She gets cast in a studio production as Emily in *Our Town*. It's her first role in a full-length play and she's excited. After a week of rehearsal she's bored to tears. Nothing happens. The Stage Manager wears wire-rim glasses and an old fedora, talks with a bad New England accent, and is supposed to be symbolic of God. The characters and dialogue seem old-fashioned, stilted, and clichéd. Emily is a complaining Goody Two-shoes. Maybe this is why the director gives her line readings. She doesn't *get* Emily. She doesn't *get* Grover's Corners. She doesn't *get Our Town*.

Ten years later, watching Paul Newman in the play on cable she realizes she *really* didn't get it. It is devastating. It is about not knowing and never recognizing the perfection of the moment when it's in your hands. It is about death and eternity. She cries, not wanting to know or think about why she is crying.

She is in the middle of a social sciences class when she gets her first panic attack. It's as if a switch abruptly flips inside her and all of a sudden terror is moving through her in waves. The air vibrates and she can't breathe. Voices have turned to menacing whispers. Faces look blurred and satanic. Somehow she excuses herself and races to the girls' lavatory, which is thankfully deserted. The feeling of nameless dread passes. That will never happen again, she thinks. The next day, in a crowded school corridor, it does. And the day after, seemingly sparked by the clatter of keyboards in the computer room at the library, it does again. Both episodes send her running out of the building desperate for open air.

The attacks become a daily occurrence. They can happen anytime, anyplace, but usually it's when she is surrounded by people. Their chatter lights the fuse and begins the countdown to kickoff. Evenings are especially bad, the weekends worse. She starts going to bed early, hoping to escape the feelings of dread through sleep. Her roommate, a black girl who likes to party, resents the lights going off early and tells her so. She also tells her that she talks in her sleep — "crazy shit, girl! Don't believe me? Ask anyone on the floor 'cause I charge admission when you go off!"

One evening, at the roommate's insistence, she takes a shot of tequila hoping it will take the edge off the day's growing anxiety. It doesn't. But the fourth one does. She begins drinking on a regular basis, not so much to get drunk but to keep calm. She discovers that alcohol makes her social. Even outgoing. She has never had friends. It has never bothered her. She can't picture herself going through life as anything but alone. But now she can actually be with people for more than the usual half hour at a time without losing interest and wanting to walk away. On the nights she doesn't drink, her brain feels like it's shooting off sparks. She sits by herself in the library pretending to read magazines or she watches television in the student center, wanting to bang her head against the wall to stem the rising tide. She wonders how long she can go on like this. She wonders if she should talk to someone about it. She wonders if she should kill herself and just get it over with. But no — she's actually curious as to how it will all turn out.

Her roommate, something of a pal now,

calls her unknowable. And she is. Even to herself.

26

Leo brings cookies.

He is a stealth bomber. He is a commando. He is a closet gourmet and home chef armed with *La Pâtisserie de Pierre Hermé,* English edition.

"These are for Mike," he says.

"Don't tell me, tell him," says Rose.

"I can't 'cause he's not in yet," says Leo, stating the obvious.

Rose, who doesn't like the obvious being sprung on her, least of all by Leo, looks up from the computer. "Shouldn't you be at the job?"

"I'm on my way."

"You're late on your way."

Making it sound like it's a regular occurrence, thinks Leo. Man, it's tough to be appreciated. "I'm just dropping these off. For Mike. And I don't want you eating any of 'em."

"Any what?" says Rose, her attention back

on the computer screen.

"These cookies." They are in a shiny aluminum tin, one-pound capacity, made by a shipping supply specialist. Leo has found they keep the air out, the freshness in.

"Cookies," says Rose as if she's not exactly sure what cookies are.

"Cookies, yeah," says Leo. "Homemade cookies."

"Homemade as in *you* made them?"

"Yes, as in me, as in I made them."

"What kind of cookies would you make, Leo?" Rose sounds skeptical, sounds as if she knows for a fact that Leo has a hard time boiling water.

So much for what you know.

"For your information, Rose, these are chocolate-chip butter-pecan maple melts. I took sugar, a teaspoon of vanilla, almond extract, unbleached flour, baking soda, ground nutmeg, maple syrup, chocolate bits, half a cup of toasted pecans, and I made these cookies. Did I mention the pound of butter?"

The recipe is actually Donna Hay, not Pierre Hermé. The chocolate bits are Leo's addition. Twisting the lid, Leo opens the tin.

"You wanna try one?"

He offers the tin to Rose who hesitates, starts to reach — Leo dangling the tin ever closer — and then abruptly pulls her hand back.

"You're such a liar, Leo."

Rose pushes her curly dark hair back behind her ears, a gesture Leo finds painfully erotic. "A liar. How?"

"You didn't make these."

"No, Rose, no, I didn't. I got 'em in the frozen food section at Costco." Leo clamps the silver tin shut, a silver tin that he would like to tell Rose cost eighty bucks he couldn't really afford at the time, but hey, you get what you pay for when it comes to cooking.

"What's going on?"

Leo turns. The outer door to the office has opened and Michael is standing there.

"Nothin'," says Leo. "I gotta talk to you about something. In private. And I brought you cookies." He holds out the tin.

"Cookies," says Michael as if he too isn't quite sure what cookies are.

"Yeah, for you and Jamie," says Leo, sounding exasperated. "Doesn't anyone know what cookies are?"

"Great. I'll take 'em home with me."

"Good," says Leo. He turns back to Rose. "At least somebody'll appreciate 'em." And putting the tin down on Rose's desk, Leo proudly turns and disappears into the inner sanctum.

"What was that all about?" Michael says to Rose.

"Never mind," Rose says. "A disagreement."

Shrugging, Michael moves into his office and closes the door behind them.

"The meeting with the guy, you never told me how it went." Leo has lowered his considerable bulk into the office's old straight-backed chair. It squeaks in protest.

"The guy. What guy?"

"The rich guy."

"That guy, oh, yeah. If he has a toilet to unplug," says Michael, moving around his desk to sit, "he might give us a call." He tries to keep his voice light. It hasn't been easy to lately.

"Aw, shit, we can do that job, Mike. In our sleep we can. Did you tell 'im that?"

"I should have known better than to even ask."

"So what's next then? After we finish dickwad's place."

"I have some irons in the fire. We'll find something."

"Meaning we got nothing."

"We'll find something, Leo. We always do."

"We're small potatoes, Mike."

"Yeah, but we're good potatoes. We taste great."

Leo rises. He suddenly feels trapped in the small room. The photos on the wall — photos of remodels, additions, cabinetry work they've done, work to be proud of — suddenly seem depressing.

"I need some money, Mike. I'm behind."

The words hang there, plaintive and pathetic, even to his own ears. He adds the last word — the dog-shit icing on a crap cake.

"Again."

"How much you in for?" asks Michael quietly.

"A grand."

"That's a lot."

"I know. I keep thinking, the circumstances and all, they'll give me a break. They don't."

"I can give you an extra two hundred . . ."

"That's not enough."

". . . a week. For the next five weeks."

"Can I get four up front?"

"I'll see what I can do."

"It won't happen again, I swear."

"No problem."

It kills Leo that the look on Michael's face

says he's heard it before. But what the hell. He has.

Damn you, Leo.

The tin keeps calling to Rose, making work impossible. The cookies were three-inch round disks, golden brown and puffy, with flecks of chocolate and pecan floating just beneath the surface. When Leo exposed them to the light, the office suddenly smelled like a bakery. Perhaps that's all she needs. To smell them again, yes. She will certainly not give Leo the satisfaction of eating one. She has heard the rumors. Leo makes fancy, full-course dinners for friends. He went to Luis's very own house and cooked Luis's father the world's best *menudo* for his birthday. Everyone tells him that he should open his own restaurant someday. Rose, who is on a Nutrisystem diet to help manage her hyperglycemia, is of the opinion that food is a weakness. Still, it is one she has a tendency to get overly excited about. She doesn't want to even think about the fact that Leo's beard smelled of butter and powdered sugar as he leaned over the desk.

Rose reaches for the tin.

It is surprisingly heavy. Obviously the contents — the cookies — are denser than they appeared. Leaden perhaps. Dry and soggy. Yes, probably both.

Rose opens the lid.

The rich smell of pecan, chocolate, butter, maple, and sugar envelops her like perfume. She feels faint with hunger. There is no way they can taste as good as they smell. She lifts one gently from its bed. There are brothers and sisters, each more beautiful than the next, underneath. She takes a small bite, careful not to spill crumbs on her desk. Saliva, sweet as nectar, floods her mouth and she feels like swooning.

¡Le consigno al infierno, Leo!

I consign you to hell.

27

Pulling into the country club parking always reminds Neal Beacham that he needs to get the damn car washed. It's a gray Lexus LS, five years old, still high-end, but undistinguished when compared to the brand-new Mercedeses, BMWs, and sports cars that dot the members' parking lot. Neal Beacham doesn't really give a rat's ass about cars, but still, there is such a thing as keeping up with his fellow club members, even if the majority of them are pompous nitwits, upgrading their cars as often as they do their golf clubs. What Bob Moses, who's in his mid-seventies, needs with a Ferrari is beyond him. And that pretentious prick Jay Bellemy can stick the silly Corvette with its U.S. Naval Academy decal and all his flying missions in Vietnam up his ass.

We lost. What good did you do?

As to the dusty car, maybe he'll ask Anita to take care of it. It's not that she has anything better to do. Hanging around the house, sitting by the pool, making coffee in the kitchen.

Puts my damn teeth on edge.

"Your mother and I would like to know your plans."

"She would or you would?"

"All right. I would."

"I don't have any."

"None."

"At the moment nary a one."

"There are such things as jobs."

"Mmm, maybe I should become a banker."

"I don't think you're funny."

"You never have, Dad."

"You may not stay here indefinitely."

"Gee, I have an idea. Maybe you could buy *me* a condo."

Children a man can brag on. Is that too much to ask for? Apparently, yes.

Heading toward the clubhouse, Neal waves perfunctorily at the group on the first tee. Karl Van der Grew with his banal sex jokes. Dave Bundy who insists on plumb bobbing every damn two-foot putt on a course he's played a thousand times. Robert Caulfield with all his so-called financial savvy and advice. As if a wart doctor knows the first thing about the workings of a private bank, knows the first thing about the regulations that demand your money, time, and resources, knows about the big boys constantly sniffing around and hovering, looking to gobble you up, knows about foreclosures, weak loan demand, and the low interest rates that pinch your lending profits. Neal Beacham prays daily for the next inevitable real estate meltdown. He's quietly and carefully positioned himself for it. And when it happens and the lemmings go down with the ship he will buy Robert Caulfield out a dime on the dollar.

"Neal B!"

"Come on, Neal-meister! We need a fourth!"

"Bring your wallet!"

"Not today, you buzzards! I already have a game!" Ha-ha. Ha-ha-ha. Ha.

He wouldn't piss on any of them if they were burning. He's playing with George Frost today — George, a retired dentist and a twenty handicap who out of sheer ego calls himself a nine and so will go down in flames to Neal Beacham's solid ten. Should at any rate. Coming around the corner of the pro shop, Neal Beacham feels disoriented, as if he is walking down an uneven, echoing passageway. His game has been . . . *off* lately. As he stands on the tee, his heart will start to beat out of control. His arms and shoulders feel stiff even when he hits the simplest iron shot. There seems to be a tremor in his hands when he holds his putter or signs his scorecard. Sometimes he feels like sitting down and not getting up again. Stress. It must be. And no wonder.

My wife is no better than my daughter.

"She's going through a difficult time, that's all."

"When hasn't she?"

"Now you're just being mean, aren't you."

"There comes a moment when one has got to cut bait."

"That's a lovely cliché. Who'd you get it from?"

"It's the truth."

"Yours perhaps."

"Just don't blame me if she becomes totally unstable and you know who I'm talking about."

"Neal?"

"What is it."

"Plan on eating alone tonight."

Love me, he wants to say. For once in your life, for once in our life together, just love me. It would all be so very different if you would.

That'll be the day.

By the time he enters the quiet of the

215

men's locker room, Neal Beacham has come to the conclusion that both his wife and children are ruining not just his golf game but his health and well-being as well. He doesn't deserve it, not any of it. He's a reasonable man who does far too much for too many and now, as usual, is going to be forced to do it again.

They're all damn lucky to have him.

III. Coastal Phase: Navigating within 50 miles of the coast or inshore of the 200 meter depth contour.

28

"Hello, this is Dr. Akrepede."

"Hey. You're a hard person to get ahold of," says Michael. He is in his truck and is fumbling to get the Bluetooth in place, the headset which always makes him feel like an old-fashioned telephone operator. The voice on the other end hesitates a moment.

"I'm sorry, I've been terribly busy at work."

"If I was a patient, I would have had to call 911."

Not the best of jokes. It's bothered him that she hasn't called back, that she seemingly has so little interest in what's been happening in his life.

"And I was at a conference," Fari now says, more an afterthought than an excuse.

"You too busy to go out Saturday night?"

"Are you sure? If it's not yet a good time for you . . ."

"It's fine. Back on track. And I want to

see you."

"All right. Saturday is fine then."

"Around seven? We'll go to dinner."

"No," Fari says. "I'll cook."

"Let's make it six then."

"Why?"

"Because I love" — Michael pauses for effect — "your *cooking*."

"Indeed," Fari says, pleasure in her voice.

Two blocks later and driving, Michael realizes any disquiet he was feeling is gone and that he's humming to himself. It's a song by the Beatles. He remembers seeing the video once. John, Paul, George, and Ringo, young, bearded, and long haired, wandering around the English countryside with their lady loves. Lennon, or maybe it's Harrison, singing about whether love will grow or not. He doesn't know. But the song's melody makes it seem likely.

29

"What a' you got today?" asks Leo.

It is past noon and the crew has broken for a well-earned lunch. Jose and Bobby have set a board on two sawhorses and, between bites of takeout burritos, are discussing the two things they share in common — internal combustion engines and women. Bobby likes motorcycles and strippers, Jose pines for souped-up Toyota Corollas and tattooed virgins. Too old to be interested in either one, Luis and Leo eat lunch on the dropped tailgate of Leo's truck.

"Tortilla soup," says Luis, opening his thermos. "Ham san-wiches and flan."

Leo peers into his brown paper bag. Podagra in his big toe, more commonly called gout or rich man's disease — which is unfair because he is anything but rich — has Leo on the third day in the latest of innumerable diets limiting the meat, fish, butter, and red wine that Leo dotes on. To pretend he's actually eating he has brought beautifully cut, fresh crudités for lunch — crudités at least being *French* for raw vegetables — cucumbers, radishes, broccoli florets, celery and carrot sticks. With the smell of tortilla soup wafting, a different name doesn't make them taste any better.

"You're gonna get fat, Luis, you keep eatin' like that."

"Then I look like you."

Leo scowls. He takes a bite of carrot. He has nothing against vegetables, even raw, sauceless ones that taste like kindling, still, the least Luis could do is share his soup.

"The problem is you're ignorant, Luis."

"*I* am?"

"You don't even *know* what makes you fat. Read a newspaper sometime. Turn the radio dial to something other than mariachi music. Learn what's going on in the world."

"You know what's goin' on in the world, Leo?" Bobby calls out, having heard the tail end of the diatribe. Today, Bobby has gone for the *carne asada,* which also has the potential to put him on Leo's shit list.

"Damn right I do. CBS evening news, every night."

"Yeah, well, from what I hear it's the Bunny Ranch and sports center."

"Fuck you," says Leo, laughing. Truth be told, he likes an occasional tour of the Bunny Ranch, which is a silly documentary show about a Nevada whorehouse. The girls are all giggly airheads, apparently untroubled and unscarred by their profession, and the owner of the bordello, whom they all seem to adore, is overweight like him. Leo isn't sure but he thinks the show is on the Fantasy Channel. The broccoli florets are suddenly tasting pretty good. Laughter does that to food.

It's not fair, thinks Luis as he digs into his *sandwich de jamón.* Bobby and Jose can laugh at Leo. Maybe it's because they haven't worked with him for ten years and still think he's funny. They probably don't read papers and listen to the news any more than he, Luis, does but Leo doesn't give them *mierda* about it. The truth is, the few times Luis has tried to look at a newspaper it has seemed obvious that the news is all about poor people getting shot, bombed, arrested, imprisoned, deported, and generally given the short end of the stick. What's new about that? And as for *el mundo,* from what Luis can tell, the rest of the world makes America seem like *una dulcería* — a sweet shop. Is it any wonder why people come?

"Ignorant, Luis. Ignorant."

There are days when Luis would like to ship Leo off to a foreign country and throw away the return ticket. Maybe he *is* ignorant. Maybe all poor people are. Luis has never quite understood how rich people make money. As a laborer, you do a service and you get paid for it. Or you make something somebody wants and they buy it. And yet it seems sometimes as if the people who do nothing and make nothing own everything. From what Luis understands, they buy and sell paper to do this. Not only that, they pay people to buy and sell this paper for them. Luis would love to know what the paper is or at least what's written on it. He's never seen it. He's not sure he'd trust it if he did. Regardless, if most of the news is about poor people getting fucked over, the rest of the news is about rich people exasperated that there are poor people in the world.

They all stop eating and quietly and collectively groan as Michael drives his truck onto the worksite.

"Aw, shit," says Jose. "Don' he got better things to do?"

"*Coma* your *almuerzo,*" says Leo. "Eat your lunch." Like Jose, Leo knows what's coming when Michael doesn't park on the street. He too wishes his boss could find better things to do with his free time, play tennis maybe or go to a movie. He just doesn't want to hear it coming out of the mouth of a kid enamored with souped-up Toyotas. He tosses his carrots aside, rises, and starts forward as Michael gets out of his pickup and starts stripping off his shirt.

"You're workin' with us this afternoon, huh?" Leo sounds somewhere between skeptical and resigned.

Michael reaches into the pickup for a leather tool belt. "Thought I would," he says, smiling, obviously a man, thinks Leo, who's had a good lunch. "You mind?"

"Just don't expect us to keep up," says Leo. "We're pros, we pace ourselves."

Michael reaches back into the pickup. "Here," he says, "consider it a bribe," and he tosses Leo a bag from Jack in the Box, the king of fast food. Oil from the fries has already begun to stain the paper and Leo, suddenly feeling faint with hunger, reaches in and pulls out something warm and wrapped. He knows, having been long intimate with its comrades, that it is an ultimate cheeseburger, two quarter-pound patties, three kinds of cheese, and a special sauce that should be outlawed as an instant heart attack.

"Workin' food!" crows Leo, and he bites into the burger, wrapper and all.

An hour and a half later, Leo is burping something that tastes of wax paper, ground beef, and ketchup into his mouth. As feared, Michael is setting the pace, working like a man happily possessed. He carts two-by-fours onto the deck, four at a time. The table saw screams, covering his bare torso with sawdust. The pneumatic nail gun fires like an automatic pistol in his hand as he nails a panel to a stud. The others, not to be outdone, pick up their pace. Michael's enthusiasm is contagious and at the end of the day they are builders and builders build. This is their craft and their art and Michael has them in the zone where an hour of hard labor goes by in a minute.

Even Leo.

He complains bitterly and groans piteously — "You're killin' me, Mike!" — but he matches them all nail for nail, header for header, stud for stud. His cuts are straight. His corners are flush and square. His top lines are true. Hawking and spitting specks of onion and ground beef, he helps Michael lift a ten-foot section of wall into place. He stares at it, panting with satisfaction.

"Hey, Leo!" Bobby calls, with a grin. "I thought all you did was doughnut runs!" Normally Leo would sentence the kid to cleanup for such impertinence, but not today. "I am the franchise!" he bellows, and he raises his arms and flexes his meaty biceps for all to see. An hour later, his big toe throbbing, he trips over some boards and falls off the platform. Bruised and tired, he is out for the rest of the day and Michael sends him on a 7-Eleven beer and Slurpee run. All are pleased with him. They know in their hearts that for once, he didn't fuck up on purpose so as to get some rest.

"Ey, boss. *¿Puedo hablar con usted?* Can I talk to you?"

Michael is nailing plywood sheathing to an exterior wall as Luis approaches, He is surprised. Luis rarely stops work and it's even rarer for him to initiate a conversation. The first two years they worked together, Michael wasn't sure Luis spoke at all. It took three years to realize he spoke passable English.

"Sure. *Por supuesto.* What's up?"

Luis stares off into space for a moment, both his jaw and mind seemingly chewing on something tough and gristly. A measure-twice, cut-once kind of guy, thinks Michael, if ever there was one.

"I'm not a man who asks favors," Luis finally rumbles, his voice a monotone.

This is an understatement. Michael was on the job one day when Luis cut his hand on a circular saw. He watched as the big man silently wrapped the bloody hand in a cloth. "Maybe we ought to get that checked out," Michael finally said, as the cloth turned crimson.

" 'Eez nothing," Luis had replied.

"Luis," Michael had said. "I insist."

A shrug. "You the boss." The cut had taken twenty stitches to close, several yards of gauze and tape to bandage, and even though Michael had offered him the rest of the day with pay, Luis had insisted on returning to work.

"You're a man people ask favors of," Michael now says.

A small tired sigh. This is true. "I always say no."

"You say no but you do the favor."

The tiniest of you-got-me smiles touches Luis's lips. "My wife. She likes to brag about my good deeds, not my good looks." Luis, the driest of comedians. *"¿Qué es un hombre que hacer?"*

"Exactly," says Michael, trying to be equally straight-faced. "What's a man to do?

So what can I do for you?"

Pulling the sixteen-ounce hammer from his tool belt and ten pennies from his nail pouch, Luis sets and bangs a nail into the plywood — tap, bam, done — one blow, the old-fashioned way. Michael can't remember if he has ever seen Luis bend a nail. "My sister, Carmen. Her boy, Eduardo. He's smart, you know? Graduating top of his class from the high school." Tap, bam. "His mother? Dumb as a soda can. But the boy?" Tap, bam. "*Muy inteligente.* And now he wants to go to college."

"That's impressive, good for him," says Michael, wondering how far Luis ever got in school. He'll have to ask Leo about it.

"Not any school. He wants to go to the Stanford. You heard of it?"

"In passing," Michael says.

"It's a tough place?"

"Yeah. But it's a good place, the best."

"Mmm."

Tap, bam. Tap, bam. Plywood secure. The nice thing about having a conversation with Luis, however minimal, is that things get done.

"So what's he need, your nephew? Money?"

"*Recomendaciones.*"

"You mean letters?"

229

"He got some from teachers, one from his priest. My sister, she say he needs some from white people."

"I don't think my recommendation is going to do much for him, Luis."

"Not you. Someone *importante.*"

It shouldn't wound but it does. It shouldn't make him wince inside but it does. Why? There are movers, there are shakers, there are people with connections, and it's abundantly clear of late, he's not one of them. He is a banger of nails and he doesn't even do it as well as the man standing across from him.

"You mean someone who might actually make a difference," Michael says, grinning to take the hurt away.

"Not my idea, my sister's."

"I'm a little short on those kind of people right now, Luis. But if I think of anyone."

"You do what you can."

"*Sí.*"

"*Bueno. Esto era el favor que preguntaba. Gracias.*"

"*De nada.*"

Meaning you're welcome. Meaning it's nothing. As Luis, in his torn jeans and dusty, worn work boots, lumbers away, Michael remembers that three or four weeks after Anita left him, the man showed up on

230

his doorstep with a bottle of tequila, a six-pack of Bud Light, and a large bag of *chich-arrónes* — Mexican pork rinds. *"Es béisbol en televisión,"* he said. The baseball is on television. With Jamie asleep, they sat, they drank, they watched the Padres. The house was a calumnious mess and at the seventh-inning stretch, Luis rose from his chair and began casually picking up. Chagrined, Michael joined him. They swept and vacuumed, drank some more, and changed the soiled sheets on the bed. Michael showered and shaved, the first time in days. They drank, ate pork rinds, did dishes, and washed clothes. Jamie woke, crying, and Luis watched as Michael bottle-fed him and rocked him back to sleep in his arms, at one point murmuring, *"Se necesita un hombre fuerte para hacer trabajo de la madre."*

It takes a strong man to do a mother's work.

Michael remembers the night as the first step on the road back to reclaiming himself.

Gracias, Luis.

De nada.

At the end of the day when the others leave, Michael and Leo stay, and as they drink beer, spirits revived, Michael tells him all about the woman he's been seeing, about

231

Anita who has returned, and about the new doctor in Jamie's corner. Leo, in turn, listens intently, feigns surprise and disbelief when necessary, and offers encouragement when needed. They toast Luis who they both agree is the best of men. They toast each other. It's so simple really. Life is. A cold beer. Some guy talk. A woman who cares about you. Atlas, a working man, held the sky on his shoulders. He endured.

"I need a sitter Saturday night, Leo. You available?"

"What's wrong with your mom?"

"She burned her house down. I need a sitter for her."

"What time?"

"Around six."

"Tell Penelope I'm makin' pizza."

They split the last beer. It's what best friends do, never even thinking twice about it, and when they finally walk to their respective trucks to go home, they are satisfied with the day and as in love with each other as any two heterosexual males can be.

30

He has decided on a wide, thick, flat-shaped board of eight feet, one ideally suited for small and slow waves.

It has taken most of the morning to plane and rough-shape the balsa blank and now, sweating and covered with dust, Michael, blue bandana tied over his mouth, carefully uses a power drill with rough sanding disk to further smooth the soft wood, working from the centerline to the edges. He should know better than to have his shirt off. Even with sawdust as opposed to foam, he's going to be itching for days. He should probably be wearing the breathing respirator as well. A wooden surfboard is like a ship. Ribs and stringer form a skeleton, the upper surface is the deck, the undersurface is the hull. The blank he is working with will be a chambered board. The balsa timbers have been precut and spot-glued together into a blank form. After the rough shaping of the blank is completed, Michael will break it apart and begin the painstaking job of chambering the timbers. The more wood he removes, the lighter the board will be. Once chambered, the planks will be permanently glued back together and the final shaping will begin.

He sees it in his head. The grain of the wood, the finish. He already knows that the skeg or skegs — he hasn't decided how many there will be yet — will be long and placed toward the tail. Round rails and more curve in the line will make for smoother, speed-conserving turns. Better for a beginner. But who will *teach* the beginner, that's the question.

Earlier in the week, spur of the moment, he has taken Jamie to the public pool for an impromptu swim lesson. A pool, with its calm, clear water and lifeguards close at hand, feels safe enough. In the shallow end, Michael teaches Jamie drown-proofing, how to lie facedown in the water, head, arms, and legs dangling, letting the body's natural buoyancy keep him near the surface. Need to breathe? A small simple stroke and kick toward the surface, raise the head, inhale, and relax again. See? First steps, baby steps, call it a day.

"The only thing to be afraid of, bub, is

being afraid," he says, wishing he believed it himself.

"Oh-kay," says Jamie, already loving the water, reveling in its gentle pressure on his entire body. Pulling his goggles down and taking a breath, he is away like a pollywog, arms reaching, gathering and pulling the water in handfuls, legs wildly kicking. He comes up, thrashing, takes a fast breath and goes under again. A natural, thinks Michael, and having no choice, he follows his son toward the deep end, keeping his head above the once familiar medium, afraid to get his face wet.

And now this. A surfboard. The whole idea was probably insane to begin with, but insane or not, once started, it's now hard to stop.

"Is this a stickup?"

He turns. Beyond the open garage door, Anita is standing out in the driveway, has been for who knows how long, watching him. Out by the curb, a small car that wasn't there a minute ago is now parked. That's the problem with energy-efficient, battery-operated cars — you can't hear them coming.

He pulls the blue bandana down. He tries to look stern. Think of this as one of the guys on the job.

"Didn't we say you were going to call first?"

"I did. You didn't answer."

"My cell's in the house."

"Is that my fault?"

Uninvited, she comes into the garage. The problem is she doesn't *look* like one of the guys on the job. She wears a light blue cotton T-shirt tucked into beige jeans. Leather belt and sandals. Hair pulled back, no makeup. A Ralph Lauren model, classy and conservative, like the mom in the photo. The mom that does porno.

"Haven't lost your figure," says Anita, her eyes moving from Michael's breastbone up to his eyes.

He suddenly feels naked. "I'm working on it." Turning, he puts aside the drill and reaches for a block covered with coarse sandpaper. As he does, Anita reaches out and touches the scar that's on the small of Michael's back just above the belt line.

"This is new. What happened?"

He turns quickly as if she's touched him with a hot match. "Nothing. I backed into a piece of rebar."

"What's that?"

"A steel rod."

"That was dumb."

"Actually I liked it so much I do it on a

regular basis."

"That's the masochist in you again."

"Ha-ha."

Anita looks in toward the house. "I thought I might take Jamie shopping, buy him some clothes or something."

"He doesn't need any."

"For me, Michael, not for him." As if stating the obvious. Like he should *know.*

"He doesn't really like shopping."

"Would you just ask, let him decide?"

Michael sighs to himself. He'd like to tell her it's not supposed to be like this. Just showing up. There are rules. But then he'd have to tell her what it *is* supposed to be like and what the rules actually *are* and he has no idea yet. Not a clue. He's winging this.

Besides, how risky can shopping be?

"HEELLLPPPP!"

Jamie has gone crazy, thinks Anita.

"Help! Help me!"

They are in front of the Disney Store. The fucking Disney Store of all things, and Jamie won't stop screaming. He won't be comforted, won't be talked to. The kid — *her* kid — has gone dipshit, goggle-eyed nuts.

"Ahhhhhh!!"

It's as if there are banshees in the air.

Coldhearted, bloodthirsty banshees, wailing of dismemberment and imminent, unavoidable death. People, of course, instead of running for shelter, are staring at them.

"Help me!! Help me!! Helppp!"

"Jamie," Anita pleads, trying to put a hand on his shoulder, trying to get him to at least look at her. "It's just a store. See? There's Woody in the window. There's Mickey and Stitch! And that's *Dopey.*" Who, thinks Anita, beginning to lose both hope and patience, is *probably fucking autistic as well!*

"Hellllp!" Jamie screams.

It started off all right. They parked, they got out of the car. Anita doesn't particularly like malls, doesn't particularly like *shopping,* but the thought of buying Jamie something, anything, is like candy. And speaking of sweets.

"Ice cream, Jamie?"

"No."

"You don't like ice cream?"

"Only at night."

"I'm sure it'd be okay."

"I don't want to."

Oh.

They go into Abercrombie & Fitch, which Anita has heard is popular with teens and preteens and which she immediately realizes is a huge mistake. Enormous black-and-white portraits of half-naked adolescents gallivanting in the woods in bisexual bliss are everywhere, making Anita wonder for the first time what exactly *is* the erotic imagination of an eight-year-old boy, let alone an autistic one. Do they even *have* fantasies yet? If so, of what? Do they get erections? Masturbate? A mother should know these things. Jamie, thank goodness, seems bored and uninterested and asks no questions.

They retreat across the outdoor concourse to Eddie Bauer's, which Anita, recognizing it as the place that supplies most of her father's casual clothes, immediately despises. She can see though that Jamie is growing restless and so they browse.

"Do you like these cargo shorts, Jamie?"

"No."

"I think they're cool."

"I hate them."

"How about these? You want to try them on?"

"I want to go home."

Even the toy store with its superhero figures and its puzzles, its bottled bubbles, and its toy cars on tracks draws a negative response.

"I don't like it."

And then there it is. Uncle Walt's familiar

signature logo. Every kid in the world wants to go to Disneyland. Okay, Anita didn't but every *other* kid.

"Come on, Jamie, let's go in!"

"Noooo! Help!! Help me!!!"

He recoils in horror, suddenly shrieking, as if the place is a haven for rodents who devour children. Maybe it is.

"Okay! Okay, Jamie, we'll go home." Anita, desperate for him to stop now. "It's fine, listen, I'll take you home!"

"Hey, lady, is this your kid?"

The man is Latino and in his mid- to late twenties, powerfully built or chubby, it's hard to tell in the baggy Chargers football jersey. Certainly well-meaning but Anita doesn't have the staying power for any kind of interference right now.

"You think I'd put up with this if he wasn't?"

Incredibly, the guy ignores her and turns to Jamie. "Ey guy, is this your mom?"

Jamie immediately turns to him, wild-eyed. "My mom ran away. She *ran away!*"

"Jamie!" If half a dozen people were watching, now a dozen are, looking at her like she's a child snatcher. The Latino guy doesn't seem nearly so well-meaning now.

"What's he talkin' abou', lady?"

"Who knows what he's talking about? I'm

his mother, all right? Get out of here!"

"Help me!" calls Jamie, his eyes going from face to surrounding face. "Helpppp!"

This can't get worse.

"Jamie, stop it! Listen to me! We're going home right now!" It's as Anita is trying to grab for his fluttering, flapping hand that she sees the uniformed security guard approaching.

The photo is of Michael and Jamie, taken at Halloween. They are dressed as pirates. Jamie is the captain, with eye patch, hook, and curling wig under three-cornered Jack Sparrow hat. Michael, kneeling next to him, scar crayoned on his cheek, is his attending Smee.

Disney, thinks Anita, thoroughly blaming the old bastard now for this debacle of an afternoon. She watches as the uniformed officer carefully studies the photos and IDs that are on his desk in front of him. She glances at Michael who stands next to her, patiently waiting. She looks over to the bench where Jamie sits, murmuring to himself, contentedly playing with the plastic parachute man Michael brought for him. He *ignores* Anita. As does the uniformed officer.

God.

Okay, yes, maybe she *has* spent the last forty minutes mouthing off, threatening and complaining. But better that than breaking down into tears which is what she's been wanting to do ever since being quietly but firmly escorted into the mall's security office in questionable possession of her son. Thankfully this time Penelope answered the phone and went and got Michael in the garage. Thankfully Michael dropped what he was doing and came right away, not even stopping to wash the sawdust from his hair or change his clothes. Thankfully —

Still ignoring Anita, the uniformed man hands Michael back the ID and photos.

"Just wanted to be careful."

"Not a problem," says Michael. "Thanks for your help."

Help, thinks Anita.

Some help.

She turns quickly for the door.

She is wiping at her eyes with a Kleenex when Michael and Jamie come out of the office. "You all right?" Michael asks, knowing and not necessarily displeased that she isn't.

"Why wouldn't they believe me?" she says, her shoulders and chest jerking with each contraction of her diaphragm. Michael remembering with some odd sentimental pleasure that she doesn't cry like most people. Tears are always accompanied by intense and continuous hiccups.

"You didn't have proof."

"Oh, for God's sake — l-look at us, Michael. The p-proof is — is in our — f-faces!"

She's right, of course. The same blond-streaked hair, the same deep green eyes. Seeing the two of them together just makes it that much more obvious.

"Good but not enough."

Michael wonders whether he should tell her about Legoland. The end of the day and Jamie wanting to go on the raft ride for the fifth time, Michael refusing and Jamie, just like today, screaming bloody murder. Next thing you know, Michael is trying to convince half a dozen security guards he's not kidnapping his own son — and the son *not* helping. Which is why —

"I always carry pictures," says Michael.

"Let me see."

He hands them to her so she can look at them again. Michael and Jamie. Father and son. Captain Hook and Smee.

Proof.

Anita pays for the Nikon Coolpix camera at the outdoor kiosk with cash. She discards the box into a trash bin along with the damp Kleenex. "Here, make yourself useful," she says, handing the camera to Michael. She turns to Jamie and kneels. "Jamie, would you let Daddy take a picture of you and me?"

"Yes, I will," he says, his face serious.

She gently pushes the hair off his forehead. There's something syrupy in her throat — the hiccups have turned to phlegm maybe — and she has to swallow a few times to get rid of it. She turns Jamie toward Michael and the camera. "Fire away."

But then —

"Wait."

Because Jamie has put his arm around her waist.

Oh, God.

"Mom is crying," says Jamie.

"No, Mom is hiccupping," says Michael.

"No, she is — n-not," says Anita, her body quivering with each throttled blip. "Mom is — as h-happy as a clam at — h-high tide." Wiping her eyes, she puts her arm around Jamie's shoulder. "Proof. Like we need proof."

"Smile," says Michael.

"Hiccup," says Anita.

Michael has brought Abigail with him and

so they drive in separate cars to North Beach, adjacent to the racetrack, where the San Dieguito River enters into the sea. It's a dog beach, a leash-free zone, and it's hard to tell who's having more fun, the packs of racing dogs or the laid-back dog owners, some walking barefoot in the low tide, some sunning on the coastal bluff above. At the water's edge, they roll their pants up, and as Jamie runs on ahead, Michael and Anita follow down the beach together, watching as he throws a tennis ball he's claimed for Abigail. It's an awkward, clumsy motion, almost girlish, and the ball balloons up into the air, not going more than ten feet. The dog bounds after it, young again, barking with excitement.

"Tell me something about him I don't know," says Anita.

"He can't throw, that's for sure."

"Why?"

"Must be your side of the family."

"Be serious."

Michael shrugs. "Developmental coordination disorder. Comes with the territory."

Anita watches as Jamie throws the ball again. Better this time though not much. But who really cares. "What else don't I know?" she says.

Michael muses a moment. "He likes

pickles. Kosher dills. The more sour, the better."

"I do too," says Anita.

"I know," says Michael, making her smile. She lived on them when pregnant with Jamie.

"What else?"

"He has a hard time telling you what he's feeling. I think a lot of times he just doesn't know."

"I don't either," says Anita.

"I know," Michael says. "Believe me, do I know."

They go to Rubio's for fish tacos where Anita discovers it's not just sour pickles that she and Jamie share a fondness for. "Eat this," he says, putting a dollop of dark red house-made habañero sauce on the back of his hand and thrusting it at Anita.

"Is it hot?" she asks, knowing it is.

"No," he says. "It is not."

She slurps it noisily off his hand. "Hmmm. Pretty mild." Taking the hot sauce, she puts a small puddle of it on the inside of her wrist and offers it to Michael. "What do you think?"

As Jamie squirms with delight, Michael takes her hand and sniffs it cautiously. "This isn't going to hurt me, is it?"

"Stop being a chicken and set an example for your son."

Michael licks, tasting her as much as the sauce. His eyes grow wide with feigned alarm. "Holy shit!" he cries and he grabs for his Tecate. Anita hasn't heard Jamie laugh before and the sound fills her like warm air.

"Tell Mom about the time — tell her about the time — tell her —"

The food or the company, probably both, thinks Michael, has turned Jamie into a raconteur who refuses to talk, instead insisting Michael do it for him.

"Why don't you, bub?"

"No. You."

And so Michael does. He tells Anita of the little boy who never took naps in bed but, rather, dropped to the floor or ground wherever and whenever the need took him. He tells her of the three-year-old who danced the Macarena naked in the driveway, of the four-year-old who walked into the neighbor's house and surprised her sitting on the toilet. "I've come for the cat," he said ominously. Michael tells her of the child who solemnly referred to himself in the third person. *A boy.* Because *a boy* needs to, wants to, hates doing, should be

247

allowed to, doesn't have to eat, bathe, dress, undress, brush his teeth, comb his hair, come inside, go outside, get up, go to bed, wear the same T-shirt three days in a row, use a napkin. And when it is of particular importance, *a boy* resorts to collective bargaining. This is because *a boy* is a *human being* and *human beings* need, want, hate, and should be allowed to, et cetera, et cetera, because *human beings are people too*!

"Ain't it the truth," says Anita.

Mom and Dad are laughing. Jamie doesn't know why but Mom and Dad laughing makes him feel good. Especially Mom. Mom laughs different from Dad. Dad laughs loud. Mom laughs quiet. Like he, Jamie, does. Maybe there are other good stories to tell Mom.

Tell her about the time.

Jamie suddenly remembers last year and immediately he wishes he didn't because it is not a good story. He is out in front of the house on the wooden deck. He is doing what Dad calls stimming — holding and shaking a thin piece of broken stick, his stick, his special stick, the one he made, in front of his face. He's not supposed to do it but it feels good to do it. To shake the special stick. That he made. It makes Jamie feel quiet inside. You look at nothing but the stick. The part where it's broken. The way it moves. The way you move it. Everything else goes away and you feel quiet. It's always so noisy and bright and hot and itchy, but moving the stick, the stick that you made, makes it all quiet.

"Time to come in now," Dad calls to him.

"No," Jamie says. If he goes in, he'll have to put down his stick and then it won't be quiet anymore. He feels angry at Dad for saying words.

"Time, kiddo. It's getting dark."

"No!"

Dad moves to him, takes the special stick from his hand and lifts him to his feet. "Let go, little man," says Dad.

He screams at Dad. He screams as loud as he can. Dad has taken away the stick — Jamie's special stick — and he screams. "Ahhh!" he says. He pulls away from Dad and throws himself down onto the wooden deck. It hurts but he doesn't care. "Ahhhh-hhh!"

"Jamie, stop."

But he doesn't stop. He's so angry. The quiet is gone and he screams and he is so angry at Dad. Then Dad picks him up. He loves Dad but he hates Dad because Dad is not letting him be. He hits Dad as hard as he can and he kicks Dad. With his arm around Jamie's waist, Dad carries him into the house. Because hitting Dad doesn't work, Jamie begins to hit himself. He hits himself in the face and in the stomach and the head as hard as he can. Dad grabs and holds Jamie's hands to stop him.

"No!" he yells at Dad. "No, no, no, no! Leave it! Leave me — leave —" Inside the house Dad closes the door and puts him down and he scrambles back toward the door and he bangs at the door and he digs with his fingers to open the door but the door won't open and so Jamie throws himself down on the floor and screams. He screams now because his body feels so hard and pulled tight it's going to break and he kicks at the air and he slaps at himself and his teeth are trying to find something to bite.

Where is the stick? Where is the quiet? Gone.

Dad holds him down and lies on Jamie so he can't move or kick, holds him, holds him and is still. Dad is heavy and it feels good. It feels good not to be able to move or hit or kick or bite. It feels like a thick blanket all over his body. After a while the blanket makes Jamie feel quiet like the stick makes him quiet. It doesn't hurt so much to breathe now. The loud sounds, the sounds he has been making, the crying sounds, are going away. Jamie lets everything else go with them.

"Jamie?" Dad says to him after a little while of the quiet.

"Yes."

"You okay?"

"Yes."

"What happened there?"

"I don't know."

" 'I don't know' is not an answer."

Dad says this sometimes. So does Mrs. McKenzie. It means it's important for Jamie to say something about what he's really feeling. Sometimes he doesn't know.

"I had a hard day."

"You want to talk about it?"

"No. I want to go to bed now." He does. He feels very tired. Bed will feel good. The blankets, the real blankets, will feel good too. It will be quiet and warm and dark in bed.

"How about some *Jungle Book*?" Dad asks him.

"No." He likes *Jungle Book*. He likes it when Dad reads to him about Mowgli, but Mowgli is tired too.

"Okay. Come on, I'll tuck you in."

And because he's Dad, Dad does.

No, thinks Jamie. He won't tell Mom this

story. It might worry Mom and he doesn't want Mom to worry. He won't tell Mom that he has no friends and doesn't want any, that he only likes to talk to adults. He won't tell Mom that he forgets to look at people and that he only likes asking questions because when you ask questions, people answer and then you don't have to. He won't tell her that sometimes he forgets to look when he crosses the street and he only likes to pay with a dollar because he doesn't like to make change and if left alone he'll sit and he'll flap his special stick if he has one for as long as you let him, and even though it feels good, Dad says this isn't okay. Dad worries about him. He doesn't want Mom to worry about him too. So, no, he won't tell her any bad stories. Only good stories.

The bad stories will happen all by themselves.

When Anita opens the truck door for Jamie, he clambers in, seemingly oblivious to his still damp and sandy clothes. The dog, equally covered with salt and sand, squeezes past Anita and leaps in beside him.

"Bye! I will see you, Mom!" A question and a statement.

"I will see *you*," says Anita. She hesitates,

wanting to kiss him but decides against it. She closes the door and looks across the hood toward Michael, who's been so wonderful.

"Sorry about your seats."

"It's what a truck's for."

He's looking at her. He has been. And now he seems to decide something.

"You want to pick him up one day after school?"

She doesn't hesitate. "Yes."

"Call. We'll set it up."

"Thank you."

Michael shrugs. "One less thing I have to do."

"I meant thank you for today."

That look from him again. As if this, her simple gratitude, is something else he needs to consider, has to decide if he can trust or not. She'd like to put his mind at ease. She'd like to tell him she's not expensive, in fact, is easily affordable, and that even with the wear and tear and bad parts, offers good dollar value. But she knows she'd be lying.

Give it time.

"Well," Anita says.

A well is a hole in the ground. It's also something to say when it's time to disappear into the sunset and you can't think of anything else. "See ya."

Michael watches as Anita turns away and moves up the sidewalk toward her car and unlocks and opens the door. He waits for it, knowing it will come. The look back, the small, seemingly surprised smile, the familiar quick wave. The dark blond hair catches and reflects light. He raises his own hand in careful nonchalance. And then she's in the car and the door is closing behind her.

"Dad?"

Michael turns to the open window of the truck.

"What is it, little man?"

Jamie is sitting quietly, his seat belt buckled. He is staring straight ahead through the windshield.

"Is it okay if I like Mom?" He sounds worried about it.

"Sure it is." Michael hesitates, then decides to tell the truth. "I do." There, he's admitted it. Ahead of them, the car pulls out from the curb and into traffic, and though Michael knows it's his imagination, there is the confounding taste of lavender and hot sauce on his tongue.

The truck comes up the street and pulls in the driveway. As Michael and Jamie get out, Leo appears at the gate, a thick slice of pizza in hand.

"Where you been?" Leo says, his mouth full. "You said six."

IV. Ocean Phase: Navigating outside the coastal area in the open sea.

31

It's not like him to be late. It's not like him not to call. Her, not him. She's the one who doesn't return his messages. She's the one who goes out for a run without her cell phone, trying to pretend she's forgotten it, left it on the counter on the way out the door. She's the one who opened the expensive bottle of white wine she'd bought for them and, thinking he'd arrive at any moment, poured two glasses. Thirty minutes later she's the one who had inexplicably drunk them both. Inexcusable. Out of character. The running is punishment.

Fari often tells patients that if the mind were an internal combustion engine, anxiety would be water poured in the gas tank, responsible for the ensuing shudders and stops. She encourages them to describe their greatest fears, to be as dramatic and emotional in the telling as possible. She then asks them to start over and tell her again.

By the third or fourth time, it all becomes a bit silly. A lipstick-marked, helium-filled balloon. Something to laugh about and move on from.

She doesn't feel like laughing and she's finding the moving difficult. She both likes and hates running. The bouncing makes her breasts hurt, but the fatigue calms her. So why isn't she calm? She's known this day was coming. She's known that what she began, she would inevitably have to end.

The need for control is most often a reaction to the fear of being at the mercy of others. Discovering the source of the fear — early abuse, abandonment, emotional neglect — is often the key to confronting the issue. Stupid words for which she's paid several hundred dollars an hour. Better the simple truth.

My father, whom I loved and trusted, sent me away to a private school when I was twelve, then brought me home to marry a venal, woman-hating shit.

Most mental health professionals, Fari knows, are at least as crazy as the general population they treat. Sigmund Freud, the father of modern psychoanalysis, was a neurotic who convinced himself he was going to die at age fifty-seven because that was his street address. She loathed the boarding

260

school in England. She could hardly breathe enough to cry. The girls called her Princess Jasmine. The only way to deal with them was to be better than them.

It frightens her how much she's missed Michael these last two weeks. It seems like months, years, since she's seen him, touched him. The longing for him has made her angry at herself. And at him. It doesn't bode well for a future without him.

How could you have been silly enough to put yourself in this position?

She's never met his mother. Though he's mentioned him to her any number of times, she's never met his son. When he called to tell her they had both almost died in a fire, she acted as if he were talking of strangers. "Of course, Michael, you must do what you need to do. I'll be here when the air clears." She had wanted to run to his side. Support him. Be with him. Why didn't she?

Because you're a control freak with intimacy issues.

Guilt, of course, is unforgiving. She's not naïve. She knows she has held on to her loveless, long-distance marriage because it is a good excuse for keeping others at a distance. It's an escape hatch. Affairs can only go so far. It never occurred to her that

Michael might have his own escape hatch as well.

What nerve you have telling people anything at all about what to do with their lives.

Michael looks up from where he's sitting on the front stoop as Fari comes out of the gathering evening shadows. He rises from the steps, feeling relieved that she is in running clothes. He left the house without changing, showering, or shaving. He smiles gratefully as she approaches, wondering now why he felt in such a panic to get here.

"I am *so* sorry. I lost track of the time. I tried to call." It comes out in a nervous rush.

Fari looks at Michael as if surprised.

"I forgot my phone. Why? Did we have plans?"

It is Michael's turn to look surprised. "You were going to make us dinner."

"I must have forgotten."

"I guess there was no reason for me to rush then."

There is suddenly every reason in the world for Michael to have rushed and they both know it.

"Well, it's not so late, would you like to come in? I think I have something in the refrigerator. And there's an open bottle of wine."

It's the white Burgundy. Left out, it's now at room temperature. Fari pours it into a long-stemmed wineglass anyway and hands it to him. He takes it.

"Aren't you having any?" he asks.

"No, I don't think so."

Michael looks at the fragile crystal glass a moment. Riedel Vinum Chablis. She gave him a pair for Christmas. It will make any wine you drink taste better, she told him. He quietly sips. The wine doesn't taste good at all.

"How's your mother?" Fari is moving through the living room, not so much picking up as incrementally moving things that don't need to be moved.

"She's okay." Another sip of the too-warm wine.

"It will take time to get over her loss."

"I guess it will."

"And your son, how is he?"

"What is this, a shrink session?"

"I'm just asking, Michael."

"He's all right. He's good."

"Has he seen his mother?"

"Yeah. Today." Michael hesitates. "I got pulled in as chaperone. That's why I was late."

"Ah. And did it go well?"

"Will you please stop talking to me like a

263

shrink?"

"You don't usually complain about my tone of voice, Michael."

"You usually look at me when you talk to me."

Fari raises her eyes. "I'm looking at you now and all I'm asking is how it went today with your wife and son."

"Ex-wife. And it went just fine."

"Good. I'm glad."

Michael takes a gulp of wine. Glass or not, it tastes worse than ever, hot and sour. "So how you been? Long time no see." There is an edge to his voice. The hinge of his jaw feels tight.

"I'm all right. Busy, as I said."

"Good! That's just *great!"*

"Why are you being sarcastic?"

"Why aren't you being honest with me?"

"I'm always honest with you."

"No. You never lie to me but you never tell the entire truth. And you never *forget* anything." Michael puts down the glass. "What the hell's going on?"

She is silent. She is lost.

"Do you want me to leave?" asks Michael.

"Only if you wish." Not looking at him again. Knowing if she does, she'll never recover.

"Okay. Sure. We'll do this another time.

When we're both in a better place."

Michael can feel what's coming as he turns for the door. He should be moving faster.

"Michael."

He stops and turns back, not wanting her to say it.

"I don't think we should see each other anymore."

He takes a breath, fighting for composure. "Why?"

"You care for her, Michael."

"You know that, huh?"

"It's in your voice. Your look when you speak of her."

"How do I look when I look at you?"

"Michael —"

"What do I sound like then, huh?"

"Don't make this harder than —"

"You are reading something that's not there."

"Even so." She takes a breath, retreating further inside herself from his growing anger. "This was bound to happen sooner or later."

"This. What is *this*?"

"Our lives catching up with us. Yours now. Mine eventually. You need someone who sees you more than once a week, Michael."

"I'm not asking for more."

"You should be."

"Yes. All right, yes, maybe I *am.*" He fights now to keep his voice calm. *Control. Always having to be in control.* "But not her . . . not her."

"Are you so sure?"

Is he? Is he sure about anything anymore? He has no idea. "Fari." He doesn't want to beg. He begged once before in an earlier life, it didn't do any good. "Don't do this."

"It's already done."

Fari listens to his truck start up. She is in the entryway where he first took her, where she allowed herself to be taken. She leans back against the door. The sound of the truck fades far too fast as he motors away. Her legs are suddenly weak and she slides to the floor, reminding herself that the day she almost hit him with her car, he was the first one to get to his feet.

We're different people.

He repeats this to himself over and over again as he drives down the boulevard.

A doctor of psychology and a contractor — what a joke.

It would be except they don't even laugh at the same things. Correction. She doesn't laugh at all. It'd be beneath her.

She's a good lay, that's all.

"You have this need to save women," Anita once told him. "It's a gift from your mother." She was talking about their relationship and she didn't mean it as a compliment. "Chivalry, Michael, means you do all the work."

No more. I'm done.

Burn me once, shame on you, burn me twice, shame on me. Well, shame on me.

Because I lied to you.

He didn't forget the time. He knew where he was supposed to be. It was a test. They failed.

I did.

Deep in his stomach, something heavy as a stone, something Michael thought was long gone, begins to hurt again. Pulling to the side of the road, he puts the truck in park. He sits, unable to drive, for what seems like a very long time.

Beware if you make a woman cry because Allah counts her tears.

He read that one night, longing for her.

Heading: the direction in which a vessel is pointed at any given moment. Heading changes constantly due to sea, tide, wind, and steering error.

32

Michael watches as Jamie floats through the air in a silk drape. Tightly nestled in a hammock swing tied at the top, he is being pushed by Julie, the plain-faced, deep-breasted goddess of wounded children. Michael has been sitting in the observation room for the past forty-five minutes watching through the one-way glass as she directs three boys, Jamie one of them, through a series of games and exercises played over a soft-form obstacle course — pits filled with hollow plastic spheres, foam barriers, tire and platform swings, miniature trampolines, tumbling mats, exercise balls, and resistance tunnels.

"Help Todd and Nicholas across the forbidden zone, Jamie! Nicholas, why do we call it a forbidden zone?"

"You can't cross it alone!"

"Yes, we have to help each other! What do we tell Jamie when he's doing a good job,

Nicholas?"

"Good job!"

"What do we say to Nicholas, Jamie?"

"Thank you!"

"Thank you who?"

"Nicholas, thank you! Todd too!"

"Todd, what do we say to Jamie?"

"D'no."

"We say you're welcome."

"Welco!"

"That is so good! Todd, ten jumps on the trampoline! Jamie and Nicholas, we have to get on the platform swing before it leaves for the moon!"

Play-based occupational therapy like this, Walter Seskin has explained to Michael, coupled with applied behavior analysis, teaches spectrum kids how to interact, how to cope, and how to problem solve. "A kid's *occupation* is playing and learning. We want to get them communicating and developing social skills in small groups. The other physical stuff is gravy."

It's like watching someone herd cats.

"Todd, you're not jumping!"

"Can't!"

"Yes you can! There's no such thing as can't! Jamie, you and Nicholas have to swing together!"

"He won't!"

"Then you have to help him! Todd, are we jumping?"

"Wan' jooze!"

"Five more minutes and then juice!"

"Arrgghh!"

" 'Arrgh' is not a word, Todd!"

"Which one is yours?"

Michael turns. The woman is Asian. He knows from having seen her with her African-American husband in the waiting room that the family is military. "One hundred twenty-five an hour, twice a week," the uniformed man said to Michael, talking about the cost of OT. "Thank God for Obama-care."

"Jamie. The little guy on the swing."

"Mine is Todd." The woman points as if Michael might have trouble picking out the only child of color in the OT room. Todd, the least communicative of the three boys, the one prone to noises, sudden grimaces, and gaping-mouthed, bug-eyed faces.

"Your son is handsome." The woman has a soft, Asian accent. Michael has no idea which country it might be from.

"They're three good-looking kids," says Michael, lying. Jamie and Nicholas at least look normal. Todd looks like the village —

Oh, you bastard, how dare you go there —

"Maybe Jamie and Todd have playdate.

We pick up."

"That'd be great," says Michael, knowing Jamie will refuse. "Maybe we can get all three of them together sometime soon."

"Todd like Jamie and Nicholas very much."

"Thanks. I'll be sure to tell him."

It's the fourth week of this and if swinging and climbing and doing obstacle courses is making a difference, Michael has yet to see it. And yet . . .

"Way to go, Jamie! Way to go, Nicholas! Good job!"

Michael sees now that Jamie and Nicholas are swinging on the board in unison, back and forth, back and forth, giddy with success. That's new. And at home, he's not drifting off into his own little world quite so much, the world of toy soldiers and plastic superheroes.

"Let's practice our handwriting, bub."

"Oh-*kay.* Which hand?"

"Mrs. Andersen says you're a lefty."

"Like Mom."

"Yup." Anita once telling him, in her mother's opinion, left-handed children were behaviorally challenged. Sinister children, Tisha Beacham called them.

Thank you, Grandma.

"Todd, Jamie, Nicholas! Who's going to

274

tell me how to climb to the top of the climbing wall! Jamie, what do we do first?"

"We spot each other!"

"Yes, we help each other stay safe!"

Jamie is pink cheeked and breathless when the session's over. Spent.

"What'ja think, little man? Did you like that today?"

"I had a good time."

"Sure looked like it."

"I have friends."

"You sure do."

"Are we coming next week?"

"We can come twice a week if you want."

"I want to."

Why not, thinks Michael. For a good time with friends, not to mention a woman who laughs and encourages and has beautiful breasts, one twenty-five an hour is cheap.

33

"You seem particularly edgy today."

"Do I? You don't."

In the five weeks that Anita's been seeing Fari Akrepede, not once has she noticed so much as a dark strand of hair out of place. Makeup — check. Clothes — check. Expensive shoes — check. Unruffled mental and emotional state — check and double check. What must it be like to be so composed, so imperturbable, so regulated?

I'll never know.

"Yeah, I am a little edgy. Maybe you could give me something for it."

Whatever you're on.

"I can't prescribe medication but I can recommend somebody who will. Right now, though, I'd rather talk about what's making you feel this way."

Questions, questions, always questions when what you're looking for is somebody to give you some answers. Anita rises abruptly from her chair and moves to look out the window. She can see the ocean in the distance, the ocean that always makes her think of Michael.

"I've always felt this way."

"What way is that?"

"Like . . ." She turns to look at this maddening sphinx of a woman. "Like I'm going to start chewing on my arm, if I don't stop thinking all the time."

"What is it you think about?"

"Lately?"

"Please."

Fari watches as Anita Beacham hesitates, then moves back to her chair to pick her bag up off the floor where she's left it. She opens the purse and, after rummaging briefly, takes out a small photo. She offers it to Fari who takes it.

"This is my son."

It's one of those posed school photos. The boy, blond, possibly five or six, is in a blue T-shirt. He stares blankly at the camera without expression.

Something familiar.

Fari hands it back. "He looks like you."

"He's autistic."

"I'm sorry. That must be difficult."

"You know some people think autism is caused by uncaring mothers? Refrigerator moms. Great, huh?"

In over a month, two sessions a week, Fari has yet to see Anita Beacham cry. She suddenly wonders if today will be the day.

"They're mistaken."

"Are they? Are they really?"

"I'm not an expert on autism but it's my understanding that genetics and environmental factors play the most important role."

"Great. I gave him defective genes and should have stayed away from bars and toxic dumps while pregnant."

"Am I supposed to laugh at that?"

"I don't care what you do."

Fari is silent as Anita turns her back to her again. Some patients can't talk if you're looking at them. Anita is one of them.

"I *was* a refrigerator."

"I'm sorry?"

"A refrigerator mom. I might as well have been. I used to wake up every morning, dreading the day. I'd get out of bed, Michael'd already be gone . . ."

Fari forces herself to keep breathing.

". . . and I'd be alone in the house, staring at walls. And then he'd start to cry. Jamie. And no matter what I did, feed him, hold him, change him, rock him, I couldn't make it better. I couldn't. I started hating

278

him. My own baby and I hated him. And then I was afraid I was going to hurt him. That I was going to hurt me."

A racing heart means adrenaline has kicked in. Adrenaline, Fari knows, allows you to use all your strength at once — but only once. "What you're describing, Anita, is an extreme form of postnatal depression. Were you seeing anyone about it?"

Anita shakes her head. Her eyes are shiny pools. "I didn't want anyone to know."

"You mentioned a Michael. Who is Michael?" Good. Her voice was matter-of-fact. Even casual.

Anita turns from the window and again goes to her purse. She takes out and offers a second photo.

"This is my husband."

Fari takes it. The snapshot is probably ten years old. A man and a woman in their twenties. Arms around each other. Smiling. Sun kissed. Radiant in their love. What a shame, thinks Fari, that innocence has only one season.

Something has happened and Anita isn't sure what. Dr. Akrepede's hand trembles slightly as she hands both the photos back. Her eyes are blinking rapidly. Anita watches as the woman carefully composes herself.

Maybe she isn't always as together as she appears to be. It's an encouraging thought.

"Tell me how you met," Dr. Akrepede softly says to her. "Tell me all about your husband."

Though the smile is still distant and professional, Dr. Akrepede's voice, thinks Anita, is suddenly that of a dear, long-lost friend.

34

She has completed her freshman year of college and she has come home for the summer. Anxiety paralyzes her. She spends her days sitting by the pool, trying not to think, and her nights using a fake ID to drink in local college bars. Though asked out, she doesn't date. At the bars, she goes home with no one. She feels indifferent to anything in her life except the panic attacks. Her parents consider her objectiveless and lazy.

Dougie Nash's parents are in Idaho and he and his older brother, Jack, have decided to throw an impromptu get-together that will turn into a bacchanal for over two hundred underage partyers. Tim "Time" Warner is one of them. A freshman linebacker at the University of Arizona, he is drunk, baked, wired, and cranked and is in the company of several other boys who aren't much better. Tim Warner has always made her nervous. Senior year of high school he would stare at her as she passed in the hallways, the muscles in his jaw and forehead working, as if furious at her. Dougie Nash has told her that "Time likes you." Great. An ape with a violent streak and a crush.

Having downed several solitary shots of vodka, she is outside by the pool, chatting with a group of unsteady girls, feeling it might be time to go home soon, when Tim Warner approaches. He stops, sucks on his beer, and stares at her. The underwater lights of the pool are on and the surface goggles like warped glass.

"Hi, Tim," she ventures, knowing without a doubt that it really *is* time to go home.

"You think your shit's too good to eat?" he says to her. She recognizes the expression on his face. Recognizes the tone of voice. It's her father confronting her mother after more than several drinks. It means she is in jeopardy. There are people who try to break what they want and can't have and, like her father, this boy is one of them. As she turns away from him, he grabs her arm.

"I'm talking to you, cunt."

She dislikes the word in general but especially hates it coming out of this ugly mouth. She pulls her arm away and slaps him hard across the face.

"Don't touch me," she hisses.

Tim Warner grunts as if he's been waiting for an invitation to a party and it's finally come in the mail.

"Bitch."

He grabs her arm again. She cries out as he twists and bends her to the side and down. And then a boy she has never seen before is wedging between them, as tall as Tim Warner but without the immense blocks of muscle.

"Time, hey! How you doing, dude? You getting out much?" The boy has a short, curly beard. Sun-streaked, woven dreadlocks fall to his shoulders.

Tim Warner's eyes narrow. His brow furrows as if it hurts to make his brain work. She is aware that everyone in their immediate vicinity has gone silent as if the wrong sound or gesture will detonate a bomb.

"Get the fuck away from me, Hodge."

The boy doesn't seem to hear. "Arizona Wildcats, huh? You and Doug. Very well done." The hand is off her now. She is aware that the tall boy is slowly edging the aggressor away. "Come on, man, I'll get you a beer, you fill me in."

"I said get away from me, motherfucker!" Tim Warner swings a huge forearm at the boy's chest. The boy takes the blow on his own arms and, instead of backing away, pushes into Tim Warner, grabbing him and pulling him off balance. A moment of struggle and then the two of them go back over the edge and into the deep end of the pool.

It has happened so fast.

She moves to the side of the pool along with all the others — the babbling girls, the boys shouting out in excitement — to watch the two bodies locked and wrestling deep beneath the surface of the brightly lit water. Later she'll remember that she is afraid for the boy. She knows he is going to be killed because of her. The bodies twist and tangle. The water flumes. Moments pass.

"They're drownin'," says a drunken voice, as if it's amusing. She is suddenly aware that Tim Warner has stopped fighting and is trying to get to the surface, but that the other boy isn't letting him, is holding on, dragging Tim back, keeping him under. She can see Tim's face just beneath the clear shell of the pool water. His mouth is open. His eyes are wide with terror. His huge arms pull frantically and to no avail. She *is* going to get to see someone die. How interesting. But no, they break the surface together, Tim Warner gagging water, flailing and shrieking for breath. Behind him, the other boy, his nose streaming blood, has one arm across Tim's chest, the other tight around his neck.

"Don't make me take you back down!"

Tim "Time" Warner struggles weakly, coughs and sags. The boy pushes him toward the side of the pool, where Tim grabs the edge and holds on, exhausted. Blood drips into the water around the tall boy's bearded chin. She watches as he dunks his head. When he comes up and flings his matted hair back, the blood is gone. He turns and with two imperceptible strokes glides into the shallow end. Standing, he walks toward the steps. His T-shirt is ripped off his shoulder and in the reflected light of the pool she can see the welts of fingers and fists on his wet and glistening skin. Some other boys she doesn't quite recognize, obviously the boys he came with, are waiting for him as he comes up and out of the pool. They sing congratulations, offer high fives, praise him with their laughter. The boy — no, the young *man* — is obviously somebody to them. He turns now, glancing back in her direction. She doesn't look away. She knows that now that he's finished slaying the dragon, he will come to claim her. He nods slightly. He turns back to his friends. He accepts a towel and a fresh beer. Twenty minutes later, she watches from a distance as he and his friends depart. After several more shots of vodka, shots that do nothing for her, confused and disappointed, she goes home.

Several days after the party, she feels enough time has gone by to ask Dougie Nash about him. They are in his air-conditioned bedroom, under the covers. She has come not so much for sex as for information but one thing has led to another.

"The boy who went in the pool with Tim Warner. Do you know him?" Her voice is casual, the question posed as a curious afterthought. The pretense is probably wasted on Dougie Nash who is well into a postcoital doobie and is stoned.

"Whoa, you were there that night, Neeta?"

"You invited me."

"I was wasted."

"No kidding. Who was he? Hodge something." He is like an image embedded in her brain. Sun-bleached Rasta hair and blood in the water.

"Hodgkins!" says Dougie Nash, delighted. "Yeah, it was him. Close bud with my bro."

"Hodgkins? Like the disease?"

"No. *Duh.* Michael *Hodge.* Like an awesome surfer? Looking to go pro."

She dislikes surfers. She dislikes the

jargon, the no-worries attitude. She associates surfers with slackers. They are nerds with wet suits and boards rather than computers.

"Why, you into him?" says Dougie Nash. He makes a stupid face, makes panting noises. She decides on the spot he will never so much as touch her again.

"Don't be an asshole," she says.

She isn't *into* anybody. But she is curious. Why did this Michael Hodge help her if not to hit on her? Why protect her if not to claim the reward?

"If you see him, say thanks for me, okay?" She's dressed now, ready to go. It feels good to know she won't be coming back.

"For what?"

"He'll know."

"Sure you don't want the intro?"

"Don't be stupid."

But she drives by Wind and Sea the next three nights running, wondering if one of the bobbing heads out in the water is him.

She sees him seven months later at — where else? — the Nashes' Christmas party. Families. Her mother and father, sister and brother. The Nashes and their children. Neighbors. Michael Hodge. The beard and dreads are gone and his thick hair is cropped close to his head. She likes him better this way. A gladiator. She is more aware of his eyes, how clear and steady they are. When he sees her, he immediately comes over.

"Hey," he says, smiling.

"Hey," she says, pushing the water glass of vodka off to the side.

"Merry Christmas."

"To you."

They don't ask each other's names. They don't acknowledge that this is the first time they've actually met. It's as if there's no need to waste time on getting to know each other. They keep sharing looks and tiny smiles that suggest secrets only the two of them possess. They take a single glass of white wine into the backyard. *He* does. She has decided not to drink any more tonight and is already regretting it. But then he inadvertently spills and, eyes locked with his, she takes his hand and licks the wine off his finger and it's just enough. The imminent sense of dread seems far away.

"All right," she finally says.

"All right what?"

"All right thank you for what you did that night."

He shrugs as if it were no big deal. "Glad I could help."

"You never said anything after."

288

"I know."

"How come?"

"I was seeing someone. If I'd started talking to you, I would have had to stop seeing them."

"Smart. Are you seeing anyone now?"

"If I was, I wouldn't be talking to you."

"Good answer," she says. The pleasure she's feeling she knows to be illogical and impermanent. Still, she would not lose this moment for anything.

A week and half later, without saying a word about what they both know is happening, they go down to the beach with a six-pack of beer and a sleeping bag. They have been inseparable. Coffee, movies, walks, swims, and meals. There have been kisses. There has been the holding of hands. There has been some minor touching. It is cold on the beach and the night is a canopy of stars overhead. She would consider it romantic if she believed in such things.

"Tell me what you like," he says to her after a while.

"I like everything you're doing," she tells him.

"You get to a place and you stop," he says to her a while later.

"If you don't think I like this, like being here and doing this with you, you are so wrong." She feels anxious that she's not pleasing him. It's certainly never been an issue before. But they start again and it all goes okay. Better than okay. Fake it to make it, her mother has told her. She was talking about dinner parties but it obviously applies to sex. And in pretending to have some kind of monster orgasm for him, in a way, more emotional than physical, she does. She feels she's in a cocoon with him, safe from the world, possibly changing. She feels the wetness in her and on her and, realizing they haven't used protection, she wonders if she'll get pregnant. It doesn't seem like it would be such a bad thing.

Despite her parents' protests, three days later, just before she is to depart, she refuses to go back to school. Eight months later, despite apocalyptic opposition, she and Michael leave for Australia. She doesn't experience a panic attack again until the day she leaves him eight years later, and when she does, she feels she deserves it.

35

As he drives up the hill to the country club, Michael finds himself thinking of his father. Thomas Hodge considered the occasional father-son round of golf together quality time and they were, at the very least, always memorable. Familiar with them now, Michael wonders if his father didn't have autistic tendencies because when not compulsively searching bushes and hazards for lost balls, Thomas, oblivious to situation, yardage, playing partners, and score, would hit his favored TopFlite in all directions with one of the six ancient clubs he carried, no rhyme or reason to the club selection, then obsessively hole out every putt, collect every broken tee, and fill every divot, while Michael, as calculated as his father was unconscious, would work the ball down the fairway and onto the green, often scoring bogey or better, delighting Thomas Hodge to no end.

"That is called talent, Ensign. You cannot teach that. A little practice, you'll be out on tour and I'll be caddying for you, happy to do it."

"Sounds like a plan, Pops."

Only it wasn't. Thomas Hodge, as confident and energized on an aircraft carrier as an astronaut on a space station, would often come down with a case of what Penelope Hodge called the melancholies when home.

"Where's Dad?"

"Swimming, darling. He's gone swimming."

Like the father in the play Michael's class had been forced to go see in the sixth grade, Thomas Hodge was most comfortable with family at a distance. And then, Michael discovered surfing.

"Ten o'clock tee time at Sea and Air, Ensign. Ready to take the old man down?"

"Rain check, Pops. Four-foot break at Blacks."

"Roger that." Pushing glasses up his nose. Frowning slightly. "Another time then."

Only there wasn't another time. Michael kept surfing and Thomas Hodge kept swimming.

As Michael pulls into the club parking lot, his truck, like his father, a fish out of water, he wishes yet again that life, like golf, gave you mulligans.

"Ten o'clock tee time at Sea and Air, Ensign. Ready to take the old man down?"

"You're on. But it'll never happen, Pops."

And it didn't.

Neal Beacham looks up from his *Wall Street Journal* as Michael is led to the table in the men's grill by a Mexican waiter.

"You're supposed to wear a shirt with a collar here."

Michael, wearing a button-down band-collared cotton shirt with his khakis, stops, staring a moment.

"Well, I guess I can leave or you can buy me one in the pro shop, Neal."

Neal glances at the dispassionate waiter, wondering if there is such a thing as a Caucasian standoff. He puts aside his paper. "Hell with it. Sit down." Neal gestures at the empty glass in front of him. "Another one of these, Ramon. Michael?"

"Iced tea."

"And bring him a menu. I've already ordered."

Nodding politely, the waiter moves away. Michael glances around. The men's grill might as well be an old folks' home for moldering, dissipated white males. One hopes the Mexican waitstaff is trained in

293

CPR. Everywhere Michael looks he sees gray hair, rheumy eyes, and pink-flushed faces. All that's missing are metal walkers and, hell, maybe there's a check room for them somewhere. The view out the picture windows, though, is remarkable. One hundred and eighty degrees of blue Pacific Ocean racing toward the distant horizon, the village with its thoroughfares and squares of buildings and neighborhoods, all spread out like an expensive board game. It could be the South of France, where Michael once competed in a crazy barrel surf contest, only the short, vicious tube rides counting. Neal Beacham, of course, has his back to it. So do most of these satisfied old farts.

"How you been, Michael?" says Neal, reaching into a bowl for a package of saltines. "We don't see you much. Not that we should."

"I'm getting by."

"Need to do better than that. Too many people in this world just get by."

"Maybe not all of us have your advantages, Neal."

The package of crackers freezes in midair. Neal Beacham stares. "Sarcasm, Michael?"

"Not capable of it, Neal. Not smart enough."

"Hmm."

Michael watches as Neal Beacham opens the saltines and begins aggressively munching. "You know, Michael," says Neal Beacham, spitting crumbs, "I always thought Anita was a fool to bail on you the way she did. You deserved better than that."

"She had her reasons."

"Did she? Explain them to me."

The waiter puts down their drinks. The tea is dark and cold looking, in a tall, frosted glass. Neal Beacham's drink is clear, comes with olives, and is on ice. Looking at it, Michael realizes he's never had a noontime martini, and certainly not a second one, in his entire life. Just another reason to avoid country clubs.

"Is that why you asked me to come by, Neal? To explain your daughter to you?"

Neal Beacham sips his drink, surprised that he doesn't want to throw it across the table. He remembers now that he likes Michael. Not smart but levelheaded. Ingenuous in his lack of respect. The kind to do a lot with nothing. His own son, Neal Jr., could learn a thing or two from him.

"A one-hundred-fifty-unit housing project was recently cleared for one of the last large tracts of land in North County. The developers are trying to get their financing through the bank. We think it's feasible. They haven't chosen the contractor yet."

"A hundred and fifty houses?"

"Roads, sewers, community center — all high-end construction. Think you could handle it?"

Michael hesitates, then nods. "Yes."

"No, you couldn't, not in a million years. But if you took a position with the company the developers *do* choose, in a couple of years, you *would* be able to oversee a job like that yourself."

"You could set this up?"

"I wouldn't be talking about it, if I couldn't."

"What's the catch, Neal? Why me?"

Neal Beacham fortifies himself with another sip of cold gin. "Do you love Jamie, Michael? Of course you do. A man loves his children. Well, guess what? I don't. Each and every one of them has disappointed me. And now my daughter, who I'd like to point out is still legally your wife, has moved back home and seemingly has no intention of leaving. I want her out of my house and I want to stop worrying about her."

"I take care of her, you take care of me? Is that it?"

"Something like that." A different waiter — *what's his damn Mexican name?* They all look alike to him — puts lunch down in front of Neal Beacham. He's ordered the veal chop today. It comes with potatoes, and mixed vegetables. He picks up a shaker and salts the meat heavily. He looks up to see Michael staring at him.

"Aren't you going to order?"

"What if she doesn't want to come back," says Michael, ignoring the question. "You ever thought of that?"

"Oh, come on. I'm not looking for guarantees. I just want to know you're open to the idea. And because you are, when the time comes, you'll act accordingly."

"Do I get a bonus if I propose again?"

"Don't get snippy with me. I'm not asking for much and you know it."

Michael stares at the old man — the old man who calmly cuts his meat, sticks a piece in his mouth, and chews, as if all they were discussing is tiddledywinks, the old man who grunts and reaches again for the salt, the shaker trembling slightly in his hand.

"What about my people?" says Michael. "I have a foreman, workers. They depend on me."

The saltshaker stops and hovers, vibrating above the plate. "You're the one who needs a job like this, Michael. I wouldn't worry about people." The veal is tough. The vegetables are tasteless. It's *people,* thinks Neal Beacham, who can't get anything right. "Well, what do you say?"

"I'll think about it," says Michael.

Neal Beacham smiles tightly. "Fine. You do that."

Pushing the menu aside, Michael rises.

"No lunch?" Neal Beacham seems surprised.

"Not hungry." Something is gnawing at Michael and he realizes what it is now. "You know one of the reasons she left, Neal? She's never believed anyone could really love her. She has this feeling she's not worthy of love. Where do you think that came from, the feeling she isn't worth giving a shit about?"

"Is this your idea of a lecture?"

"You asked. Thanks for the iced tea."

Neal Beacham watches as Michael turns away and crosses the dining room without looking back. Not liking him nearly so much now. Maybe it would be easier to buy his daughter a condo.

A small one.

36

Michael comes home to find his mother systematically rooting through garbage.

He has left the country club and Neal Beacham so unsettled, he goes to Trader Joe's to do some grocery shopping. Michael has always found the act of buying food, not so much hunting but gathering, a pleasant passage of time, and it doesn't hurt that the local Trader Joe's is next to a 24-Hour Fitness and the store is most often teeming with attractive young women in workout clothes buying premade salads and two-dollar wine. Always invigorating. Michael also likes the prepackaged meals. It's nice to have a place to go to that more than once has put exotic items like tikka masala and chicken pasta Alfredo on the kitchen table for Jamie to refuse, then reluctantly taste, and then say, finally, "I like it." The alternative would be burgers with fries and ketchup seven nights a week.

He is checking out the ingredients in a frozen lasagna — should the beef be organic? Or is it just the kale? — when a voice assails him.

"Michael, Michael. Oh my God, Michaelllll . . . !"

Shit.

It is Beth Beacham. Michael can never remember her married name. She is making her way toward him, grocery cart in tow, skinny jeans turning her into a plump sausage stuffed into a too-tight casing.

Here a Beacham, there a Beacham, everywhere a Beacham-Beacham.

"Beth," he says, forcing a smile. "Hey, good to see you."

The wrong thing to say, far too intimate, because Beth throws her arms around him and in the middle of the frozen food aisle, in a voice husky with emotion, tells all within yodeling distance, customers, fitness trainers, and employees, "Oh, Michael. She's back, Michael. She's back, she's back."

Beth. Sweet and somewhat goofy when sober. A drama queen with even one glass of wine inside her. And obviously it's already been cocktail hour somewhere in the world today.

"Oh, Michael, Michael, Michael . . ."

"Yeah, I know, I know," Michael murmurs, not knowing anything, but nudging her back a bit, trying to establish a bubble of space.

"She's home," says Beth fervently. "She is home for good this time. You know that, don't you?" Still nose to nose with him, bubbles be damned.

"Yeah, maybe so," Michael replies.

"She is doing so much better."

"You'd know that better than I would."

"No, Michael. No." As if horrified at the thought. "No one knows her like you. No one."

"Yeah, well . . ."

Why isn't he wearing a watch when he needs one? You glance at it — oops, running late, you say. Hard to do when you've put your father's Rolex in a bureau drawer for safekeeping and these days you tell time with a cell phone. Has Neal put her up to this? He suspects a setup.

"We have just got to get together, Michael. We need to put our heads together. We need to put together a game plan, the two of us."

"You're right, we should do that."

Michael remembering the first time he was ever alone with Beth. It would have been the kitchen at her parents' home, with Anita in the adjacent family room watching television. Beth had pushed him up against the refrigerator, pushed a clumsy leg into his crotch, and proclaimed her availability whenever Michael wanted because "no one has to know."

"Your sister's a little aggressive," he'd said later to Anita.

"She always wants what I have," Anita had said, unconcerned. "If she comes on to you, hit her on the nose with a rolled-up newspaper."

"I am killing myself, Michael, I am killing myself."

Michael is pulled back from his reverie by the thought of Beth's imminent suicide.

"Sorry?"

"That little boy of yours? Jamie? Oh, so sweet. We have just *got* to have him over to play with Bebe and Everett. We have just got to. And you too. Because you know how Bob feels about you. He admires you so much."

This is news to Michael. He and Bruin Bob have said less than one hundred words to each other in their entire lives, most of them consisting of "hi," "how ya doing," and "bye."

"I know! We'll have a barbecue. And we'll invite Anita. And Mom and Daddy too. It'll be family again, Michael."

Michael, reminded of Anita's joke that if

you ever find yourself thinking your family is crazy go to a state fair. And if that doesn't work go to the Beacham house.

"We'll see how it goes, Beth."

"You're right. First things first. You have my number?"

"I'm sure I do."

"We'll put our heads together. We'll solve this."

"I'm sure we will. I gotta get moving, Beth."

"I do too. Oh, Michael. So good to see you."

"You too."

As Michael finishes the rest of his shopping, he is aware that she is never too far away, in fact, seems to be tagging along. They hit checkout at the same time, he at one register, she at another. "We've got to stop meeting like this," she says, making it sound like it's his idea. They walk to the parking lot. At her request, he helps her load her groceries into the trunk of her car, and when Beth abruptly hugs him and kisses him on the cheek to say good-bye, she somehow misses and tries to stick her tongue in his mouth.

"Beth . . ."

"I'm sorry, you're right, you're right . . ." she says, almost whimpering. And then she leans close and whispers in his ear. "But Michael, if you ever want to . . . because I'm unhappy, Michael. And I've always cared about you so very, very much."

And now his mother is sorting through garbage.

Taken from the bins, the plastic kitchen bags are on the driveway, uniformly spaced, their contents spilled into awkward piles of refuse on the cement. The dog, Abigail, is wolfing down carrot peelings.

"What are you doing, Mom?" he asks, hoping it's something as simple as retroactively separating the recyclables but knowing it's not.

"Nana lost her money," says Jamie, who seems to be engaged in a spastic, one-man parade around the periphery of the driveway, skipping, hopping, and flapping. "We're looking for her money in the garbage!"

"There was fifty dollars in my purse," says Penelope, dumping another plastic bag out onto the cement.

"Are you sure you didn't spend it?"

"Of course I didn't spend it, Michael. I'd remember if I spent it, wouldn't I?"

Would she? Three days ago she arrived home in a police car, having been picked up, wandering up and down the boulevard.

"I wasn't wandering, Michael. I was *lost.*

There's a complete difference."

She'd gone off to see the remains of the old house. To say good-bye to it, as it were.

"The problem is I *walked.* I'm sure if I'd driven, I'd have remembered *exactly* where I was going."

"Mom, just ask me, I'll take you wherever you want to go."

"Oh, really, Michael, I don't need or want you to do *everything* for me. Besides, there are things one must do oneself. And if you can't understand that, there's really not much at all I can do about it, is there."

She had been on the verge of tears.

"Besides. It was the coming back *here,* darling, that was so difficult. I found the old place just fine. The lovely bones. And I said a prayer and I left a little something there. A bit of spirit, I think. And in return, I took any number of precious memories with me. Now give me one good reason why after all that I wouldn't get a bit lost."

Knowing he had any number of good reasons but none that would satisfy her, Michael hadn't answered.

"Mom, why do you think your fifty dollars is in the garbage bin?"

"Because where else would it be? Do stop asking stupid questions, Michael, and help."

And so he does. He hunkers down and

digs through eggshells, cucumber and carrot peelings, and coffee grounds, through open sardine cans . . .

"Who doesn't like sardines, darling?"

. . . and old, cooked spaghetti, Abigail at his hip, tail wagging expectantly, stomach gurgling with expectation . . .

"Do not feed her, Michael, she's a pig!"

"I *know*, Mom."

. . . until, finally disgusted, he excuses himself, goes into the house, and pulling out his wallet, puts two twenties and a ten into Penelope's purse.

"Mom, look, your money's right here in your purse."

"What? No. Really?"

"See? Fifty."

"But — I know I checked."

"It's all right here, Mom."

"And I could have sworn it was a single bill." Penelope doesn't look so much suspicious as perplexed.

"Mom, what difference does it make? It's fifty bucks and it's in your purse."

"Oh, maybe I *am* getting just a bit forgetful." And taking the money she goes into the house, leaving him to return the garbage to the bags, the bags to the bins, and the bins to the side of the house.

Uu-unck — hu-uck — hoo-unk!

Michael turns. The dog is vomiting. Spewing carrot peelings and chicken bones, kibble and green bile onto the driveway.

"Abbie's puking money, Dad," says Jamie, pointing at the wadded and sordid fifty-dollar bill. He giggles in happy disgust as Michael carefully picks up the bill.

Would that the fucking dog could.

"Abbie is buying us Bahia for dinner with this," Michael says, naming their favorite Mexican takeout.

"Yay!" says Jamie. Together, they turn and head into the house, Michael determined to open the first of what will be several cold beers. What's worse? he wonders. Crotchety old men, unhappy women, or puking dogs?

At least it didn't come out its ass.

Holding the bill by the edge, he shuts the gate, intent on putting the day and all things Beacham behind him.

37

As Fari prepares herself dinner, she tells herself yet again that she has done the right thing. For him, yes, of course, but mostly for her. She had no choice. Her upbringing, her education, the values and morals she holds herself to, what little remains of her religion — all dictated her decision.

Still.

When she lets her guard down, she feels sick with the knowledge that Michael is no longer in her life. She wonders if this is what being in love is — to feel physically ill at its loss.

She has turned to what has always been important to her. She has worked extra hours, seeing more patients. She runs, she shops, she meditates. Music has been proven to have a therapeutic effect and so she listens to the radio, mostly classical stations. Even though food seems to have no taste, she cooks, she sets the table, she opens good wine, she eats. She watches some television. She reads before bed. Her mind keeps constantly going to him. She berates herself for it.

Pain is the gateway to lasting happiness, she tells the people who come to her for advice, for help, for solace.

Easy for you to say.

She goes to visit friends in Los Angeles. Fellow Iranian expats. Successful and well educated. So very stylish and sophisticated. She feels like a performer in a play with characters she no longer knows. They arrange a date for her. He is an orthopedic surgeon, a bit older, divorced, brilliant, part of the "brain drain" that left Iran in the nineties, the kind of man she used to be in the habit of having affairs with. He has family in Tabriz who refuse to upgrade to mobile phones and he jokes about how bad the landline service is in Iran. He has been back recently. It is all double-digit unemployment and sky-high inflation, he says. No one in their right mind would live there. He proceeds to tell her all about women's knees, and when he conspiratorially compares a lateral meniscus to a beautiful vagina, she smiles politely, excuses herself, goes out to the parking lot, gets in her car, and drives back to San Diego. She cries the entire way, telling herself it's perfectly natural to feel what she's feeling, not believing it for a second. She wonders, not for the first time, if she's afraid of happiness. She reminds herself that the conflicts associated with the human condition can often impact one's capacity to accept and enjoy love. When we feel cherished and admired by a loved one, we place greater value on ourselves and therefore we face more pain related to the loss of that person. Consciously or unconsciously we may pull back from love.

Blah-blah-blahshit.

She spends the entire fourth weekend unable to get out of bed. It's not so much grief and longing anymore. It's not even about Michael. It's that her life seems like a gilded, empty house. All façade. No roots. Nothing real inside. She feels helpless to do anything about it.

The phone rings while she is eating dinner. For a moment she wonders if it's him. Don't be silly, she thinks. But she lets the answering machine take it anyway.

"This is Dr. Fari Akrepede. If this is of a professional nature, please call my office at 858–555–0971. Otherwise, leave a message and I will get back to you as soon as I can."

Fari likes it that the voice — *her* voice —

sounds well trained and very professional. It betrays nothing. She will be back to that place soon.

I have to be.

The machine beeps, she hears the faint voice of her mother, and she rushes to the phone.

38

The library is dark. Something about shelves lined with old, unread leather-bound books makes a room quiet. Provides soundproofing. Has a certain smell. As do old cushions and silk throws. When in the throes of a migraine or a panic attack, Anita has often sought refuge here. Curled up, closed her eyes, and feigned sleep.

Sessions with the dark-haired Dr. Akrepede aren't doing anything. It's all too vague, too harmony-speak. The good doctor recommends books and articles to read. All recommend mood diaries, positive thinking, meditation, tapping, and deep breathing, and Anita feels a need for something far stronger. Like an exorcism. Like a memory wipe. Like a drink. It's exhausting when the past is constantly confronting you.

Constantly.

The day she leaves them, she leaves *knowing*

she is leaving. Before Michael goes to work, she hugs him. She holds him tight and kisses him.

"What's this about?" he says.

"Nothing," she says.

Later in the morning after putting Jamie down for a nap, she calls Penelope and asks if she can come over. "Errands to do," she says. Her bags are packed and in the trunk when Penelope arrives. Starting the car, she falters, panic welling up in her, suddenly not sure she can do it. But then she does.

She drives north to L.A. and checks into a mid-range hotel. She fully expects — *wants* — to feel guilt, despair, and self-loathing. It's only fair. But she doesn't. She finds the solitude a balm. For the first time in she isn't sure how long, she feels at peace. No one is asking anything of her or expecting her to be what she isn't and feels she never can be. It's so easy to deal with people at a distance, even those you love. You can make it *their* fault.

On the fourth day, slightly concerned she might not ever come out of the room, she calls her mother. Tisha is not so much frantic as she is indignant.

"What do you think you're doing?"

"Michael and I have separated."

"Have you told him? He's beside himself

with worry."

"I can't go back."

"And your child?"

"He's better off with Michael."

"There's no talking to you on this, is there."

It's a statement not a question and Anita says nothing.

"Where are you?" asks her mother.

She drives up and in three days moves Anita into a small, one-bedroom apartment in the flats of Beverly Hills. Furniture is purchased at Ikea. Kitchenware, towels, and linens at Walmart. "You can leave it behind at a moment's notice," Tisha says.

"Don't tell Michael where I am," says Anita.

"I'm not the idiot," says her mother, departing. "You are."

As she gains courage, she ventures farther and farther out from the apartment. She walks to the grocery store for food. She goes to the Verizon store where she opens a new account and buys a new, virgin phone. She goes to Rodeo Drive where she finds the people more interesting than the clothes. She's hopelessly out of style, hasn't so much as tried anything new on in years. Like her mother, she shops, quickly and efficiently, knowing instinctively what's a fad and what will last. "You make anything look good," says a salesgirl, wistfully. She smiles politely, goes back to the apartment, stuffs the new clothes in the closet, and closes the door.

She is in Starbucks on Beverly Drive when a guy — inevitably — hits on her. He is an actor. Is she? Why not, yes. Is she working, does she have an agent, who is she studying with? No, no, and no one. He makes recommendations. He gives advice. When he asks for her phone number, she makes one up on the spot. Call me, she says and goes home.

But a week later she does enroll in an acting class, not because she is all that interested in acting, but because it will make her feel as if she's working toward something. A goal. A noble endeavor. Actors are artists, artists make sacrifices. Family, friends, relationships. Artists tend toward crazy. They can't be held accountable for a fucked-up muse.

She attends the classes. She watches. She listens. It's impossible to take sensory exercises and emotional recall seriously and she thinks of quitting. She does a scene from a Neal LaBute play with another woman. She kills. Unlike Thornton Wilder, she *gets* Neal LaBute. Cynicism, anger, and self-loathing are right up her alley. The teacher recommends her to an agent, the agent sends her out on some casting calls, and she finds herself sitting in rooms with a throng of young women who were, without a doubt, the most beautiful girls in their own hometowns. She feels happily lost in the crowd. She doesn't care if she gets cast or not and so of course she does. A walk-on in an episode of a TV series — third whore from the left. A commercial, both film and print, where she pretends to be — *are you kidding me?* — a blissful mother. The bar girl with no name who gets picked up by the star, then shot to death, naked in bed, twenty-six seconds of screen time later. She moves up the pecking order. She is the drug lord's mistress in a pilot that doesn't get picked up. She is the Navy SEAL's philandering wife in a pilot that doesn't get picked up. She is the oncologist in a medical pilot that *does* get picked up and is killed in the third episode by the scalpel-wielding wife of the brain surgeon she's having an illicit affair with. She comes to realize that while the bits and pieces of lives portrayed on screen might seem interesting and dramatic, the making of those pretend moments, the countless takes and ten-hour turnarounds, is tedious and boring to the point of brain death. She decides that someone who never goes to movies, never watches television, and doesn't have the patience to sit through even a one-act play, has no business being an actor, and she quits the profession for good.

Pretending in real life is another thing entirely.

The woman from the class who has become sort of a friend calls one day to ask if she'll emergency sub for her at a restaurant — a hostess position. She does and finds it busy and fun. Flirtation with strangers. A faux social life. A paycheck that she has automatically deposited into a savings account in Jamie's name — automatic because the actual setting up of the account sends her into a sinkhole she can't climb out of for a week. Automatic means you don't have to think about it anymore.

Within a year she's named an assistant manager. It's more money, more responsibility, and more hours, and after three days, she quits and takes another hostess position for less money at a different restaurant.

She drinks. Not too much at any one time but constantly and consistently, effectively creating a state where she's never quite drunk but never exactly sober. She likes to think of herself as a dentist using Novocain to dull a throbbing tooth. She offsets the alcohol with exercise. She runs, she spins, she does yoga — often all three in one day. She goes to clubs and dances till the early hours of the morning. Exhaustion also dulls painful teeth.

She occasionally sleeps with men. She very occasionally sleeps with women. Usually not more than once and never at her own place. Almost always it feels like an athletic event she's supposed to be good at and isn't. It makes her self-conscious. It makes her uncomfortable. Talking afterward is still excruciating.

At least a dozen times she gets in the car and drives south, determined to confront her past, to admit her mistakes and failings and beg forgiveness. Invariably she gets there and immediately turns around and goes back, not even stopping for gas.

She wakes up one morning. Alone. It's three years later. It's Christmas morning. She thinks of Michael. She thinks of Jamie. She longs for a warm, safe place. By four that afternoon she's in the emergency room at Cedars-Sinai. She has consumed a quart of vodka, gotten into her car, and crashed it head-on into a telephone pole. The doctor on call tells her she's lucky to be alive and then asks her out.

At last, she thinks. The bottom. Never

once considering it's not.

The black phone on the nearby side table suddenly rings, startling her and sending waves of nausea through her gut. The damn thing — *is that actually still a rotary?* — jangles again. And then again. And then it stops.

Thank God.

Anita settles back on the couch, pulls the silk throw up and over her face. She hears the approaching footsteps out in the hall. Not what she needs right now. And then, the door to the library opens and her mother is standing there, somehow making drab pants and a man's cotton shirt look chic. Not for the first time, Anita wonders if her mother isn't secretly from another planet.

Which means both of us are aliens.

As if reading Anita's mind, Tisha Beacham frowns in annoyance.

"Oh, for goodness sake, Anita."

She moves across the room toward the heavy drapes. With hard jerks, she pulls them open.

"Let in some light."

Bright sunlight pours in, filling the room with dust motes. Anita moans and winces in pain. Tisha turns to her.

"You know these headaches of yours are purely psychosomatic. You only get them when you want to avoid things."

"Thanks for the sympathy."

"You don't need sympathy, you need two Tylenol. Now please, pick up the phone. Your *son* is calling."

"Hi, Mom, this is Jamie."

As if it could be anyone else. His voice is excited. He sounds pleased. Which thrills her to the bone. The landline — this rotary phone — is a wonderful invention.

"Hi, baby, I'm so glad you called."

"I know. Mom, can you play soccer I gotta go now bye."

"Can I what? Jamie? Are you there? Hello?"

"Guess who?"

The who being Michael. It makes her smile. "What's going on?"

"He's playing soccer this afternoon and he wants you to come and watch."

"I didn't know he played soccer."

"He has never," says Michael, "played soccer in his entire life."

"Sounds like an occasion."

"You have no idea. Why don't you come by the house around noon and we'll all go together."

Ten minutes later, in the shower, washing her hair, Anita realizes her headache is gone.

39

She sees immediately that it is more than just a soccer game. It's not just the tents and banners that line the wide swathe of green that is Presidio Park. It's not the groups and families manning the grills and sitting on blankets and beach chairs and playing volleyball. And it's not the parents and grandparents and coaches and volunteers.

It's the children.

Anita doesn't need a program to tell that some of them are retarded, that some have Down syndrome, that some with their flapping hands and vacant expressions are severely autistic. And there are so many of them. They're everywhere, all ages, some bawling inarticulately, others twisting and moaning, their parents and siblings — *handlers* — encouraging them, restraining them, calming them with words and hugs and caresses.

Apprehensive in the most sedate of crowds, Anita feels her stomach churning like a pit of bubbling mud. She watches as Michael finishes tying the laces on Jamie's new soccer cleats, the laces he was helpless to tie himself.

"Lookin' like a star, bub," says Michael.

"I know," says Jamie.

Star of what? Anita wonders. Jamie, like many of the children, has been given a soccer shirt. SPECIAL NEEDS FAMILY FUN DAY is emblazoned like an advertisement across the chest.

Why advertise?

"All our soccer players! Let's get you over here!"

They turn. Near the first field, a man in a baseball cap is waving people to him. A group of older boys and girls, college-age volunteers, all of them tanned and athletic and smiling, are gathered around the man, holding soccer balls. All wear T-shirts with the SPECIAL NEEDS FAMILY DAY logo.

"Come on, who wants to play some soccer!"

The young volunteers cheer, such a wall of warmth and support that Anita can only assume they're Mormons.

"You ready to play, little man?" says Michael, kneeling.

Anita sees the sudden hesitation in the boy, the uncertainty. Good, maybe they can leave and go to lunch, just the three of them. But Michael puts his hands on Jamie's shoulders and speaks softly, warmly.

"We'll be right here waiting. Just like when you're in the therapy room with Bridget."

Jamie nods. "I'm ready," he says, and turning away, he hurries to join the other children, Anita noting again that his left arm flaps with excitement as he runs, that his stride is full of intermittent skips and hops. She feels embarrassed for him. And then upset at herself for feeling it.

"Hey."

She realizes Michael is looking at her.

"He's glad you're here."

"Me too," she says. She smiles, hoping she's doing a better acting job than she did for Little Mary Sunshine. Mounties and petticoats and an audience of parents and peers didn't give her half as much stage fright as this.

The game begins and Anita and Michael join the other parents and families on the sidelines to watch. Most of the children have one of the college kids standing close by, instructing and encouraging. Shadows, Michael calls them.

"No headers!" shouts the man in the baseball cap. Meaning don't hit the ball with your head, Michael explains. Not that any of these children would. Most of them are skittish about the fast-moving, flying ball. Even the older ones flinch, put up their hands and shy away. And it's quickly obvious to Anita that most of them know even less about the game of soccer than she does. One boy picks up the ball and dribbles it as if on a basketball court. A painfully thin girl, wearing ballet slippers and a tutu with her soccer shirt, spins in circles and falls down on the grass. A child holds a ball and, wailing, refuses to give it back. Some children, upset by the noise and crowd, don't wish to join in at all. They rock, they run away, they stare into space, lost in their own worlds. But some of the children, Anita sees, do try to play, and their enthusiasm, as well as that of the parents and volunteers, is enormous. Just making contact, foot to ball, is a reason to applaud, and a kick that actually sends the ball in the right direction is cause for a celebration. And when Jamie breaks away from the middle of the field, chasing the ball toward the near goal, Anita is suddenly beside herself with excitement.

"Go, Jamie, go," she screams.

Almost falling, Jamie kicks the ball down

the field toward the goalie, who stands in place looking confused.

"He's going to score," says Michael.

And he is. As Jamie runs after the ball, the goalie leaves the net and comes out to meet him.

"Oh, please," whispers Anita. "Please."

And then she gapes as instead of booting the ball past the goalie, Jamie picks it up and offers it to him. Smiling with pleasure, the goalie takes the ball, turns, and heaves it into his own net. "Score!" shouts Michael. He's laughing. Everyone is. The crowd begins to cheer as Jamie and the goalie raise their hands above their heads to slap clumsy high fives.

"Are you crying?" Michael asks her.

"This is laughing," says Anita.

"You're doing both then."

She is. Anita has been to sporting events before, usually begrudgingly, but in no stadium or arena or ballpark has she ever heard a crowd cheer louder.

For her son.

They picnic afterward. Tents and tables have been set up selling food and drink and Michael goes to one of the community grills and comes back with hot dogs and chips and Gatorade. They sit together on the soft grass, eating from paper plates.

"I did *very* well," says Jamie, yet again.

"You did just great," says Anita.

"You were fabulous, little man," Michael says.

It doesn't seem quite so disconcerting now. The rocking children, the wordless sounds, the tics and spasms. Anita is more aware of the patience and devotion of the parents. They're like Michael. She wonders if you learn this with practice. She wants to. She needs to.

"Michael!"

A middle-aged man is approaching, stepping carefully through the picnicking families. AUTISM ROCKS! proclaims his T-shirt. A pale young man with a bad complexion is with him.

"Walter, hey!" says Michael, rising to his feet to shake hands.

"Jamie, you did great out there."

"I *know,*" says Jamie.

"Mr. Modest," says Michael, grinning and ruffling Jamie's hair.

The man, now identified as Walter, glances at Anita, nods quickly, and turns back to Michael. "Michael, this is my son, David. David, this is Mr. Hodge and his son, Jamie."

No response. No words. The young man

shifts uncomfortably and looks away. I'm being rude, thinks Anita, and she tries unsuccessfully to rise, her brain saying one thing, her body stubbornly doing another.

"It's been a big day for him too," says the man called Walter. "Huh, David?" The young man, now identified as David, seems to be listening to a voice deep inside his head.

Not meaning to, Anita clears her throat.

"Oh," says Michael. "This is Jamie's mom, Anita. Anita, this is Walter Seskin. He runs the autism lab at the university. Jamie's been doing some therapy there."

Mom. With a title now and reason to be here, it's suddenly easy for Anita to get to her feet. Easy to hold out her hand. "Hi. Anita Hodge." The married surname comes out by accident, unplanned and blurted. Impossible to take back. She glances at Michael who, if he's heard it, doesn't let on.

"Dad! Dad, look!"

It's Jamie and he's pointing. Across the grassy field a man wearing a blanketlike poncho and a wide-brimmed straw hat has arrived and is leading a string of complacent, oddly gaited animals behind him. "Autistic horses" is what flares, unbidden, into Anita's head. Now it's her brain that isn't obeying her.

"Llamas!" says Jamie. "The man has llamas! Dad, those are llamas!"

"Ah-mahs!" cries the young man, David, his dark eyes now wide and intent, his body suddenly shivering.

"What do you think, guys," says Michael. "Wanna go see'm?"

"Yes!" says Jamie.

"No!" blurts David, his face suddenly frightened. "Too many."

"Too many llamas or too many people?" says Walter Seskin.

"Pee-puh."

Anita watches as Walter Seskin leans in close to whisper softly into his son's ear. "You can do it. You're my big guy. Go on. Go with Jamie."

Like Michael.

At the sound of his name, Jamie grabs the older boy's hand. "C'mon, David! Let's go see the llamas!" He tugs, pulling David after him, the bigger boy reluctant at first and then less so, following the smaller boy.

"Ahmas! Go to see ahmas!"

"Incredible," says Michael, shaking his head.

"Cool," says Walter Seskin, as if it happens every day.

"I'll make sure they don't burn the place down." And with that, Michael is off, following the boys across the field.

No. He didn't have to learn anything, Anita thinks. It's who he is. She envies him for it. With a start, she realizes Walter Seskin is looking at her and she forces another smile. She's begun to feel as if she's selling soap door to door. "Well, what a special occasion this is!" Sounding just like her mother.

The alien.

"You have a great little guy there," says Walter Seskin.

"Thank you. I think so too."

She wonders how much this man knows of their circumstances, of her title of absentee wife and mother. Lately she's been telling people, the old acquaintances she invariably runs into, that she's been off on deployment. "Oh, yeah, overseas. Serving God and country." You can see in their faces that the joke doesn't fly. They know the truth. Absent and abandoned are two different words, two different worlds.

"You seem a little uncomfortable."

It's Walter Seskin speaking again.

"No. Not at all." Uncomfortable doesn't begin to describe what she's suddenly feeling. The mud pit in her stomach is sending toxic fumes into her esophagus.

Across the field, the children are gathered

in a mass around the pack animals. Michael is carefully running David's hand down a llama's flank.

"I hope they don't bite," Anita says.

"As a matter of fact, they do. They also spit. But it's life on life's terms. You learn from it. And that's worth it, don't you think?"

"I'm sure it is."

Looking back across the field, Michael sees Anita and Walter Seskin standing together and he wonders what they're talking about. Perhaps Anita will ask questions, perhaps Walter Seskin will fill her in, bring her up to speed. Make her realize, as he's beginning to, that the autism is a challenge not a death sentence. Perhaps. But probably not. She comes from a family where anything atypical and less than standard is considered a character flaw. It's no wonder she's never been able to talk honestly about herself.

"Hi," he heard her say. "Anita *Hodge.*"

Whoa, Nelly.

Yet again, he asks himself if he's making it all too easy for her. The answer is the same. No, not if it makes his son happy.

"We could invite her if we wanted to." It was both a question and a statement.

"We could."

"She will want to see me play." Again, question and statement.

"She might. Shall we call?"

"You."

"Uh-uh. You. I'll dial, you talk."

"Yes, I will."

And so he called and Jamie talked on the phone. A first. She came for him. She cheered for him. And look at him now. Getting ready to ride llamas with a friend. Let it go, thinks Michael. Forget the rules. Enjoy the moment.

He is.

"You know," says Walter Seskin, "when you first have kids, you think it's going to be like a trip to Italy."

"Italy?" Anita has no idea what he's talking about it, but it sounds like it's going to be either advice or a lecture and she's not in the mood for either one.

"You know, sunshine, good food. The kids are going to grow up happy and when the time comes, they'll move on to a life all their own."

"I'm not sure I'm following," says Anita, not sure she wants to.

"My point being that for a lot of us here" —Walter Seskin gestures in a way that takes in the families and the entire field — "the tickets got screwed up and we ended up in Iceland."

"Iceland."

Seskin smiles. "Actually in the literature it's Holland. But I've been to Holland and Holland is a pretty sweet place. Iceland, on the other hand, with its volcanoes and steam fields and black sand, is not what anyone expects."

"Unless you're from Iceland."

Walter Seskin laughs. "Good, that's good. You're right. But not many of us are."

Across the field, the children have formed a line, and those in the front, Jamie and David among them, are being helped by the splendid, shining-bright college kids onto oblivious llama backs.

"The point is," says Walter Seskin, "give it a chance and I think you'll find Iceland has its moments." Again, the expansive gesture. Is he talking about the families, the field, or the llamas?

"Good advice."

"Stop by the lab sometime, see what we're doing."

Experiments. You can run tests on me.

"I will. Thank you."

"And read the T-shirts."

"The shirts?"

"Special Needs Family Day. Emphasis on

family. We're all in it together."

"I'll remember that."

As Walter Seskin turns and walks across the soccer pitch toward the llamas and waiting children, Anita finds herself forcing yet another smile. Like Walter Seskin's gesture, it takes in everything. The people, the pitch. It feels fake and fearful and Anita is sure if she holds it too much longer, her face will break.

Iceland. I'm living in Iceland.

The effects of waves on a ship vary considerably with the type of ship, its course and speed, and the condition of the sea. The set and drift of ocean currents are of great concern to the navigator. More than any other single factor, waves are likely to cause a navigator to change course to avoid damage to a ship.

40

It's book buddies and Jamie hates it. He hates Ben Shapiro who seems to think he's being helpful when he corrects Jamie's pronunciation when they read out loud to each other. Jamie, who reads slowly and spells phonetically, thinks his pronunciation is just fine. As his friend Luis, who is no one's book buddy, has confirmed to him more than once, it's the words that are wrong.

"*Inglés,* Jaimito. Nothing looks like it sounds."

But Ben Shapiro won't listen. Ben Shapiro thinks he's so smart. Ben Shapiro is a farthead.

"Jamie, are you all right?"

It's Mrs. McKenzie, who's nice and who looks out for him but makes him do book buddies. He must be doing something wrong for her to ask if he's all right. And then he sees it. The other kids are putting away their papers and scissors and getting their books from their cubbies and he isn't. He's not moving. He's sitting by himself. Which is how he'd like to spend book buddies.

"I'm all right."

Mrs. McKenzie smiles at him. Mrs. McKenzie is nice and looks out for him, but still, she makes him do book buddies.

"Let's put away our things."

"Okay."

"Mrs. McKenzie — Mrs. McKenzie!"

Mrs. McKenzie turns away because Sara Rollins who has red hair and freckles which Jamie likes is calling for her. Jamie wishes Sara Rollins were his book buddy. Sara Rollins wouldn't tell him how to pronounce hard words. And even if she did, Jamie wouldn't mind.

The classroom door is open.

Ben Shapiro, whom Jamie avoids without thinking, is nowhere to be seen.

The classroom door is open.

It hits Jamie that Ben Shapiro, who gets sick a lot for no reason, hasn't been here all day. Which means he's absent. Which means Jamie will have to read with some other book buddy who won't be Sara Rollins who never makes fun of him.

The door is open.

Mrs. McKenzie isn't looking. Everyone is busy getting their books from their cubbies except for Jamie who is sitting. He rises from his desk and slips out the door.

It's quiet in the hallway and Jamie doesn't know where to go so he goes down the hall and around the corner to the boys' room because he's been holding it all day. He doesn't like going to the boys' room with the other boys when they go on a bathroom break. One time Kyle Bush told him it would be cool to flush a T-shirt from lost and found down the toilet and Jamie flushed. Only the T-shirt got stuck and the toilet overflowed and the boys laughed. Jamie tried to laugh too but he couldn't because it was the kind of thing that gets you into trouble and it did.

"What were you thinking, little man?" said Dad.

"Next time flush *Kyle Bush* down the toilet," said Nana.

What was even worse was that Mrs. Mc-Kenzie called a class meeting where she talked about the A-word. Meaning they talked about *him.* On the outside he tried not to pay attention but on the inside he did. Mrs. McKenzie said it wasn't nice to make fun of people. Would you make fun of a blind person? Would you make fun of someone who couldn't hear? Jamie isn't blind or deaf and he hates it when people talk about him. The only thing worse is when they talk *to* him and then he has to answer. Sort of like book buddies.

He enters the boys' room, hurries into a stall and closes the door. He has to go so bad. He drops his pants to the floor and he sits. He likes the boys' room when no one else is here. The tiles are cool. It's quiet. No one is talking all at once like they do in class and at lunch and at recess. His mind can look at pictures. He doesn't have to remember what he's supposed to be doing. Or what faces are saying. It's all so tiring and confusing all the time to try to understand what faces are saying and what words mean, but in an hour he can go home.

Jamie flushes. He reaches for toilet paper. There is none. Jamie's right hand begins to shake slightly as he tries to figure out what to do.

She has to admit it. Sometimes Karen McKenzie's favorite time of day is when the last bell rings and she can go outside on the playground and wave children good-bye.

"Bye, Mrs. McKenzie, bye!"

"Good-bye! See you tomorrow."

She loves her job, loves teaching, but

sometimes the energy and patience it takes to keep twenty-three second-graders organized and on task can be overwhelming. And they keep getting old so young. Cell phones. Miley Cyrus. The Walking Dead. It is Karen McKenzie's opinion that the vast majority of parents should be arrested for reckless driving and sent not to traffic school but to a parenting academy where they would be forced to learn lessons in protecting their children.

"Good-bye, Mrs. McKenzie!"

"See you tomorrow, Sara!"

Sara Rollins. One of the good ones. As is her mother, Liz, a working single parent. Just like —

Karen McKenzie looks around, puzzled. The playground is still busy but is beginning to empty. Some boys are shooting baskets. Aftercare is beginning at the outdoor tables. Children who will be picked up later. Karen McKenzie calls toward another teacher. "Helen, have you seen Jamie Hodge?"

The young woman, Helen Fowler, kindergarten, turns from where she's putting out after-school snacks.

"No, did he get picked up?"

"I don't think so."

"It's usually his father or his grandmother."

"I know. They meet him at the gate." Karen McKenzie turns and walks toward the playground entrance.

There are three boys and that's too many boys to say anything. They're yelling and laughing and flushing and running the water and making noise. If they know he's been sitting there with no paper and a stinky bottom they'll make fun of him. They'll tell people. He's probably already in trouble for having left the classroom. Mrs. McKenzie will *not* be smiling. Not only that, Mom is picking him up today and he was supposed to tell Mrs. McKenzie but he forgot. But maybe Mom will be smiling. Maybe she will think it's funny. An adventure even. Maybe he and Mom will make up a story about it and it will be a good story, not a bad story, and it will be fine.

Maybe.

In front of the school, the sixth-grade monitors are escorting children across the crosswalk. Cars, there for pickup, line both sides of the busy street. Karen McKenzie looks up and down the sidewalk, worried now. She knows from both study and experience that children on the spectrum tend to be runners. They're drawn to water, fascinated by road signs. They're hit by cars, they drown. She knows of a high school special-ed teacher who used to hide a particular student's shoes with the hopes of slowing him down.

How could she have taken her eye off him.

She's about to turn back into the school yard when a woman hurrying up the walk sees her and breathlessly approaches.

"Excuse me? Are you Mrs. McKenzie?"

The woman's hair is twenty shades of blond. The eyes are deep green. Karen McKenzie knows without having to ask that this is Jamie's mother.

"Yes."

The woman exhales in apparent relief. "Oh, God — great. I'm Anita Beacham. Jamie Hodge's mom? I'm picking him up today. Only I had a problem finding parking so I'm late."

A problem parking. To Karen McKenzie, a problem parking has always seemed a little too much like the dog ate my homework. Parents are supposed to know it's busy and arrive accordingly. Yet, the woman does seem flustered. Karen McKenzie can forgive beginners.

"I really hoped to get here early. Jamie told me all about you and I wanted to introduce myself. He's not worried, is he?"

"I'm not sure," says Karen McKenzie. "We can't seem to find him."

In the boy's lavatory, Henry Dominguez enters and hurries to a washbasin because if he wants an after-school snack, and he *does*, Miss Fowler says his hands must be clean. Henry turns on a faucet, hits the pushy nozzle thing that delivers soap, and begins to wash.

"Paper," a voice says.

Henry turns, his hands full of suds. "What?"

"I need paper," says the voice.

"I don't have any," says Henry Dominguez, and in anticipation of animal crackers, he departs the lavatory, drying his hands on the seat of his pants as he goes out the door.

In the closed stall, Jamie sits, his pants around his shoes. He has found one of his toy figures in the front pocket. He waves it in front of his face. He is nothing if not patient. Dad says this is a good thing.

Michael knows he should be working. He should be canvassing local architects, he should be talking to local real estate agents to see if any of their clients are discussing remodels or teardowns. Enrique Paz has gone back to Mexico and he should be looking for a new tile subcontractor. At the very least he should get off his *own* ass and go over and help Leo and the crew. Lose himself in hard, physical work and feel like he's accomplished something worthwhile. But he's just sitting at his desk. Sitting in his office. Staring into space. It's as if his brain weighs a ton.

The cell phone on his belt, turned to silent, vibrates, then vibrates again. Michael pulls it from its small plastic holster. He feels like an idiot, carrying it there — like wearing a plastic pen holder in a shirt pocket — but if he doesn't, it will be lost in an hour. He checks to see who's calling, already deciding he's not going to answer. Seeing who it is, he does.

"Hey, hello."

"Michael," Anita says. "Jamie's missing."

Michael feels his heart turn over, feels a sudden pain just above his groin.

"I came to the school to pick him up and I was late and now he's not here and they can't find him, they can't find him, Michael."

"Wait, slow down. What do you mean, can't find him?" Stupid question. Find is find, can't find is lost.

They've lost him.

Anita's voice, already shaking and strident, begins to further rise in pitch and tone. "I don't know they can't find him he's not here they're supposed to look after your kids aren't they that's what they're supposed to do, right — ?"

"He probably got tired of waiting and walked home. Did you try the house?"

"Yes, I tried the house I talked to your mom he's not he's not there he would be shouldn't he?"

Michael is moving out of the office now, past Rose who's aware that something is wrong, heading for the door because beyond the door is the truck and it's one foot in front of the other, one step at a time, that's how you get places, that's how you get things done. Not by feeling sorry for yourself. Not when people — when *he* — is depending on you. Get the keys out of your pocket.

Wake the fuck up!

"Is Mrs. McKenzie there?"

"Who?"

Don't raise your voice. Keep your cool.

"His teacher, Anita."

"Yeah, she's right here."

"Let me talk to her."

It's all going to be fine. Keep calm, keep

346

focused.

"Michael, it's Karen."

Be like Mrs. McKenzie who is a rock.

"How long has he been missing?"

"We're not sure. I know he was in class around two o'clock. No one's sure they've seen him since."

"When did you call the house?"

"As soon as we knew. Your mother's been there all afternoon. She'll call us if he shows up. We've informed the police, Michael. They've sent out a car."

"I'll be right there."

He disconnects. He's driving now and it wouldn't do to get pulled over for being on a cell phone. The police have more important things to do.

Anita remembers the time in sixth grade when Tisha Beacham was supposed to pick her and Beth up after an after-school event. Glee club or some silly thing. Waiting. And waiting. For someone who was never late. *Never.* Other parents asking if they were okay. "Yes, my mother will be here any minute." Only she wasn't. Beth beginning to cry. Anita quiet, silently daring her mother *not* to come, willing to stay in that one spot forever if she didn't.

Because this is your job and you're sup-

posed to do it. You do everything right all the time. Except what you don't do.

But of course her mother finally did arrive. An hour late, Tisha Beacham pulled into the middle school parking lot, rolled down the window, and staring straight ahead simply said, "Get in." On the way home, the ride deathly quiet, adding, "There was a mix-up." Nothing more. Not a word. Until that night, lying in bed, Anita heard her parents going at each other. Neal Beacham, who had apparently been the one on pickup duty, out of his mind with anger — "You and your expectations!" and "I work for a living!" — making it all sound like battery acid. Her mother's voice never above a murmur, a wasp attacking a water buffalo to dreadful effect. "You can leave anytime. *Leave.* We don't need you. I don't need you. Play your golf and have your little assignations till the cows come home but you'll be doing it on your own dime."

Even now, years later, Anita wonders if her mother's quiet fury was on her children's behalf or her own.

Michael pulls to a stop in front of the elementary school and gets out. There's a police car double-parked ahead of him and near the entrance he can see Karen McKen-

348

zie and the school's principal, Carol Udall, talking to two uniformed officers, one male, one female. Seeing him, Karen McKenzie excuses herself and approaches.

"They have another squad car going up and down the streets between your home and the school. They'll call in if they see him."

"Do they know he's autistic?"

"Yes. We're also calling parents to see if there's any chance he went home with one of them."

"He wouldn't." Michael reaches for his wallet. "It might help if the police have some photographs of him."

"They have them. Your wife had several."

"Where is she?"

"Out on the playground."

He sees Mrs. McKenzie hesitate. "What is it?"

"Michael, if I'd known she was going to be the one picking him up today . . ."

"Jamie was supposed to tell you."

"He didn't."

Michael can see tears glinting. Karen McKenzie may be a rock but she's a rock with a soft center.

Anita sits on the low rung of a jungle gym, a lit cigarette between her fingers. The steel bar behind her is quite literally a pain in the ass but right now pain feels good. The jungle gym is also a good distance away from the children and teachers who surround the after-school activities table. The last thing she needs right now are small voices asking questions.

"Why do they call it a jungle gym?" she once asked her mother.

"Because," Tisha replied, " 'monkey bars' is impolite."

"Why do they call them monkey bars?"

"Because," her mother answered with some impatience, "children play like monkeys." Unspoken but implied was that children playing like monkeys was unacceptable behavior at best.

The material on the ground under and surrounding the climbing bars is a heavy, soft, thick blue plastic pad, obviously there to protect a child should he or she fall. She should make a dress of it. And then climb deep into the center of the jungle gym where no one can get to her.

"There's no smoking."

Anita opens her eyes to look at Michael. "Any news?" she asks, not dropping the cigarette.

"The cops are out looking between here

and the house. They'll call in when they find him."

"When will that be?"

"They'll find him, Anita."

"And if they don't?"

"Let's not go there."

"This is because of me."

"Why, because you were late?"

"Because I insisted on picking him up. Because he doesn't even know me." Anita pushes her lower back into the metal joist, pushes harder. "Who am I? Some sleazy stranger who shows up out of nowhere and inserts herself into his life? What was I thinking?"

"Stop."

"I can't stop, I can't. If anything happens to him —"

"This is not about *you.*" Louder than Michael intended. Anita's green eyes open wide. "He was looking forward to it, Anita. Now let's just find him and then you can blame yourself all you want to later, okay?"

"Okay." Almost inaudible.

He turns away.

"Where are you going?"

"I'm not *leaving,* if that's what you're worried about."

Even though everyone is complaining of

drought conditions, Penelope feels she should water her plants. If not that, she should find something else to do, perhaps clean something, well, maybe not *that,* but she should keep busy, yes, because it's no good worrying, is it. Only she's afraid to go out back because even with the front door open and the gate open, if Jamie comes home and doesn't see her, doesn't know she's here, doesn't know she's in the back working, he might leave. She should make him a peanut butter sandwich which is what he likes after school. With the crusts cut off like a tea sandwich. Has she eaten today? She's not sure. Regardless, she's not hungry. They'll call when they find him. They'll call any minute. Of course they will.

"Abbie, here. Here, sweetness."

Petting her dog's gray muzzle, once such a rich gold, calms her. "Oh, darling, would that I had your splendid nose. I'd go searching for him myself."

Penelope rises from her chair. She goes into the kitchen. She wants to be sure the sandwiches are ready when her boys get home.

Michael enters the empty classroom. He moves to what he knows to be Jamie's desk and sees that his books are still there, that his backpack is slung over the chair. He crosses the room to the rows of cube storage units that line the wall to find that Jamie's Power Rangers lunchbox is also still present and accounted for. He should call Penelope and ask if he's come home yet. Only the little holster is empty because he's left his cell phone in the truck and really what difference does it make because he knows Jamie is all right, knows someone is going to call in to the school at any second and they'll all breathe a sigh of relief and this will be over.

"I'll get in a car. I'll drive away. I'll drive!"

A dread akin to nausea surges in Michael and he bolts from the classroom.

Not leaving, *if that's what you're worried about.*

He has every right to blame her. The right to say anything. Anita knows this. It's no big deal.

"Words are just words," as her mother would say. "They can't hurt us."

Wrong, Mom.

Words are more dangerous than jungle gyms. Words are what should be surrounded by protective padding. She wishes now she'd told Michael that it was her only cigarette, one long forgotten about and found in the bottom of her bag. And she isn't even smoking it, not really. Just letting it burn to a nub in her fingers.

Entering the lavatory, Michael strides to the row of sinks and turns on a faucet. He cups his hands, fills them with water, drinks and spits. He splashes water onto his face. Breathe, he thinks.

Breathe.

"I need paper."

He's hearing things. He must be. A child calling from out in the yard. Ghosts in the pipes. Michael turns to face the row of toilet stalls that line the wall behind him.

"Jamie?"

He hears the lock turn. He sees the stall door open a crack. The little face peers out at him.

"Hi, Dad."

Michael, moving to the stall, carefully pushes the door inward and kneels on the tiles so he is face-to-face with his son . . .

"Hi, Dad. Hi."

. . . and scoops the boy up, half off the toilet seat, pulling him close, vaguely aware that he's babbling as he does so. "Jamie, Jamie, Jesus, Jamie, what are you doing, what the hell, are you okay?"

"I have to wipe my bottom."

"You what?"

"My *akole,* Dad."

Akole. Hawaiian for asshole.

Hawaiian for me.

Sometimes you don't know whether to laugh or cry and so Michael squeezes his son tight to his chest until it draws a protest . . .

"Dad!"

. . . and just like Anita, but without the hiccups, alternates between both.

Karen McKenzie is trying to describe to a newly arrived plainclothesman what the missing boy was wearing and finding it difficult. The day, the students, clothes, and her brain all keep running together. Primary colors mix and produce nothing but brown.

"— red polo, wait, no — T-shirt, I think. Jeans and sneakers. Just like every other little boy."

"Like that one?" says the man in the suit, pointing behind her. McKenzie turns. And sags in exquisite relief. Michael is walking from the school entrance, Jamie at his side. Thank God. All is not yet quite right with the world but her heart can beat again.

"Mom will pick me up," Jamie is saying. A statement and a question.

Michael looks across the quiet playground, toward the jungle gym.

No one is there.

41

When her mother pulls into the driveway behind her, Anita realizes she has no idea how long she's been sitting in the car. It could be minutes, it could be hours, it could be days. "If you can't solve a problem by thinking about it for fifteen minutes, just stop," Dr. Akrepede has told her. "Research shows that your odds of solving it after that is nearly zero. Take a break. Move on."

"Move on to *what*?" Anita replied.

Has she even called Dr. Akrepede? She thinks she did. Yes, she got a machine. Leave a message. Call 911 if it's a real emergency. What constitutes a real emergency? The feeling you'd like to run over yourself with your own car? The desire to get quickly and quietly drunk? In the rearview mirror, Anita sees that her mother, wearing the cotton skirt and drab, sleeveless polo that Beacham women associate with golf, is now out of the car and reaching for groceries and so she quickly gets out as well. Better to pretend she's just arrived so as not to raise suspicion. Suspicion means you have to answer questions and that means you have to lie.

"Here, let me help you with those."

Meaning the groceries. Tisha glances at her in surprise. "Why, thank you." She hands Anita a brown paper bag, then stops, staring at her.

"You look pale."

"Not the best of days."

"Mmm. Will you be having dinner with us?"

"Not sure."

"Well, there's enough."

"Food or sustenance?"

"I swear, Anita," says Tisha Beacham, frowning. "Sometimes I don't know what you're talking about."

"No problem. Neither do I." She and her mother start for the house, each carrying a grocery bag.

Wow. How normal.

"By the way," says Tisha, "Michael called while I was in the car."

Was.

"What? Why didn't you —" Anita realizes she's not so much talking as spitting.

"He was trying to get in touch with you

but you didn't answer."

Anita takes a breath. "What did he say?"

"Something about Jamie. Apparently he was at the school the entire time. In the bathroom. What's that about? Are you all right?"

Her mother staring at her as if she's a fish sucking air.

"Fine. It's nothing. Don't worry about it."

"Anita, if you're not going to talk about things, don't bother talking at all."

"Good advice. I won't."

The phone is ringing as they go in through the front door.

"Yes. Yes. Well, casual game or not, rules are rules."

In the kitchen, Anita puts down the bag of groceries. Having answered the phone, her mother has taken it into the pantry, not pleased with something or someone, and so it seems a good time to open her own bag and grab for the vial.

"Well, I say it's cheating," says Tisha Beacham, biting the words.

Taking a small orange pill out of the vial, Anita moves to the sink and is about to wash it down with tap water when her mother abruptly reenters the kitchen.

"Then I doubt I'll be part of this foursome anymore," says Tisha Beacham "Good day." Anita watches as her mother disconnects, then strides to the counter and puts the cordless phone back in its cradle.

"What was that about?"

"What was *what* about," says Tisha, as she turns to unpack groceries. Her jaw is a smooth, stiff line, a telltale sign that she's upset or angry.

"Phone call?"

"Jodie Hill. She's constantly fumbling with her ball mark, turning three-foot putts into two, and I've had enough of it."

"She's been doing it as long as you've known her and it's never bothered you before."

"That's beside the point. It bothers me now." Tisha abruptly turns, glaring. "What's that you're taking?"

Idiot, thinks Anita as she realizes that both pill and vial are still in hand. "Xanax. For anxiety. You want one?" She offers the pill to her mother on outstretched palm.

"Don't be silly," says Tisha. She begins putting cans into cupboards, pulling them from the bag and thrusting them onto shelves with hard, impatient movements. "I suppose that *psychologist* you're seeing gave them to you."

"Psychologist" obviously rhyming with

"charlatan." At the Beacham house, Anita knows, mental health problems aren't problems at all, they're a lack of discipline. "No, Mom, they sell them in the candy section at the supermarket."

"Now you're being ridiculous."

"Ridiculous or silly, which is it, make up your mind."

"You have nothing to be anxious or depressed about." Turning back to the counter. Folding and then refolding the brown paper bag for recycling, hands now as tight as her jaw. Anita waiting for it — waiting. "Oh, yes, I know that's what those other pills are for. All this so-called *therapy.* Well, I've had enough of it. You're just paying someone to listen to you complain about *me.*"

"You're a trouper, Mom, you can handle it."

With a sudden, violent flail of her arm, Tisha Beacham sweeps the second bag of groceries from the counter, sending eggs, milk, and cream cartons and a box of Ritz crackers skidding across the hardwood floor toward Anita's feet, shocking them both.

Lord, may I be slow to anger and filled with love. Please fill my heart with patience. Thank you, Lord, that you are forever giving when it comes to forgiveness.

■ ■ ■ ■

Sustenance. Sustenance is not food. Sustenance is love. Sustenance is validation. Sustenance is support. You give it, Mother. Or you don't.

"Anita," says Tisha Beacham, staring into space. "If you could just accept Jesus into your life, things would be so much better."

Anita places the vial of Xanax carefully on the white counter. Her mother is right. She doesn't need them. Like everyone in the family, she knows where Neal Beacham stores his gin and vodka reserves. It's time for something stronger.

42

The board has taken on its final shape and Michael checks its symmetry with calipers. He's done it at least half a dozen times now, knows it's perfect, knows that all that's really left is the fine sanding to make sure the surface is pure and then the glassing. But he knows too that there is a part of him that doesn't want to finish. A finished board, like a ship, is a tool meant to be taken into the water and Michael is no longer sure he's even capable of teaching his son to navigate on dry land.

Lifting her head, Abigail growls low in her throat and barks once, staring out the open garage door toward the unlit driveway. And then she's up and padding forward, tail wagging as Anita steps tentatively into the harsh, fluorescent light of the garage. Anita pets her, rubs her soft ears with both hands. "Hey, Abbie. Hey, sweet girl." She glances toward Michael who hasn't moved. She tries to smile.

"May I come in?"

"You already are," says Michael, and he begins sanding the board again, not needing the chore but needing something to pretend to do. He's aware that she is moving as if in sensuous slow motion, that her eyes are wide, blank saucers. He knows these are the signs that she has been drinking heavily.

"It's coming along," Anita says, rubbing her fingers down the wood surface of the board.

"Slow but sure," he says. It's an idiot reply but he's trying to fill empty space.

"I got your message."

"Which one?"

"The one you left my mother."

"I wanted to make sure you knew."

"He was really in the bathroom?"

"Yeah. In a toilet stall. On a toilet."

"Why?"

"He had no toilet paper and he wanted to wipe his ass."

"You know," says Anita, "I bet someday we're really going to laugh about this."

"But not now."

"No. Not just now, no."

He watches as she turns away, seemingly appraising the untidy holdings and plain walls of the garage as if she were in the gallery of an art museum. He remembers the silences she'd fall into when drinking too much. Conversations with myself, she'd call them. Shoulda-coulda-wouldas. Mightabeens. Hope-to-be's.

"I really fucked things up today," Anita says softly, still staring at the wall.

"Only because you left."

"I freaked."

"I did too."

"But you didn't leave." She turns now to look at him, listing slightly. "Did he ask about me?"

"He wanted to know where you were."

"What did you say?"

"I told him you hadn't been able to make it. That's why I was there."

"And after that?"

"I brought him home, fed him. We read. I tucked him into bed."

"So he's okay."

"He's okay, yeah."

"Good." Her head bobbles as if it's momentarily lost its balance on her neck. She blinks as if trying to recall where she is.

"Anita?"

". . . uh?"

"Are you okay?"

She'd like to tell him that the façade of

balance she's been so carefully maintaining all day has finally left her. So have any semblance of words. It's not a bad feeling. It's just that the cement floor, unsteady now beneath her feet, is going to hurt when she falls.

As if in a dream, Jamie hears his mother's voice. But then, he's always heard her voice. He just didn't know it was her voice until she came back and then he remembered. It's good that Mom's come back. He wasn't sure it was at first but he is now. For some reason, Jamie doesn't have to work to tell what Mom's face is saying. There are things there he doesn't understand but he doesn't need to. Mostly her face says she loves him. Her face makes him feel it back. Now if he could only find the right words for that so that if his face can't say it to Mom, his words can. Dad will know. Jamie will ask him and then he'll know too. He falls back asleep hearing Mom and Dad whisper his name.

Anita awakes, alone in bed, head throbbing, first morning light coming through the windows.

Their room.

The same chair. The familiar bureaus. The

framed photos that feel like old friends. She can't remember how she got here. And then she does. Michael. Catching her as her legs gave way. Carrying her into the house. She, in no position to walk anymore, let alone drive home. Bringing her down the hall past Jamie's room and into the bedroom, lowering her to the bed. Taking off her shoes. Her jeans and shirt. Stopping her as she struggled to take off her bra, to push off her panties. Pulling back the spread and sheets. Her arms going around his neck as he shifted her beneath the sheets, moved her head gently to the pillow.

"Kiss me, Michael. Be with me."

"Shhh," he said, gently covering her. "We'll talk in the morning." She was asleep before he left the room.

She is increasingly aware of her hangover and how horrible she feels.

I am so out of practice.

Eyes closed, she is trying to find the coolest place on the pillow to rest her cheek when she hears the bedroom door open, then close.

"Michael?" she whispers. She raises her head. Opens her heavy-lidded eyes.

She remembers there was once a hummingbird nest outside the bedroom window. It was in the forked branch of a bush, the thin branches ensuring that the hatchlings would be protected from sun, wind, rain, or predators. Built by the female, Penelope told her, because other than copulation, male hummingbirds, like most men, want nothing to do with raising children.

She sits up in the bed that once was hers. She tries to smile. "Hi, baby."

As fragile and breakable to her as any small bird, she fully expects him to flee. It doesn't happen. He moves forward toward the bed, and pulling back the edge of the sheet, he gets in.

"I'm sleepy," Jamie says, resting his head against her shoulder.

"Me too," she says. Pulling him close, Anita covers them both and settles back.

"Let's sleep."

When Michael comes into the bedroom to see if she's all right, he sees the two of them. They are each on their left sides. Anita's arm is across Jamie, holding him against her. Her lips are near the back of his head. Both have the hushed breath of slumber. He feels he's looking at a painting, one painted in the colors of memory. When Jamie was a newborn, they would lie together like this. It seemed a private moment then and it does so now, something between mother and child, not to be trespassed on. He wishes he could leave his son to wake on his own and feel the graceful place he's in. But no.

"Jamie." A touch. "Time to get up. School."

Jamie stirs. Yawns. Opening his eyes, it takes him a moment to realize where he is and who he is with.

"Is Mom having breakfast with us?"

"Let's let Mom sleep, okay?"

"Okay. Sleep, Mom."

She has heard him enter. She hears them both leave. She drifts, eyes closed, sleep close at hand but far away. The headache is a friendly companion now. It allows her not to think.

Penelope is in the kitchen when she hears the front door open and then close, and even though nothing was said, not so much as mentioned before Michael left taking Jamie to school, she knows who it is, knows that Anita has spent the night and now is leaving. She heard Michael carry her down the hall, heard Anita's soft, plaintive, slurred voice.

"Le' me go home, Michael, I should jus' go home."

369

"This is home," Michael had said.

She heard him come back down the hall shortly thereafter. He was asleep on the couch, still dressed, just a blanket over him, when she arose in the early hours. She resolved not to wake him. So many burdens on her son's shoulders. Herself not the least of them. Not fair at all. But then, who ever said it was supposed to be? You accept the bad with the good and you soldier on. There's no doubt she's becoming increasingly forgetful. When last she saw Dr. Curtis he asked her to count backward from one hundred by sevens. She was lost at eighty-six. But the truth is, it feels as if it's only unpleasant things she can't remember, and as for math, she was never good at it to begin with. Some of the better poetry has gone missing and that's sad. Penelope's early education emphasized learning by rote and her mind has long been stockpiled with miscellaneous quotes pulled from any number of different texts. People, she was taught, are what they learn, even if the lessons do not relate directly to their own lives. Having said that, she has come to realize that most of the verses and passages she memorized are useless in the modern world, and other than the pleasure she's always taken in them, they will not be missed.

Penelope wouldn't be a young person these days for anything.

She rises and goes to make the beds. It's the least she can do.

Anita calls him in the early evening.

"Michael? May I try again? Picking him up? At school?"

The voice is soft and vacant and he wonders if she's drinking again. Or if she even stopped.

"I'll ask him."

"If he says yes?"

"Then you can pick him up."

He waits for her to say something else. Maybe she needs help. He reminds himself that she's never asked for it in the past.

"You still there?"

"Michael?"

"Yes?"

"Would you change him? Would you change him if you could?"

He finds himself nodding into the phone. "Yes," he says. "But I can't. And if I could, would it still be him?"

"Michael?"

"Yes."

"I love the way you love our son."

She hangs up so softly it's a moment before he realizes she's gone.

■ ■ ■ ■

"I'm pregnant," she tells him.

They are in the living room. He has just arrived home, filthy and exhausted from work, to find her sitting on the couch, a blanket around her as if cold, staring into space. The look on her face suggests terminal cancer not impending motherhood. She has never wanted children, has told him so more than once.

"I said, I'm pregnant, Michael."

"I know. I mean . . . did you stop taking something?" He doesn't know what birth control method she uses. He *should* but doesn't. He just *assumes.* This has never happened before, not even so much as a scare.

"I don't take anything," Anita says. "I never have."

They are in their twenties. They are mad for each other. They make love as much as they eat, breathe, and drink water. It seems impossible.

"Why now then?"

"I don't know," she moans. "I didn't think I could."

"Wow," he says. Thinking it but not saying it — *divine intervention.*

"Yeah. *Wow.*" Nothing heavenly or divine about it.

Michael realizes he's still standing and he sits down on the couch. Close to her but careful not to look at her until he can judge the place she's in. It's harder than ever to do these days. It's like loving someone who alternates between two seasons. You adore the spring with its light and warmth. You're not so much afraid as you are sad for the winter with its darkness and frozen silence. It was easier when they were traveling. Her with not so much time to think, him with not so much time to notice. Coming back to the day-to-day existence of one place, the part-time college classes, working for an antiques dealer friend of her mother's to stay busy, has created an inertia in her. She gets lost in unexplainable places, places he can't go with her to and doesn't understand. It makes him ache for her.

"Nothing. Not you. Not your fault," she'll say. "Now go away." Or even, "Just leave me the fuck alone!"

But then the veil suddenly lifting. To come home and find her humming to herself, glowing and happy, eyes bright with humor and intelligence, arms and bed welcoming. It's the equivalent, his mother would say, of the kettle being on.

"What would you do without me?" she'll say to him as if confident he'd be lost.

"Which you we talking about?" he'll respond, teasing her back.

"This one, definitely."

Both of them knowing beyond a shadow of a doubt that this one is the real one, both of them hoping against hope that this one will stay awhile.

"You're happy about it, aren't you," she says now, looking at him. "You want this baby."

"I think it could be a good thing," he says carefully.

"Oh, God, Michael."

"I know."

"I don't think I can."

"I know."

"I barely hold it together as it is."

"You do fine," Michael says. "You do just great." Turning and reaching for her as she comes into his arms in a rush, beginning to cry now.

"I am so afraid of being pinned down," she says.

"Do I do that?" he asks.

"No. But a baby . . ."

"Would be beautiful like her mom," he says.

"Her?"

"I don't know why I said that."

"You want somebody to take care of you in your old age."

"Don't we all? You're smiling."

"No, I'm not," she says. "Stop making me."

"Since when can anyone make you do anything?"

"You can. You're the only one."

"I won't, Anita."

"Won't what?" she asks.

"Make you do anything you don't want to do."

"But you want to, don't you."

"Yes," he whispers. "And I'm not trying to talk you into anything but I think we should get married."

"Oh, God." A deep sigh. Holding her, he feels it course through her entire body. "Okay," she finally says. "In for an inch, in for a mile." Making both distances sound like a marathon. "Just remember one thing, Michael."

"What's that?" he asks.

"This isn't a fairy tale."

"So warned."

Not remotely understanding what it meant.

Carefully planning a route and using various methods to monitor the ship's position as the trip proceeds are fundamental to safe navigation and are the marks of a navigator. When the situation demands more resources than are immediately available to the navigator, a dangerous condition exists. In maritime law the responsibility of the navigator for his ship is paramount no matter what its condition. The navigator's chief responsibility is the safety of the vessel and its crew.

43

For as long as Michael has known him, Leo has lived in a modest, Cape Cod–style guest cottage, high on a bluff above the beach in Del Mar. It is the smallest in a compound of four secluded houses and Leo provides his landlord, the elderly matron in the big main house, with yard and maintenance service, from painting to plumbing to pruning, and in return is charged a well-below-market rent. He is the first to admit he lives far beyond his means. It's not just the cottage's small stone fireplace or the shaded sitting area of wood posts and vined, sturdy, open lattice he's built just off the back door, where Michael sits waiting for him. The kitchen has an old Crown stove from the early eighties with four gas burners and two ovens and Leo prizes it more than the view.

A door closes behind him and Michael glances back to see Donald Duck approaching on a background of purple and red plaid. The baggy boxer shorts, along with a huge white T-shirt, are Leo's sleeping attire. He's carrying two big mugs of coffee. Leo grinds his own estate-grown beans, uses water poured through a charcoal-carbon filter, and steams the milk.

"No sugar, right?"

"No sugar," says Michael, knowing that Leo considers spooning sugar into good coffee an insult to the coffee.

"All right then."

Leo hands Michael a mug and sits. Michael sips. He notices now there is a huge, circular purple welt on the back of Leo's calf.

"Nice. What happened?"

"Spider bite," says Leo, casually. "Brown recluse. Got up my pants. He won the battle, I won the war."

"Step on'm?"

Leo laughs. "Sat on'm."

Reaching into his pocket, Michael takes out an envelope and places it on the small table between them.

"What's that?"

"An extra two hundred."

"Only if you can afford it."

"I wouldn't give it to you if I couldn't."

" 'Cause you know I'm gonna pay you back."

"I know."

Leo is suddenly blinking tears and Michael looks away, not embarrassed for him but wanting to give him his privacy.

"It's crazy, Mike. It's really crazy."

"I know."

"I mean, it's not like Denise needs alimony. Her husband sells insurance, he prints money. But I don't pay up, I don't get to see the girls, so . . ."

"You don't have to explain a thing."

"Yeah, well . . ."

"I'll tell you one thing though."

"What's that?"

"You must have really pissed her off."

It's an old joke and they laugh. Michael knowing that Leo's ex, Denise, was an impossible woman, status conscious and demanding, wanting much more out of life than Leo could ever provide. That two months pregnant, she met, ensnared, and married the hapless Leo and that Leo gave not just his name to the twin girls but with them formed a mutual adoration society that very much excluded their mother. Which, yes, pissed her off so completely she packed her bags and girls and left, citing emotional cruelty. The girls still doting on Leo and he on them. Certainly worth any amount of money.

They've grown quiet.

"So what really brings you here on a Sunday morning, Mike? Not my problems, I hope."

"Anita's dad offered me a job, Leo. Supervising a development up near Oceanside. Hundred and fifty units."

Leo just about jumps out of his chair. "Whoa! This is fantastic. When do we start?"

"No we, Leo. Just me."

Arrrooo! Just over the bluff, a train, horn sounding, flies by on the tracks that are between the houses and the cliffs. It's a pain-in-the-ass sound, Leo has said, but one that you get used to, even begin to enjoy after a while. Certainly one you miss when it's gone.

"I haven't said yes yet but —"

"Take it."

"I'm just thinking about it."

"Take it. Me and the guys can always find work. We're good."

"Yeah, but —"

"No buts. You got other things to worry about. I'm happy for ya, Mike. So come on, I'll make us some breakfast. Ya like chorizo?"

"I like anything you make, Leo."

Nodding, Leo rises and lumbers back into the house, Michael not knowing how proud and pleased he is, Leo feeling that like a badly wounded man on a battleground, he has had the courage to tell his friend to leave him.

Run! Save yourself!

Live.

44

"Apples, peaches, pears, and plums! Tell me when your birthday comes! January, February, March —"

She is late again. She is late again because — yes, she has to admit it — she is drinking again. Shots of vodka for breakfast. Wine with lunch. It slows everything down, which is a relief, but it makes her too clumsy to parallel park. Which is a problem when you're picking up kids at school. And so, unable to wedge in between a Chevy Tahoe and a Fiat, she has ended up ditching the car a quarter of a mile away in the lot of an old folks home.

And now, hurrying to the sidewalk, she immediately passes an elderly woman, obviously senile, being pushed in a wheelchair by a woman in her fifties. "Isn't it a beautiful day, Mom?" the younger woman is chirping to the blanket-wrapped, wispy-haired, older woman. "You warm enough?"

It makes Anita wonder if she will end up like this someday, oblivious and in a wheelchair. Anything's possible, and if it is, who will be walking with her? She reminds herself that drinking can make her morose.

"California oranges, fifty cents a pack. California oranges, tap me on the back!"

On the school playground, the little girls are playing at jump rope. Each one of them a future heartbreaker. Boys and sex, jobs, marriages, and children. And then a wheelchair with one of those children, now grown, pushing you if you're not lucky enough to go first.

Careful.

Anita turns at the sound of shouting. On the other side of the playground, a group of boys, older, probably third-graders, are clamoring. The bodies part and she sees Jamie in the middle, face twisted in tears, clumsily trying to hit them. The boys are laughing and jeering and pushing and Anita is racing across the pavement before she even knows she's moving.

"Hey!" she screams. "Stop it!" The boys turn at the sound of her voice. "You little shits! Get away from him!" They scatter as she approaches, fear in their faces.

You better be afraid.

But one of them doesn't run and Anita

385

sees that Jamie is holding the boy's arm with one hand and is swinging his fist with the other. Each awkward blow elicits a shrill scream from both Jamie and the boy he's hitting. Anita grabs for him, pulls him away from the older, bigger boy.

"Jamie, stop!"

Only he doesn't. Shrieking, he turns and begins throwing his fists at her. "Ahh! — ahh!" He shrieks as she pulls him to her chest, more to protect herself than to give comfort.

"It's me, it's okay, it's Momma. It's me, sweetie."

Across the playground Anita sees that the little girls have stopped jumping rope and are staring in obvious alarm. What must they think? What would she have thought at that age?

What's with the little freak . . .

"It's okay, baby, it's okay." Her son has begun to cry now. Though it seems to calm him, the sound of it kills her. She strokes his head gently. She realizes that she too is crying.

"I hate school. I hate it," he murmurs.

"Jamie, what happened. Can you tell me what happened?"

"They called me retard," he moans.

It kills her.

386

"Oh, sweetheart."

"I want to go home. I want Dad."

It all just kills her.

45

I curse you again, Leo.

"Mike in?"

Leo has come bustling through the door, all hustle and male body odor, as if he has other places to go, people to see, a busy man, in demand, no time to waste on frivolities, no sir.

"You know he's not," says Rose, not trusting herself to look up from the computer. Leo has shaved recently, lost the bushy red beard but retained an extravagant Pancho Villa moustache. The shearing has revealed a strong chin and sensitive mouth that Rose finds disconcerting.

"Now how would I know that?"

As matter of fact, Leo knows exactly that. Just twenty minutes ago, Michael has called him from the lumberyard asking if an order of scrap board has been delivered and where they are on tenpenny nails, construction ties, and cement mix.

"Did you see his truck outside?"

"Maybe it's in the shop."

"Leo, you should be in the shop."

"Okay, okay, just give this to him, okay?" Leo puts the thick tome down on Rose's desk, cover up, a swirling sun in a burning red sky over a city skyline. What did the librarian tell him? London. As in England. Oh.

"This." Rose looks as if a small, furry animal with rabies has suddenly appeared on her desk and plunked itself down for a nap.

"Yeah," says Leo. Casual.

"*This* book?"

"It's a good read," says Leo.

It's *Gravity's Rainbow*.

"What's a book really, really smart people read?" Leo asks the librarian, and after determining that Leo is thinking fiction and not theoretical physics or analytical philosophy, the librarian, a wizened woman with a thick, waist-length braid of gray hair, has recommended Thomas Pynchon. Taking it home, Leo prepares English breakfast tea, puts on comfortable pajamas, props himself up with pillows on the couch, and begins to read. After three minutes, he gets up to go to the bathroom. He never returns to the couch. The book is undecipherable. It's as if it's written in code from the very first paragraph. It's not Thomas Pynchon's fault. Leo knows he's no genius. He knows he is lacking in big thoughts and meaningful insight. He is opinionated and occasionally belligerent for no other reason than annoyance at human imperfection, especially his own. One does not have to be smart to want things to somehow be better.

"You actually read this," says Rose, sounding skeptical.

"Yeah," says Leo. "I don't think it's his best but . . ."

"His best." Rose now looks as if she doesn't know whether to spit or swallow. Leo hopes it's the latter. "Okay, tell me what it's about, Leo, this book, his best."

"What?" says Leo as if offended. "It's about determinism, the reverse flow of time, and the inherent sexuality of mechanical devices." Whew. Good. He's got it out without stumbling. Copying it off Wikipedia took two minutes, memorizing it took hours.

"Fine, Leo," Rose says coldly. "I will give this to Michael. I'm sure he'll enjoy it very much." And with that, Rose turns her golden eyes back to her computer screen.

Failure. Always failure. The whole charade suddenly feels ridiculous. If women only knew what guys do for them. Cook. Read.

Shave. Leo turns for the door. And suddenly annoyed, not just annoyed, *pissed* — at himself, at Rose, at Thomas Pynchon whoever that is — he turns back.

"You know what, Rose? You want to know the truth? The only books I enjoy reading are cookbooks." And just like that, he has her complete and total attention.

"Cookbooks."

"Recipes? Food?"

"I know what a cookbook is, Leo."

"Oh, really," says Leo, thinking Rose is not the only one who can cross arms across an ample chest. " 'Cause I was under the impression you didn't even like to eat."

"Would I look like this if I didn't eat, Leo?"

By God, he has her on the defensive. "Yeah? What's your favorite dish? What kind of food you like?" He's on familiar ground now. Unless it's Martian cuisine, Leo has cooked it.

Rose hesitates, as if searching the data banks. "New Orleans," she finally says. "I like New Orleans–style food."

Score, thinks Leo, whose copy of *The Picayune's Creole Cook Book* is worn and tattered with use. "Yeah? Cajun or Creole?"

"There's a difference?" For the first time in Leo's experience, Rose looks nervous.

391

"Creole uses tomatoes, Rose, Cajun doesn't."

"If you say so." Make that very nervous.

"I know so. What about jambalaya? You like jambalaya?"

"I don't know. What is it?"

"It's like a paella. Beans and rice. Shrimp. Andouille sausage and ham. Sound good?"

"I guess."

"Good," says Leo. " 'Cause I'm gonna make you some."

"Get out of here, Leo."

"I am. A whole big pot of it. And we'll talk about books while we eat it."

"I'm not going out with you, Leo."

"Not out. My place. Rose, c'mon. What's a little food, wine, and fine literature among friends?"

"Leave me alone!" screams Rose, frightening Leo out of his shorts. "For the last time. I'm not your friend. This is sexual harassment, and if it happens again, I will tell Michael and he will have no choice but to boot your ass out of a job. Now take your recipes and your books and your cookies and your stupid *bigote* and get out of here." And then Rose is on her feet and moving across the room to the office's single restroom, graceful for a big woman. Open, close, click of lock. Done. Over.

"I'm sorry," whispers Leo, staring into some vast, empty space. "I'm sorry and I promise I won't bother you again."

From the solitude of the tiny bathroom, Rose listens to Leo leave. It pains her to act like this. Rose has heard that Leo is a devoted father with a faithless ex-wife who puts her own selfish needs ahead of her children, the thought of which makes Rose think, *esa perra mejor no cruzan mi camino* — that bitch better not ever cross my path. But really, enough is enough. Time to put a stop to this nonsense once and for all. Leo is getting too close for comfort.

Rose pulls up her dress, hops up on the throne, and sits. She regrets she doesn't have a book because her mind immediately goes to New Orleans, a place she's read about but never visited. What was it Leo called that dish again? Made with beans, rice, shrimp, and andouille sausage. Or was it ambrosia sausage? Aphrodisiac sausage? Rose's stomach gurgles mournfully and involuntarily she farts.

Oh, just damn you, Leo. Damn you to hell.

46

Michael drives north on Interstate 5. It's mid-morning and any residual commuter traffic should be going in the opposite direction, but still, both sides of the highway are packed and it takes him a good forty minutes to get to Carlsbad. Getting off the highway, he drives east toward San Marco, past industrial parks and shopping centers featuring Costco, Home Depot, and Target, the land flattening out and opening up, turning drier and more desolate, the flats giving way to foothills, the foothills to mountain canyons. Ten miles on, he comes up and across a ridge and in the distance sees housing developments spread out in large clusters, the mortar of canyon, chaparral, sage scrub, and conifer separating them. Planned suburban living pushing against nature. Nature resisting, if not pushing back.

Resting Palms is a relatively new development where each modest house with its attached garage and small postage stamp of lawn is a complete clone of the one next to it, a place, Michael muses, where you could come home drunk at night and find yourself searching for your front door as if it were a lost car in an immense parking lot. There is a community center. There is a clubhouse with a pool. He sees no one, not man, woman, or child, on the sidewalks.

At the northeastern edge of the development, a new row of houses are under construction. The land has been plowed flat and shaved clean of any kind of vegetation. Trenches have been dug for what will be plumbing and sewage lines. Where will the water come from? Michael wonders. To drink, to flush, to wash. Do the developers include the cost of it in the sale price? Or do the happy new home owners discover the cost of living in a drought area when the first bill arrives?

At the end of the already paved road, foundation footings and slabs have been poured and framing has begun. Michael notes that the workers are using lightweight steel, strong, easy, and fast to assemble, but hard to insulate. A steel stud conducts ten times as much heat as dimensional lumber. Questionable when the temperature gauge on his dash tells Michael that it's now fifteen degrees hotter than it was on the coast. He doesn't want to think what it'll be like working outside here in the summer. Not yet anyway.

And then nothing. The road ends and he stops.

Dry ground. Piles of rubble. Surveyor stakes topped with red plastic ribbons denoting where the next phase of construction will begin. Beyond it, charred hills and wasted chaparral, evidence of the last wildfire that took out almost seven thousand acres in east county. Nature pushing back hard. You buy your ticket, you take your chances.

Michael has never thought of himself as having any kind of an aesthetic. Architects draw up the plans. He executes. He makes suggestions, sometimes they're picked up on, sometimes not. But there has always been something unique about each project. Something about the finished result he liked and was proud of. This job will be like working on an assembly line. Like Model Ts, the houses will be identical to the ones behind him. They will be code compliant and have fire-safe landscaping. Unlike his own haphazard bungalow, they will have high-end kitchens and marble baths. They will be prewired for cable and Internet. They will have all the latest conveniences. They will be commuter friendly and have easy access to the interstate. But to Michael's mind, they will say nothing about the people who live in them. Nothing about the people who built them.

Ah, progress.

Neal Beacham was right. Michael couldn't handle a job like this in a million years. But he'll learn. He has to. People are counting on him.

The problem is he's been spoiled by the sea.

47

"I'm getting that feeling again."

Anita is pacing the small room, unable to sit and unsteady on her feet, so much so that Fari wonders if she's on something.

"What feeling is that?" Fari asks.

"I don't know, I don't know, like — *ahh-hhh.*" Anita feigns biting her arm. "Like I'm gonna go crazy if I don't get moving."

There is a hardness to Anita's eyes Fari hasn't seen before, as if the brain behind them weighs too much.

"Moving."

"You know. Get away from here. Away."

"Will that make you happy?"

"I don't know."

"Has it in the past?"

"I don't *know,*" Anita says, agitated. Drinking is making her thoughts both fierce and clumsy. It never used to be this way. A drink made things clearer. Or at least calmer.

It's too much. It's all just too much.

"What would make you happy, Anita? Do you really even know?"

"Oh, for — don't you ever listen to me? Do you ever really hear what I'm saying? I don't know what being happy even is. I never have."

"I'm sure that's a very difficult feeling."

"Yeah, sure. Like you'd know."

Drinking never used to make her angry either. Her father, not her.

"More than you might think."

"Okay, let's go down the list then. How about worried all the time. How about guilty. I fucked up as a wife, okay? I fucked it up as a mother and I have a hard time living with that. Do you know what kids called Jamie at school the other day? You want to know? They called him a retard. And I didn't know what to do about it. His mother, and I didn't know how to make it better for him. How would that make *you* feel?"

"Not very good."

"Now *there's* an understatement. But who cares. He didn't want me anyway, he wanted Michael. And he should." Anita knows now she's going to cry. She's going to cry any second. In front of this sphinx-faced woman who is so like her mother, both of them women who never feel anything.

"I — I think I should leave. This isn't working. It's all just so stupid."

"I wish you wouldn't."

"Yeah? Why?"

"Because you're in distress. And it's my job to help."

"Your job. God forbid we should make it personal."

"It is personal."

It is very personal.

"Anita, I've been doing some reading. Do you know there are autistic people who can tell you what pi to the twenty-thousandth place is off the top of their heads?"

"Really? Great. Now tell me how that makes for a meaningful life."

"A woman taught herself to speak Latin in a week. I find that meaningful. An autistic child in Japan wrote a best-selling novel. I find that very meaningful. People on the autism spectrum are brilliant scientists, they're tech geniuses, they're experts in finance."

"I'd settle for normal."

"What is normal, Anita? Is it being like everybody else? Is anybody like anybody else? Are you? The only thing that's normal is that we all share the same imperfect human condition."

Words, thinks Anita. People think words are a cure for everything.

I'm done.

"Look, the problem is this. I'm not sure this mom thing is gonna work out, okay? I'm not cut out for it. I never was. I should just accept it. I mean, I'm not even sure parents make that much of a difference. I had the classic American upbringing, alcoholic father, emotionally distant mother, and look at me. I turned out just fine."

It's a good line. She's used it before and has always gotten an amused reaction. She wants Dr. Akrepede to laugh or at least smile before she leaves for the last time, but instead the woman is looking at her with disapproval.

Not you too.

"You abandoned your husband and child once, Anita. It's caused you nothing but pain. If you're looking for excuses to do it again, I'm not the one who can give them to you."

The stricken look on Anita's face makes Fari sad. She has wanted so much to help this woman. And in doing so, help Michael. She hasn't. She's failed both of them. "You know, I think perhaps you're right. This isn't working. It really might be best if you do look for another therapist," says Fari. Her voice sounds hollow. "I'll be happy to recommend some."

"That hopeless, huh?" says Anita, suddenly not wanting to go anywhere.

"No. It's my fault. Boundaries are a crucial element in patient-therapist interaction and I've crossed them."

"I don't understand."

"I should have told you from the very beginning. I know your husband."

"Michael?"

Fari nods. "And because I do, I'm finding it harder and harder to be objective with you."

"Just how well do you know him?"

The room seems very quiet. Fari suddenly has the terrible feeling that there are telltale spots in the rug.

"Ever run over a guy in your car?" Anita asks softly.

"The session," Fari says, "is over."

48

The weather, thinks Luis, has gone crazy. Temperature in the eighties. Hot, dry winds coming out of the west, *Aliento del Diablo* — Devil's Breath — blowing dust and palm fronds everywhere. Fine for tourists with nothing better to do than go to the beach in their air-conditioned cars but brutal for men working construction. Even the boss, Miguel, on the second deck, nailing plywood with the pneumatic nail gun, is shirtless. And maybe it's the heat as well but Luis is finding Leo and his nonstop opinions tough to take today.

"This ain't the friggin' Dark Ages, Luis. Your wife wants to work, you let her work."

"A wife of mine, she don't work."

"Why? 'Cause she has to make you lunch every day?"

Maybe it isn't the heat. Leo has been out of sorts of late. Women on the brain. Luis has certainly had his fair share of trouble

403

with women. Fortunately, he learned at any early age to pay no attention to the pretty ones, not when their less attractive sisters were more attentive. Unfortunately, the pretty ones, realizing they were being ignored, could still cause you problems.

Luis looks up as a Mercedes pulls into the entryway and *el gusano,* the pale earthworm, the homeowner, Caulfield, gets out. He looks around a moment as if lost and then he sees Michael up on the beams.

"Mike! Hey, Mike, can I talk to you?"

Luis wouldn't be a boss in a million years. Working is one thing. Dealing with *idiotas* is another skill set entirely.

"Leo, how you doing?" the man calls out as Michael climbs down the ladder.

"Fine, yeah, thanks," grunts Leo, head down, face dripping with sweat. His friend really is off, thinks Luis. Normally a greeting from *un propietario* would be a reason to stop work entirely.

"Great day, huh?" says Robert Caulfield as he and Michael make their way down the sidewalk.

Since being hit up for back wages and unpaid bills, Robert Caulfield has been a friendly and careful client. On several occasions, he's stopped by bringing pizzas and soda for the crew. Much to his surprise, Michael is tentatively beginning to like the man. "It's why we live here," says Michael.

"Exactly. And it's why everybody wants to move here."

Michael is silent, waiting for the shoe, whatever style it is, to drop. He's read recently that it costs seventy-five-thousand dollars a year to support a family of four in San Diego. Even with nice weather it seems like a lot of money. Maybe that's why people are living in cookie-cutter housing developments in east county.

"So, listen," says Robert Caulfield. "I was really sorry to hear about your mother's house. What are you going to do?"

"We're not sure yet," says Michael, surprised the man would know anything about Penelope or her house. The weekly village newspaper. It has to be. "Right now, it's sitting."

"It's a heck of a piece of property. Shame not to do something with it."

So that's it.

"What's your point?"

"Isn't it obvious?" Caulfield seems surprised. "I want to buy it, Mike. I checked it out. We could put a high-end, six-, seven-thousand-foot house on that lot. This area, this market? We could sell it in a second, double our money."

"We," says Michael. The thought of anyone checking out the remains of his mother's house, even if it was from the sidewalk, feels a bit like trespassing.

Caulfield stops and turns to Michael. "You'd be my contractor, Mike. I put up the money, you do the work, we split the profits down the middle. Simple. Sweet."

"It's my mother's house, not mine."

"It's not a house anymore, it's an empty lot. And it's sure not doing your mother any good. With what you'd clear on it, you could move her into a nice, furnished condo."

"She'd hate that."

"How do you know?"

"She has Alzheimer's." It's popped out of his mouth. They don't even know if it's true yet. She's getting old, that's all. "At least, she might."

"Oh, God, Mike, that's a bitch. But frankly? I've been there, and let me tell you, it's even more reason to act. You move her into a home, get her the best possible care, twenty-four seven. You'd have the money to do that. To give her what she needs."

What does his mother need? Michael wonders. They should have had this conversation by now. He's been avoiding it. Waiting for yet another problem to solve itself without him having to think about it.

"Look, I don't want to push," says Robert Caulfield. "You've obviously got a lot on your plate. But the property's going to be yours eventually, right? So why not do you and your mom and your son a favor and take advantage of it? Strike while the iron's hot."

The guy's a salesman, no doubt about it. Funny, how the wrong answers can suddenly seem so rational.

"I appreciate the advice. I'll think about it, okay?"

"Fine," says Robert Caulfield. "Get back to me whenever."

"And now, there's something else I want to talk about," says Michael.

49

"God grant me the serenity to accept the things I cannot change, the courage to change the things I can, and the wisdom to know the difference."

Anita recites the serenity prayer to herself by rote, not really thinking about it anymore. This local chapter of AA meets in a building upstairs and behind a church, has been easy to find, and is very much like all the others she's ever attended. Outside the room, people are drinking coffee and talking. Inside, others are already seated in the semicircle of chairs, some together, some quietly alone. As usual, she takes a seat close to the door, the better to make a quick exit. As more people enter and take seats, some of them nod at her, a few say hello, inviting conversation. She nods and looks away. She likes it better when people keep to themselves.

As always it seems to take forever to start.

The first meeting she ever went to, the one in Brentwood, the wait was so interminable, she left. It was only when she got to the car that she realized she'd been inside all of five minutes.

A tall man on the other side of the circle is staring at her. This is why she likes the women-only meetings. Men have a tendency to want to be "helpful." They seem to believe a drinking problem makes people compatible.

Finally a well-dressed, middle-aged man takes a chair into the center of the circle. Funny, thinks Anita, he doesn't look like an alcoholic. She's gotten over being surprised at how few of them do, especially when it's a meeting of so-called professionals. This man looks like he could be a stockbroker or a lawyer. I wonder what I look like? A deadbeat mother? A porn star?

It was the traffic accident that got her to the first meetings. They were a waste of time but she had to do them to get her driver's license back, and once she had it, she stopped. She started them again several weeks after the porn shoot, feeling she'd never have done it if she'd been in even half a cogent state of mind. Something had to be punished, so why not her good friend alcohol?

As a participant gets up, introduces herself by first name, admits to being an alcoholic, and begins to read the 12 steps, Anita still isn't sure it all fits. Not really. She wasn't and isn't powerless over alcohol. She can stop for weeks at a time, has done so regularly to prove it to herself. Did so, in fact, before coming down here. It was stress that made her start drinking again. Combined with the antidepressants, it made her lose control. She'll attend a few meetings, get a handle on this maddening desire to be blotto all the time, and she'll be out of here.

The woman in the circle is now at the part about putting her trust in a higher power in order to restore her sanity, the part that always makes Anita uncomfortable. Anita doesn't believe in God, and though she's troubled, she's not insane. Her mother, on the other hand, an infinitely sane woman, came to Christ in her forties, and immediately went nuts.

The woman is making an inventory of her life. Good for her. Anita has as well. She has done it fearlessly, and yes, she has found herself lacking in moral inventory and good judgment. Why else would she have ever thought, even drunk and on both illegal and prescription drugs, that shooting sex scenes with strangers might make for a fun week-

410

end. She is messed up, there is no doubt about it. She is more than willing to admit it and she is more than willing to have these defects excised from her character. The problem is she's still waiting. Sometimes it seems to Anita that this God, whom everybody in AA professes to believe in, really likes to rub it in.

Now the woman in the circle is tearfully making a list of all the persons she has harmed, stating she is willing to make amends to them all. They are at the crux of it. It is why Anita is really here, why she keeps inevitably coming back. If the message of these meetings is atonement and a chance for forgiveness, then she is ready to listen. She is ready to be the messenger. She is *dying* to make amends. When it's her turn, she rises.

"My name is Anita Beacham Hodge and I'm an alcoholic."

Eight people later, the meeting breaks and Anita collects the coin she came for, the coin that symbolizes her desire to start a new way of life. She has a lot of them and she hopes eventually they'll add up to something.

"Anita?"

Anita turns. It's the tall man, the one who

411

was staring at her across the room. And she'd almost made it to the car too.

"Yes?"

"It's me, Tim."

"Tim."

"Tim Warner."

Recognition sweeps through her. Holy shit, it *is* him. The boy who used to stare at her, who attacked her, now a man. Or two thirds of him. The figure that stands in front of her in slacks and a crisp navy T-shirt is as lean as a post. The hair is prematurely gray. There is something different about the face, as if it's been broken and reassembled into something both harder and softer at the same time. Abe Lincoln with a close shave.

"Oh, my gosh. Tim. Yes, hi," she says. Not sure if she should run for the car.

"I saw you inside." The voice is soft, almost but not quite a rough whisper. "I thought it was you."

"I saw you too," she says. "I didn't recognize you."

"I look a little different, don't I?" he says.

"Yeah, you do." No way around it.

"You look the same as always."

She can tell he means it as a compliment. She really should go now. She really should. He looks different, that's all. People don't change. Not people like Tim "Time" Warner. "I'm just back visiting," Anita says, still not moving. It seems important that he know this is a chance meeting, that it won't ever happen again.

"Me too. Helping my mom move into a senior residence."

"Oh. I'm sorry."

"No. It's good. *She's* good."

"Nice."

"Do you, uh . . . come to these often?" Tim Warner seems almost embarrassed to ask.

"Not really. No." Anita hesitates. "Do you?" She winces inside. Mistake. Asking a participant how often they come to meetings is like asking them how far they've fallen. Which is silly, really, because *supposedly* there are no part-time alcoholics, which means there are no partial falls.

"Every chance I get," says Tim Warner. "It saved my life."

Oh, shit.

Now she's supposed to hear his story. Now she's supposed to tell him hers. Does she want to? She's surprised she's still standing here, let alone talking to him. And all of a sudden she knows why. For the first time since being back she feels she's in the presence of someone who isn't judging her. Tim Warner looks like he's gone through

413

hell. She is curious as to what's been burned away.

"I started doing steroids and HGH in high school. By junior year at Arizona I was two sixty-five. I could bench-press two hundred twenty-five pounds thirty-eight times, did a four point six in the forty. I was going right to the NFL."

At his suggestion, they are at the old coffee shop and are at an outdoor table, mugs in front of them. A latte for her, a decaf for him. He has insisted on buying.

"Then in the second-to-last game against Oregon I shredded my knee and it was all over but for the burial."

"That must have been tough," she says, thinking of Michael. What is it with men's knees that they can so easily derail dreams?

Tim Warner shrugs. He is quiet, staring into his coffee. She waits, patient.

"I'd always partied hard. I partied harder. Twenty-four seven, anything I could get my hands on. Needless to say, I did not finish my college education."

He smiles at his own joke. A stoic, Anita thinks, also like Michael.

"I began working as a bouncer at local clubs. Still worked out, did the 'roids, still liked hitting and hurting people. I'd put you

414

in the hospital for looking at me wrong."

We're getting to it now, thinks Anita.

"One night four of us were in a car. Beyond wasted. Driver was doing a line of meth off the top of his hand and he lost control. We crossed the centerline doing ninety. Only by the grace of God we didn't take someone out coming the other way. Hit a ditch, the car flipped, went into a tree. Only one survivor."

"The driver," says Anita.

Tim Warner stares at her a moment and then nods imperceptibly and again looks down into his coffee. Again, is quiet for a while. Anita sips her coffee and waits.

"I was in an induced coma for three weeks. Head injuries. Pretty much needed a whole new . . ." Tim gestures at the sharp bones and shiny patches of his face. Anita recognizing them now as the signs of reconstruction and skin grafts. ". . . but other than that . . ."

"Did you blame yourself?"

Tim grunts and then shakes his head. "No. Could have been any one of us driving that car. But I did think to myself, it cannot get any worse than this. Shows what I knew. Bottom was still a long way down."

"It works that way, doesn't it," Anita says.

"But then I got lucky. Beat cop, guy I'd

played ball with, yanked my ass off the street and into his car one night. Took me to a meeting. You can be here or you can be in prison, he said. And brother, you will die in prison. I had just enough left up here" — Tim Warner points at his head — "to know he was right. Took a little while. Stops and starts. But now I haven't had a drink in six years. I don't even touch aspirin. I run fifty miles a week. I go to church. I go to meetings. Anybody needs a sponsor or a helping hand, I'm there. That's my life now."

"Does it pay well?"

He laughs. She's pleased that he recognizes a joke when he hears one.

"The father of one of the guys who died in that car, he gave me a job at his shipping company. I'm an actual manager. I've had more people forgive me in this life than I deserve." Tim Warner reaches across the table. His fingers stop just short of touching Anita's hand. "I hope you will too. That's all I really wanted to say."

"Not a problem. Done."

A smile creases Tim Warner's long, sad face. "I was so crazy about you, Anita," he says. "You were my dream girl and I was afraid to say so much as a word. I had no clue in the world."

"None of us ever do," she says in reply.

■ ■ ■ ■

He walks her to her car. A shuffling, shambling gait, hands stuffed in his jacket pockets as if he's walking her to class and is pleased but is self-conscious about it, trying to make it out as no big deal and failing completely. I'm glad I'm not a man, thinks Anita. And then the next thought —

He's sweet.

"Well, listen," he says. "You ever get to Tucson, I'm in the book. I have a pretty nice house. Quiet. Some land around it. Way too big for one person, so if you and yours ever need a place to stay." He is silent for a moment and then he repeats himself, "I'm in the book." It sounds cowboyish, a lonesome sheriff letting the settler woman know she's welcome at any time. She is touched. Again the thought — *sweet.*

"Thank you, Tim."

"No. Thank you."

She gets in the car, feeling at ease for the first time in days. If Tim Warner can become a real person, perhaps she can too. It's something to seriously consider.

50

Fari calls mid-morning, knowing it will be the best time to get the answering machine. The first time a woman with a brisk English accent answers the phone . . .

"Hello. Yes, hello? Anyone there?"

. . . and Fari quickly hangs up. When she tries again an hour later, she thankfully gets Michael's voice on a recording, and when she hears the beep, she composes herself with a deep breath and begins what's she rehearsed in her mind so carefully.

"Michael, this is Fari. I'm so glad it's a machine and not you. It makes it much easier this way."

Meaning she's a coward and they both know it. Meaning she is unwilling to face the surge of emotions that seeing him or hearing his voice again would entail.

"Michael, my father has died. Three weeks ago. Very fast, a stroke. Even though we had issues, it pains me. I never got to say good-bye to him. But that's another long story."

In preparing to leave, Fari has felt as if she's been putting photos that are meaningful to her into a box, not for safekeeping, but for storage, in all probability never to be looked at again. Photos, of course, are memories captured in real time. Some photos, she thinks —

— *those of you, Michael* —

— unfold like a deck of cards, a single image in the mind's eye cascading open into many. Some, those of her father, are nothing more than a single, frozen image in her head.

"My mother is now in London with my sister and I'm going to join them. For how long I'm not sure. I might even stay. Regardless, I've decided to close my practice for the time being."

Fari hesitates. She takes another breath. She goes on.

"I need to tell you that for a couple of months now I've been seeing your wife as a patient. I didn't make the connection at first and then I did. I probably shouldn't have continued but I thought I could help and yes . . . I was curious."

Fari hears Michael's voice in her head, concerned and asking the obvious question. She answers it.

"She's a troubled woman. Terrified of abandonment, both real and imagined. Her interpersonal relationships alternate between idealization and devaluation. She's subject to intense mood swings, mostly depression."

Speak English.

"She wants to go back to a place and time where she can make everything right again. She thinks this will make her whole. I've tried to tell her that a person who needs a specific other person to feel whole will never be whole and, try as they might, will always create circumstances that lead to even more damaging behavior."

She hesitates. She continues.

"You know, Michael, I have always understood why a person can have reasons to be sad. But I've never quite understood why when a person has every reason to feel joy, they don't. It's as if all the feeling has gone out of them. Perhaps they've grown tired of feeling pain and so they've decided to try and feel nothing at all. I fear Anita is like that. I'm sorry to say I've been guilty of it as well. Please don't ever let it happen to you."

The script she so carefully composed has flown from her head. She's off book now, knows it but can't help herself, knows now she wanted to be all along.

"Guess what? I'm a single woman, Michael. My husband divorced me. My father asked him to do so just before he died. It was a gift to me."

What a martyr she's being. A Muslim woman who has never married can marry any man she wants in paradise. She's blown that possibility.

"Isn't it funny? The timing of things? I can do anything I want now and all I want is —"

Fari stops. No, not funny at all. When he listens, if he listens at all, he'll probably have hung up by now.

"I leave on the seventeenth. Perhaps we'll speak before then. If not . . .

"Stay well."

It's late when Michael goes to bed. He hasn't changed the sheets since Anita slept over and he knows now he'll do it in the morning. But at the moment the faint scent of her perfume, rose and lavender, full of memories, is still on the pillows. It's as he's drifting off into restless sleep, the message playing over and over again in his head, that the fragrance changes. Rose becomes entangled with sandalwood, lavender with jasmine. The essence of one woman is somehow transmuted into two. Both women are equally vivid to him, both to be cherished, both ephemeral.

He calls to them in the dark.

"Come back," he says. "Come back."

Neither one answers. He is alone.

Storm surge. Increase or decrease in sea level by strong winds such as those accompanying a hurricane or other intense storm.

Flood current. The movement of a tidal current toward the shore.

Stranding. The grounding of a vessel so that it is not easily refloated; a serious grounding.

Umbra. The darkest part of a shadow in which light is completely cut off by an intervening object.

51

Arriving at the club, Neal Beacham scrapes the back fender of an Audi sedan as he pulls into a parking place. He spends a good three minutes wondering if he knows who the owner of the car is and, coming to the conclusion he doesn't, decides the ding is minor and that it's not worth leaving a note. Just to be safe, he parks several stalls away. Silly for the place to be crowded on a Tuesday afternoon. The damn club really should have valet parking.

He enters the locker room, in a hurry, wanting to hit balls before the regular one o'clock drop-in. His locker, one of the big ones, is toward the rear, away from the showers where a man can have some privacy.

Neal unlocks his locker and opens it. Sitting on the cushioned bench, he takes off his street shoes. It's pleasant to think they'll be newly polished when he returns after his round. He takes out golf shoes and a bucket hat. He wonders if he should take a wind shirt. As he reaches to the top shelf of the locker for a sleeve of new golf balls, something in the back catches his eye. It's a manila envelope. There is a note on it — *thought you should see this.* Puzzled, Neal Beacham opens the envelope.

In the living room at the Beacham house, Beth and Tisha are going through fabric swatches for new dining room curtains.

It's most annoying.

Tisha has felt for a time now that Beth's old ones, faded and beginning to fray at the bottom, are in need of replacing. Beth, of course, thinks they're perfectly fine. And so now Tisha has not only had to offer to pay for the new ones, she's had to go to all the trouble of finding a good interior designer, not because she wants or needs advice on design for goodness' sake, no, but rather, because designers seem to be the only ones who have access to decent fabric houses these days. It's enough to make one do all one's shopping online. Well, at least the woman's local and Beth hasn't had to drive far to pick up the samples. Still, Beth is *not* being a help. It's almost as if she resents everything that's being done for her.

"What about the silk?" says Beth, holding up a heavy cream-colored swathe of fabric. Naturally the most expensive.

"It won't stand up to the sun," says Tisha. She reaches for another swatch. "This plaid's nice."

"Why don't I just stuff a golden retriever and stick it in the hallway?" says Beth.

A golden retriever? Oh. All right, yes, thinks Tisha, the plaid *is* a bit *Town & Country.* But the attitude. "Beth, why do you ask for my advice when you really don't like it."

"It's my way of bonding. And I didn't ask for it, you're just giving it to me. I can pick out my own curtains, Mother."

"Not on my dime."

"Whatever."

Rolling her eyes like that. It's enough to —

They both look up at the sudden sound of the front door slamming hard.

"What on earth?" says Tisha.

"Anita?" Neal Beacham's voice sounds like his vocal chords have been shortened with a dull bread knife.

"Whee!" says Beth. "Daddy's home!"

"Don't you dare start."

"Aneetah!"

"Neal? We're in here!" calls Tisha. "Why are you yelling like that? What's wrong?"

They hear the heavy steps. Both hear and feel the dull thud of a closed fist against the doorjamb.

Oh, well, *that's* helpful, thinks Tisha.

The man who appears in the doorway looks like a cartoon character on the verge of a heart attack. His hair is disheveled and there is sweat on his pale face and lined forehead. The eyes are bulging with heavy bags beneath them and the mouth is twisted into a tight red line. "Where is she?" says Neal Beacham. "Your *daughter.* Where is she?"

Tisha Beacham regards her husband calmly. "I think she's upstairs. Why?"

Without answering, Neal Beacham turns from the room. "Oh, this is gonna be good," says Beth, as if pleased at the prospect of a total conflagration.

"Beth," says Tisha. "I'm warning you. Keep your mouth shut."

They quickly follow Neal out of the room.

Anita lies on the couch in the darkened library, her headache finally fading. Maybe she shouldn't have gone cold turkey on the antidepressants. This migraine was the kind that started with an aura of flickering light, a warning that the oncoming headache was going to be a doozy. A few times she's felt

428

as if she were actually floating above her own body, looking down at herself. She listens to her father angrily calling her name. What is it *this* time? she wonders. She rises and, still unsteady on her feet, walks toward the closed door.

"Anita!"

Neal Beacham moves across the house entryway and starts up the stairs. He is aware that his wife is behind him, that his daughter who seems, God help her, *amused* at all this, brings up the rear.

"Neal, you're acting like a madman. What's wrong, what has she done?" His wife, always putting the blame on *him,* making it his fault. His daughter always acting as if everything is so *funny.* On the upstairs landing, Neal Beacham turns on them both. "What has she done? What hasn't she done? Disappointing us, failing us. Ungrateful slut from the beginning!"

"Gee, I thought *I* was the slut," says Beth, as if thrilled about it.

Pushing past his wife, Neal Beacham slaps his daughter across the face. "Is it funny now?" He swings again, missing her but pushing her now, back into the wall. His daughter cries out in fear. He's hurt her, but he can't help it, can't stop, he won't. "Is it funny!? Is it?"

The sudden wild blow to his own face takes him by surprise. The next one, hard to the ear, the sharp *pain* of it, even more. His daughter, sobbing, her face that of some deranged harpy, is striking back, wildly pushing and punching — no, now *kicking* — him.

"Don't you — ever — you — ever again —"

Impossible.

"Stop it!" his wife cries, grabbing at Beth. "Stop it! Are the two of you insane!?"

It takes Neal Beacham only a moment to muster his outrage. "Talk sanity the next time you go to the club to play golf and someone sticks this under your nose!" Taking the DVD case from the pocket of his wind shirt, he thrusts it at Tisha, makes her take it.

Now she'll understand.

"Look at it! That's your daughter sucking a dick! That's her, letting some tattooed pig screw her up the ass!"

"Oh, God," says Tisha Beacham, the blood draining from her face.

"Yes! Sitting in my locker. A *friend* thought I should see it. Hah! No doubt everyone else has!" Turning, Neal Beacham screams down the upstairs hallway toward his daughter's bedroom. "Aneeetah — !"

"What."

Standing in the foyer below them, Anita remembers a lesson from an acting class. When you want focus, speak quietly. No matter the hubbub on the other side of the stage, speak softly and succinctly and the focus will come to you. And it does. Yanking something square and plastic from her mother's hand, Neal Beacham throws it down at her. She knows immediately what it is. The cover. She was never supposed to be on it. She was a participant, yes, but not a name player. How gullible can you be to believe anything people like that would tell you.

"Is this it? Is this what you are?" yells Neal Beacham. "Answer me!"

"I guess so." The lack of emotion in her voice surprises even her.

"Anita." It's her mother speaking now. She has never seen her mother look frightened before. It's not a good feeling and she pushes it away. Her sister is crying on the stairs and she pushes that away as well. "How could you? Was it money? You have money. When you need it, I give you more."

As if it's so *tragic.*

"Maybe I was tired of asking." Good. Let them think it was about money. She can see

431

the matter-of-factness of it stuns them both.

"I want you out of this house," says her father. "I want you out now."

"Not a problem."

"No —" her mother starts to say.

"Yes! After all we've done for her! All *I've* done!"

It's finally too much, it really is. "What have you ever done for me, Dad? What have you done? I'd like to know."

"Oh, don't you talk to me like that — don't you dare." Her father is shaking now as if indignant. It actually seems funny. "The strings I've pulled? To get you back what you should have never given up in the first place? Well, so much for that."

And suddenly, it's not funny at all. "What are you talking about?" she says.

"Neal, stop *now* —" she hears her mother say.

"No. You're talking about Michael. What did you do? Did you offer *him* money?" He did. She knows he did. She *knows* it.

"Hah! It should be so easy. No, I promised him a job, that's all. A real one. Thank God, he's a little more employable than you. I opened the door but once again you've managed to slam it shut. Well, good riddance this time. To the both of you. Good riddance to bad trash."

Wrong, Anita thinks. I've been so wrong.

Beth isn't quite sure what's going down but whatever it is, it's something momentous. No, actually it's something that would normally happen at *her* house.

"Shut up!" her mother screams — *screams* — at her father, her father, whom, she, Beth, has somehow finally found the guts to beat the shit out of.

Her father turns to her mother as if offended. "What?" he says. "What did you say?"

"Shut up!" her mother screams again. "You *idiot*! Shut up!"

Beautiful.

Down below, Anita is moving toward the front door.

"Anita, wait — please —" her mother calls.

Too late. Her sister is out the door. And now her mother — *will wonders never cease?* — is hurrying down the stairs after her.

"Let her leave!" her father calls after her.

"Fuck — you!" her mother screams back.

Beth can't remember the last time she heard Tisha Beacham use profanity.

Beautiful.

"You are such a pathetic bastard," she says

to her father. As she hurries down the stairs and out the door after her mother and sister she realizes, with such a sense of relief, she will never be coming back to this house again.

Tisha comes out into the courtyard just in time to see Anita slam the car door behind her. "Anita," she calls. "Anita, please!" Please *what*? she wonders. What is she saying? Please stop? Please come back? Please, I'll make it better? She feels as if there is a small metal box inside her. It is where she has put unwanted feelings for as long as she can remember and now the box is on the verge of bursting and spilling its tightly compressed contents. No, she tells herself. *No.* She stands, unmoving, as Anita drives away. She is vaguely aware of someone behind her.

"Where's she going? What are we going to do?" asks Beth.

"You are going to go home," says Tisha.

"But —"

"*Please.* Don't argue with me." The box inside her is on the brink of breaking again. *Shore it up, shore it up.*

"We've all had enough drama for one day."

"So much for curtains, huh?"

It actually makes her smile. "Yes. So much

for curtains."

She finds her husband in the kitchen. Neal Beacham is pouring himself a drink. "Would you like one?" he calmly asks. Cocktail hour at the Ritz.

"Yes," she says quietly. He hands her his. How thoughtful. She drains half of it in one swallow. "Are you happy now?" she asks.

"The truth," says Neal Beacham, "has never made me unhappy."

Tisha Beacham throws the remains of the liquor into her husband's face.

"I should have left you years ago."

No anger. No sputtering indignation. Acceptance.

"You did."

52

It's subflooring for the second story of the house, three-quarter-inch tongue-and-groove plywood glued and nailed to the first story's ceiling joists. Hard and heavy work, tough on the knees, tougher on the back, and even with Michael there to help, the work is going slowly.

"That was Bobby." Jose puts his cell phone back in the pocket of his baggy, low-riding jeans. Bobby, who has gone missing the last two days, finally calling in. "He's in Vegas. He got married over the weekend."

"I didn't know he was engaged," Michael says quietly.

"He wasn't," says Jose. "He says he met her in the casino Saturday night."

Bobby, a good kid, hardworking and reliable, but often a yard short in the brains department.

"Whata you think, Luis?" Jose is grinning now. He enjoys goading the dour older man.

"Does he stand a chance?"

Luis shrugs. "All that matters is she make him happy. Women today, they forget their job. It's what they're supposed to do."

"Yeah, I'll tell my girlfriend that. Then I'll run." Jose's girlfriend, a sociology major at San Diego State, is a retired Cerco Blanco gang sister from L.A. who could kick the shit out of most men in a fight. "Hey, you think we should send Bobby a gift?"

"How about a get-well card," says Michael.

Happy.

Hitting the brakes, Anita stops in the middle of the street. The Prius lurches forward as she opens the car door. She slams the button on the console with a closed fist, hating a car that allows her to forget to put it in park.

She can see them up on the second floor, working. Sees Michael rise up off his knees and, balancing on a beam, approach the edge of the roof, hammer in hand, tool belt at his waist. And at that moment, she realizes that she despises him — *has* for such a long time. That he chose *this* as a way to make a living. This trapped, plain-wrapped, unending *thing*. He could have been anything else. And if he had been different, she would have been different. They would have been different. All so different.

Your fault.

"Whoa. Here comes happy," murmurs Jose.

"Shut up," says Leo, his face grim. This is going to be bad, he thinks. He knows an angry woman when he sees one. All you can do is hope that they're not armed.

"Get back to work," says Michael. He lowers himself to the beam, dangles and drops to the ground.

Leaving her car in the middle of the street, Anita strides across the sidewalk and onto the rough ground of the worksite. Michael sees that her face is pinched and pale. What should be a pretty sundress seems like a rough bag of fabric on her, barely holding her together.

"Hey. What's going on? What's wrong?"

Bending, Anita picks up a piece of scrap wood and throws it at him. It bounces off his quickly raised arms, hurts him.

Good.

"What the hell —"

She grabs for other pieces of scrap, anything she can get her hands on, anything that will make for a projectile. "Damn you! Damn you! Fucking bastard, I trusted you!"

Throwing, reaching, throwing. Wild and inept and frantic.

"Anita, are you crazy? What's wrong with you?"

Nothing left to throw now. Nothing to hurt him with but closed, ineffectual fists. "Poor Anita! Huh? Needs a home and a husband to take care of her! Can't do it by herself, can she?"

"I don't know what you're talking about."

"Bullshit, Michael! Bullshit! He paid you! He paid you off and you took it! You took it!"

Oh, God, Michael thinks, knowing now exactly what she's talking about. What did Neal tell her? What did he say? Be calm. "Okay, wait. If you're talking about that job offer, no. No, I never did. I never told him yes." It sounds clumsy and false coming out of his mouth. "I never promised him a thing."

"Did you say no, Michael? Did you spell it out for him? Because he thinks you did."

Michael knowing the truth. Good intentions suddenly made bad. Conveying it with silence.

"If you didn't say no, you said yes, and that makes you the asshole in my book. Oh, God, I am so out of here." She turns quickly away, striding for the street.

Futile to call after her. So futile. Still. He does. "Anita! I would have done it anyway. I didn't need his help to make me want to try."

"Fuck! You!" she screams. Not even breaking stride. Not even listening.

He starts after her. On her quickly. He is a dog at her heels and anger is suddenly a bone in his mouth, something to grind and break with his teeth. "This is what you've been looking for, isn't it? Just waiting. Another reason to bail. Just like last time."

"Shut up!" she says. "You know nothing about me! Nothing! You never did!" A worthless response. No leg to stand on. Pitiful.

"Tell me you haven't! Tell me you haven't, Anita!"

She turns back, screaming at him, her rage now every bit the equal of his own. "Leave me alone!"

He doesn't. He no longer can. "What is it you want from me? What is it you want, period? You think I'm fine this way? That it was supposed to be like this? A fucked-up wife and a screwed-up kid?"

"Stop it," she says again. Turning away again. Beginning to cry now. "Just stop talking."

"*You* stop. I am barely getting by. I am

440

trying my best. What is your best? I haven't seen it yet. I keep waiting for the conversation we never had. The one where you explain everything to me so that I finally understand. It's never gonna happen, is it?"

Her anger is gone now. She wishes it wasn't. Anger is such a good alternative to feeling what she's feeling now. "All I do is hurt you."

"Tell me about it."

"I can't be what you want. I'm not that thing."

"I don't care about me. Not for me. For him, Anita, stay for him."

Anguish.

Anguish, Penelope once told Michael, is standing at the edge of a cliff knowing you have the freedom to throw yourself off or stay put and wanting desperately to do both. It is anguish that he sees in Anita's eyes.

"Why did you love me?" she asks, her voice a dead thing. "Why did you try and save me? You knew. Why couldn't you have left me alone?"

Your fault.

Anita turns and walks, half stumbling, into the street. Somehow she gets into the car. It starts silently. It crawls slowly away, rounds the corner and is gone.

On the second floor, Leo, Luis, and Jose

have stopped working. Who can nail plywood when two people are nailing each
other?

"Go home," Michael calls out, not looking back at them. "Everybody go home."

53

Tisha is in the kitchen, forcing herself to boil water for tea, when the phone rings. Steeling herself, she answers it.

"Yes, hello."

"It's me," Michael's voice says. "Has Anita come back?"

"What do you mean?" Tisha asks, fearing the worst.

"She came by the worksite. She was upset. Tisha, is she there or not?"

"No. She's left, Michael," says Tisha. "Anita's . . . left." She quickly puts a hand over her mouth. Something is coming up inside and it wouldn't do to let it out. "She came home, gathered up her things, and now she's gone."

"Let me talk to your husband."

"He isn't here either, Michael. He went to the club. The country club."

"You're fucking kidding me."

"No."

"What did he say to her, Tisha?"

"Horrible things. Unforgivable." The taste in her mouth is horrible. It's bile. It's vinegar. It's amniotic fluid gone sour. "Please know this is not your fault."

"Are you okay?"

"No, Michael, I'm not okay. At the moment, I'm not okay at all. As a matter of fact, I've got to go now. The kettle's boiling, I've got to go."

She hangs up. Terribly rude but she had no choice. The tears are coming. She can't stop them, doesn't really want to, and so to keep calm, she focuses on filling the teacup with them, one by one.

The truck comes into the country club parking lot and stops at the walk's bag drop, blocking the lane. Michael leaps out and rushes in.

In the golf shop, the assistant pro looks up from his magazine as this *worker* enters in dirty jeans, heavy leather boots, and sweat-streaked T-shirt.

What the hell?

"Uh — sir, can I help you?"

The grim-faced man doesn't stop. He marches across the shop past the club displays and the neatly folded sports clothes as if he knows where he's going.

444

"Hey! Service entrance is in the back!"

Too late. The man is gone. Shit, the assistant pro thinks, and feeling as if his job is suddenly on the line, he grabs a putter off a rack and holding it like a club hurries after the crazy guy.

In the card room, Neal Beacham has just been served his second vodka tonic when, hearing voices, he looks up to see Michael enter. The assistant pro, whose name Neal can never remember, is behind him, obviously having failed to halt his forward progress with — *what is the man brandishing?* — a putter. Neal Beacham feels an unaccustomed foreboding. Sitting here, playing cards with men that he thought were his friends, men that he assumes now know *everything,* has been torture. Every smile has felt colored with innuendo. Each bark of laughter has seemed like it comes at his expense.

Your daughter. I'd like a piece of that. How much?

Smirky bastards, each time they raise, stand pat, or call, they've made him feel as if he had this coming to him all along and they are enormously pleased and satisfied that it finally did.

Your wife is leaving you? What took her so

long? Ha-ha!

How could he not have known? It's so obvious. They don't like him. They never have. All of them. He'll never be able to come here again.

What am I going to do without the club?

"I'm sorry, Mr. Beacham," says the assistant pro. "He insisted on coming in. If you'd like we can call the police."

"No, it's all right," says Neal Beacham. Glancing at his cards, he throws some chips into the pot. "See you and raise you ten," he says, smiling complacently across the table at Hal Weinraub, who is staring at Michael, an uncertain expression on his face. Wimp. So, for that matter, are the other two, Ed Buchanan and Ken Klyce.

He'll show these people how to act.

He reaches for his drink. "Again, you're not appropriately dressed, Michael. Why don't you come back when you are."

"Why don't you kiss my puckered ass."

"Really? And why don't you just —" With a hard, sudden slap, Michael knocks the glass from Neal Beacham's hand, drenching him and freezing him in his chair.

"You're not talking. I am."

Neal Beacham cowers in his chair from the blow that doesn't come. Unforgivable. To forget that there are people in the world

446

who don't care about the rules, people who will hurt you, hurt you badly, damn the consequences. The others at the table are just staring in confusion, doing nothing.

"You bitter, useless old man," says Michael. "Fucking with people's lives. What did you ever do that makes you think you matter? Sitting here like you deserve something? You're lucky somebody doesn't come up here with a shotgun and show you the real world."

"Olé." It's just a murmur from the Mexican waiter but it feels like a stab wound, makes Neal Beacham realize yet again how far and quickly he's fallen.

Even the hired help.

"You come near me ever again," says Michael, "I'll put you in the hospital in pieces." He hawks and spits. The ugly, thick wad of phlegm lands on Neal Beacham's chips. "Enjoy your game." And with that, Michael turns back through the door and exits. Air returns to the room but not nearly enough.

"Well, that was an occasion," says Neal Beacham, forcing a laugh.

"Shall I call the police, sir?" says the assistant pro.

"A little late, don't you think?" says Neal Beacham, growing angrier by the moment now. If he was ten years younger, things

447

would have been different. He turns to the nameless waiter. "Clean this goddamn mess up, why don't you?"

"Wasn't that your son-in-law?" says Hal Weinraub, quietly.

"What? Yes. *Ex.* Son of a bitch. I *ought* to press charges."

"Everything all right with your daughter?" asks Ken Klyce.

Acting as if they're concerned now.

"Fine. Are we playing cards or not?"

"I think I'm done," says Ed Buchanan, rising.

"Put the drinks on my tab, Javier," says Hal Weinraub, following suit.

So that's the bastard's name.

"Tough day, Neal," says Ken Klyce. He claps Neal gently on the shoulder as he exits the card room.

Know. All of them know.

"You want another drink, Mr. Beacham?" The waiter, Javier, has picked the glass up off the rug.

"Go fuck yourself," whispers Neal Beacham, unable to rise. Thank God there's someone in the world who won't fight back. Neal Beacham's hands are shaking. There is a ringing in his ears and he feels dizzy. He'll sit here a moment and then he'll go home.

If only he knew where the hell that was anymore.

54

At Wind and Sea, the cars and trucks are parked up and down the street. And why not. Looking out the truck window, Michael sees that the surf is huge, six to eight feet, prime sets with surfers wiping out and going rag doll all over the place.

A car pulls out in front of him and, on impulse, Michael quickly turns and pulls into the parking place. He turns off the engine. He sags in the seat. The fury draining away.

Senseless asshole.

Taking your anger and pain out on a belligerent old man who probably shrugged it off the moment you left. What good did it do? What good does anything do?

"I'm tired," says Michael out loud to no one. "I'm tired." He gets out of the truck. He walks to the rocky outlook that overlooks the beach. Spectators gape and point as out beyond the reef a particularly huge wave builds and charges. In the middle zone, two surfers paddle side by side to catch it. Each is quickly up, one on the inside, close to the peak of the wave, and one on the outside. And then the inside surfer, fighting for right of way, is down and falling as if tumbling headfirst into a canyon. The water crashes over him, burying him. His board, attached to his ankle by a leash, careens crazily in the air and then is swallowed as well. Michael winces, knowing that in big surf, the leash can hold you under, that the board is like an anchor as you fight your way to the surface. That is, if you even know which way to go once the washing machine stops spinning you. Down too long and the next wave hits you and keeps you under. Another lands on top of you and there's a chance you're not coming up.

Like an avalanche, the wave continues on, submerging the parade of oncomers who are stroking furiously to get out to the heart of the lineup. On the ridge overlooking the slim stretch of sand, a lifeguard rises from his plastic chair, tense and alert. An exhausted surfer holding a split and broken board is climbing the rocks toward them. The look on his face says it's treacherous out there. There are deadly creatures lurking, waiting to feast.

Enough, Michael abruptly thinks. Enough being afraid. Enough treading the path of least resistance. Enough merely responding to circumstances. Enough killing time while time quietly kills you.

Enough.

Pulling his T-shirt up and over his head, Michael leaps the rail and runs down the ridge toward the beach. He leaps down to the soft, wet sand and starts forward. In half a dozen steps, his work boots and the bottom of his jeans take on weight and he quickly stops to take them off.

"Look at that!" cries a woman, delighted at the sight of Michael's naked white ass.

"What the hell's he doing?" another man cries out to no one in particular.

As if in answer, Michael kicks his jeans off and runs naked into the heavy surf. The freezing cold water hits him, driving him back, but he keeps his feet. And then heavy backwash from the beach takes him from behind and carries him forward into the water. His feet touch bottom and then the bottom is gone and Michael begins to swim. So easy, he thinks. So easy. His body has forgotten nothing. He used to train for surf like this. Jump rope and do pushups, run and swim distance, knowing there were going to be situations out in the water when help wouldn't be an option, that he'd be on his own.

So why is he already growing tired?

He dives forward beneath the first oncoming wave, feels its power and weight as it surges over him. Surfacing, he kicks and swims on.

How many waves to each set? How much time between sets? He should know this. Is it a rising swell or a dropping swell? He should know this too. Where does the reef begin, where are the rocks, how deep is the bottom? He has forgotten. He has forgotten how blinding the ocean can be. How deafening the ocean is. He used to know everything or he thought he did. Where did he ever get such confidence? No one has ever fought the ocean when it's angry and won.

"You got a sense of humor?"

"A guy gets hit by a rock."

"And?"

"That's it."

A wave is rising and Michael dives again. Not deep enough and he is pulled and kneaded this time as if in a giant baker's hands. Momentum lost, he surfaces. He takes a breath and chokes as froth fills his mouth and throat. He coughs, treading water, knowing he is now adrift and sliding in the impact zone, where crashing wave meets sucking undertow. He swims. Tries to. Where is he even going? Where was his father going? Out to sea? Back to shore? Michael sees the next wave peaking in front of him, and pulling in a ragged gulp of air, he starts to dive. Too late. The wave grabs him, pushes him up and back, flips him over and slams him down. Deadweight, far heavier than water, he both falls and is driven toward the bottom. The bottom, where it is peaceful. Yes, he thinks. At last. The maelstrom is overhead. All the turbulence is back onshore. Here, it is just like in the dream. Here he can drift. Here he is a clairvoyant, seeing not the future, but the present in all its different machinations. He wonders if this is how his father felt while swimming, wonders if Thomas Hodge was visiting the people he loved, as he gave himself over to the ocean.

Michael sees Fari is in her bedroom, packing a suitcase. She is taking clothes from a bureau drawer. She is surprised to find something under a blouse. It's the good-luck bracelet, woven red yarn with two tiny jade mandarin ducks. Michael bought it for her on a lark when they walked into a cheap sundries shop one evening while in Old Town. The ducks, the shopkeeper told them, represent love in Chinese culture. As far as Michael knows, it was the only time she ever wore it. She considers it a moment. She puts it carefully into her suitcase.

He sees Anita. She is in her car, driving up a long hill. Her face is vacant; her eyes are dull. Michael knows now that he had been waiting, waiting those seven years, for her to come back. He expected it, he counted on it, assuming that when she did, that all the issues would be behind her, that she would have somehow resolved them. They would be in love again and Jamie would be cured by their love. They would all go back in time together. It would be Talujah again.

So stupid. A child's dream. A fairy tale.

He sees the photo of Anita and Jamie, taken at the mall, on the sunshade of the car. And then Anita grabs it and tosses it into the backseat. Out of sight, out of mind. The car races up and disappears over the crest of the hill and is gone.

Michael sees Penelope. She is in the makeshift garden in the backyard, on her knees, talking to her flowers. "No, this won't do," she says. "You've got to grow. I know you would have done better at the old house. There were friends there, dear friends. But you owe it to them not to give up . . . you've got to grow."

"No. Quit that stuff," Michael says. "Be quiet."

And now, Michael sees Jamie. His son is behind his mother, naked and violently stimming; shaking a garden trowel, moving to an arhythmic inner music, mumbling to himself. "Even if you're not there, you love me . . . llamas! There are llamas . . . would you change me if you could?"

"Would you still be you?" Michael asks his son.

"It doesn't matter," Jamie replies. "Because you love me . . . love me . . . you love me . . ."

"How much?" whispers Michael.

"To infinity and beyond."

No.

As if waking but not in bed, Michael begins to claw his way toward the surface. The clairvoyance is acute now. On the shore, a lifeguard is running toward the surf with his long rescue board. "I don't see him!" someone screams. "He's not coming up!" another voice cries.

No, Michael thinks. *No.* He knows now without any sense of doubt that his father was trying to come home, that Thomas Hodge was swimming as hard as he could. He ran out of strength, that's all. The ocean was too much for him.

I am not my father.

Michael's head and shoulders erupt up out of the water. It takes a moment to remember to breathe and when he does he feels ecstasy. The water takes him, pushes him, holds him buoyant. He is fine now. In his element. No big deal. You go down, you come up. Even afraid, you keep swimming. What else is there? The ocean and life are one and the same thing. Calm at times, rough at times. Always beautiful. Amniotic fluid has the same composition as seawater. The ocean carries us. The ocean is inside us.

I choose this.

"Hey! You okay?" A lifeguard is approaching, paddling fast on his long board. "I said, are you all right!"

"Fine," Michael says. And he is. He is strong and weightless. He is reborn, a creature of the sea. Something has been washed away and he is newly baptized.

"Dude, you're crazy!" calls the lifeguard.

Michael laughs. "You're right! I am!" Behind him, a wave is cresting, the face rising like a smooth green wall. Michael kicks and swims forward and it takes him.

Onshore, the spectators and the beach walkers watch, pointing, grinning and shaking their heads as out among the surfers in their dark wet suits, the naked man, his body pale and white against the swell, cuts down and across the face of the wave. He careens along the bottom of it and then, angling his arms and arching, he rides up and out of it as it folds and crashes in a cloud of foam and spray.

Harbor. A haven or space of deep water so sheltered by the adjacent land as to afford a safe anchorage for ships.

55

Penelope is terrible at falling asleep of late, and so to compensate for it, she goes to bed early to give herself lots of time. It's especially difficult when Michael hasn't come home. She worries about him as if he's sixteen again and out past what Thomas Hodge referred to as "his curfew." She wonders if she should get up and go watch *Jeopardy!* It's reassuring to realize she still knows as much as the contestants. But no, the Daily Double might wake Jamie who needs his sleep.

Her two boys. It was easier living alone. One could be concerned for one's loved ones at a safe distance. But it was so solitary. She hadn't even realized she was lonely until she suddenly wasn't anymore. It would be so difficult now to go back to the old way.

At the sound of the front door, the dog, Abigail, stirs at the foot of the bed, raises a heavy head, regards Penelope for a moment, and then, groaning, puts her head back down between her paws.

"Well, no one is asking you to get up and see who it is." Without opening her eyes, Abigail grunts. *Good,* she seems to say. Penelope rises and reaches for her robe.

She comes quietly down the hallway, so as not to wake Jamie. They had salmon and boiled new potatoes for dinner. It's lovely that her grandson shares her enthusiasm for fresh fish. And didn't they have a wonderful conversation? Penelope, who comes from a long line of English train spotters and solitary stamp collectors, feels this autism thing is very much overblown.

At Jamie's room, the door is open and the light is on within. Odd. She was sure she turned it out when she tucked him in. She peeks in. Michael is curled up next to a sleeping Jamie. His clothes, Penelope sees, are patched with sand. His hair is mussed and twisted with traces of salt. He immediately opens his eyes and looks at her. Smiling, he puts a finger to his lips. "Shhhh. I'll be out in a minute."

When Michael comes into the kitchen, Penelope is sitting at the table, looking at the photograph.

"Did you do this?" she says quietly.

"No. Jamie did. I just had it reframed."

Penelope's fingers lightly brush the glass. Next to the uniformed Thomas Hodge, Jamie, solemn and formal looking, and Michael, smiling proudly, pose shoulder to shoulder. Upon seeing it, Michael was surprised at how much he looked like his father.

"How on earth?"

"He's figured out Photoshop. He scanned some old photos of the two of us and stuck them next to Dad. He said he wanted you to have all three of us in one frame. Pretty cool, huh?"

"No. Not cool. It's wonderful."

"Mom? Are you crying?"

"Yes."

"Want to tell me why?"

Putting the framed photo down in front of her, Penelope takes a deep breath. "Your father. Such a dear man, Michael. And I wasn't a good wife to him. I always liked it better when he was gone. When he was home he wanted things his way and I wanted things my way and we'd get very cross with one another. I didn't help him. I didn't know." His mother's voice drops to a sigh now. "Do you think it was truly an accident, Michael? Do you? He was such an

463

expert swimmer."

Michael hesitates, wanting to get it right. "It was an accident, Mom. He swam out too far, that's all, and he couldn't make it back. I can tell you that he wanted to. I have no doubt the last thing he was thinking about was us."

"Oh, Michael."

She feels very small in his arms when she rises to hug him. Michael squeezes softly so as not to bruise.

"We need to talk about your house."

She looks at him, her face telling him she's been dreading this conversation.

"Must we?"

"I think we should."

Penelope sits again, folding her hands in front of her. "There is no house, is there." A simple statement, telling him she's accepted the truth.

"The lot is worth something."

"Then we should sell it," Penelope says, immediately intent on the idea. "It's a good parcel and someone will undoubtedly want to build on it."

"I was thinking *we* would," Michael says. And now she's blinking at him, as if confused, as if he's going far too fast for her. "I'm pretty sure I can get an equity loan on this place. Probably on your lot as well.

464

Enough to rebuild what was there. Or make it even better. And after it's built, we'd sell this place and move in there."

It takes Penelope a moment to speak. "Of course, we'd own it together."

"If you want," says Michael.

"Oh, I do, yes, I do. In fact, I think it'd be better if *you* owned all of it outright." Very serious now. "It'll be yours someday anyway."

"We can talk about it."

Not trusting herself to speak further, Penelope reaches out to take Michael's face in her hands. And in doing so, finds it easy to speak again.

"A perfect house."

"Yeah. Something like that."

"Oh, Michael, I do love you so."

"I love you too, Mom. I love you too."

56

Michael's pickup is parked outside the office. Leo's truck comes to a stop behind it. Leo and Luis get out. Something is wrong with Leo today, Luis can tell. He hasn't expressed a stupid opinion, he hasn't ordered anyone around — when you get right down to it, he hasn't said a word. He just stares into space with a hangdog expression. Has for some days now. You'd think this would be a relief but Luis now finds himself concerned. Maybe it's Michael's unhappy wife that has Leo down in the dumps. Luis knows they are friends. Or maybe it's trouble with the ex-wife and her daughters. Leo takes fathering seriously, even if the girls aren't his, and Luis respects him for it. The thought has also occurred that maybe he was too hard on Leo the other day. You don't talk about a man's shoes until you walk in them. Or some *pendejada* thing like that.

"Leo, you feelin' okay?"

"Yeah, why?"

"Just askin'."

"Fine."

Oh, yeah, something is definitely *muy malo.* When given the slightest opportunity to complain about his gout or his creaky joints or his bowel movements, his friend Leo is usually a loud television show you can't turn off. And though Luis doesn't usually admit it, one of his favorites. In between being annoying and unconscious, Leo is often amusing and makes the workday go well. More than that, he is a friend. Luis would trust Leo with his wife though maybe not his ATM card.

The *afrijole* woman, Rosa, is working at the computer when they enter. Luis has always found this brusque, unsmiling woman and her crazy gold eyes somewhat unsettling but Leo, he knows, likes her.

"Mike here?" grunts Leo.

"His truck's outside," grunts Rose in return.

"In here, Leo." Michael calls from the inner office.

"I gotta use the bathroom," says Luis, feeling he should ask permission of the woman at the desk.

"No necesita mi ayuda." You don't need *my* help.

Nice. As Luis turns toward the bathroom, he hears the half grunt again.

"So how's Linda doing, Leo?"

¿Qué diablos? What the hell? Luis pretends to fumble with the doorknob, the better to hear what this is about.

"There is no Linda, Rose," he hears Leo reply. "You know there's not. I'm a fat pig and I embarrass myself every day. So just let it go."

Luis turns to see Leo disappear into Michael's office. The *afrijole* woman, Luis sees, is no longer working. She is staring down at her desk as if lost.

Eso es todo. So that's it.

"Hey, Leo," Luis calls out. "Can I get a minute with you out here?"

Leo comes back into the office doorway. "What is it?"

Luis turns to the sad-faced woman at the desk. "*Rosa. Es Leo un cerdo gordo?* A fat pig? Huh?"

Startled, Rose hesitates. She looks from Luis to Leo and then down at her desktop again. "No."

Michael appears in the doorway behind Leo. "What's going on?"

"Un momento," says Luis, silencing him.

"I'll be in here," says Michael, getting it and quickly retreating. *Un hombre inteligente.*

Luis turns to Rose again. "*Dígale.* Tell him."

Rose raises her crazy gold eyes to look at Leo again. "You're no pig, Leo. You're big, but you carry it well."

Leo, whom Luis would like to see carrying *anything,* stands there as if no longer understanding English. "Leo. Say something back to the girl, Leo."

"You too."

Ei-yi-yi. Luis rubs his head. This is like talking to his children, which is like talking to stubborn donkeys. "You can't do better'n that?"

"What do you want me to do?"

"Ask her out, Leo. Go on. Ask her. *Pregúntele.*"

"I do," protests Leo. "She always says no."

"So do it again now. With me here."

"Rose, you want to go out?" says Leo, looking at the floor.

"With *you?*" says Rose.

"No, with the pope," says Leo, now bristling a little as he looks up. "Yeah, with me."

It is now the stern woman who doesn't seem to speak such good English, thinks Luis. "*Chica,*" he says gruffly, knowing it's no good to be gentle. "No more bullshitting. *Este es un buen hombre.* He deserve respect. Answer him. Sí or no?"

Rose takes a deep breath. Her back, which till now has seemed bent under a heavy weight, straightens. *"Un momento, Luis?"* Give us a moment?

"I'll be waitin' in the truck," Luis says to Leo. His broad face expressionless, he exits.

"What is it," says Leo. He feels something momentous is about to happen, good or bad, he can't tell. Rose regards him. At least she doesn't seem to *actively* dislike what she sees.

"Did you know I was married once, Leo?"

"Yeah? Me too."

"My husband hurt me," says Rose. "He'd get angry, curse at me, tell me how dark and fat and ugly I was. Sometimes he'd hit me."

"You let him get away with that?"

"I was a young girl. I was crazy about him. I thought it was my fault. I thought if I could be different it would all be better. Only I never could be different enough. He left me for another woman, some skinny, light-skinned thing, and I just about died. It took me a long time to get over it. Maybe I'm not over it yet. I wasn't always such a hard-ass, Leo, but I promised myself I'd

470

never go through anything like that again."

"I understand."

"No you don't. Let me finish. I tell you you're not my type because I have no type. I'm a wide, fat half-black Mexican woman with a brain and an attitude. Whose type is that? I don't talk to men, I don't go out, I don't make love. I've forgotten all that stuff."

"I could teach you again," says Leo, hoping against hope. "Not that I'm in any kind of practice myself," he adds quickly. "But I'm patient and I try hard."

The golden eyes spark. "Are you talking about having sex with me, Leo?"

Leo shrugs. He *was* but —

"We'd be like two Mack trucks hooking bumpers."

"You're not a truck, Rose, you're a beautiful woman."

"You are *SO* full of it."

Rose quickly reaches for the box of Kleenex that's on the edge of her desk. The tawny eyes are shimmering. Incapable of casting spells, thinks Leo, at least bad ones.

"Whatsa matter, your nose itchin', Rose?"

"Yeah."

"Mine does that too on occasion."

He waits and watches as Rose carefully wipes her eyes, wads the Kleenex, and

471

disposes of it beneath her desk. She turns back to Leo.

"Okay," Rose says.

"Okay what?"

"Okay, you'll cook, we'll eat, we'll make like Mack trucks, and then I'll read a book."

"You serious?"

"About eating? Yes."

"You won't regret it, Rose."

"I do already."

Outside the truck horn blares, loud and insistent. Luis can only be so patient.

"I gotta go."

"So go."

"I'll call."

"Please do."

"This weekend, keep it open."

"Yes. Now please get outta here, I have work to do."

"Tell Mike to call me."

Leo turns for the door. It no longer seems big enough to go through.

"Hey, Leo."

Leo turns back. Rose is standing now. She turns sideways. She arches her back and touches her outthrust butt. "Beep-beep." She hisses and shakes her hand as if it's hot. And then, her dark skin blushing, she turns into Michael's office and is gone.

Luis is just getting out of the truck, intent

on going back inside for rescue purposes, when Leo comes out the door and down to the sidewalk. *Aturdido*. He seems dazed.

"You two figure it out?" asks Luis.

"Huh? Yeah, sure," says Leo. "No big deal."

"Bueno."

What else is there to say? Luis starts to turn for the truck. Before he can, Leo throws his arms around him, pulling him close. Leo's a head shorter, so his ample stomach presses awkwardly against Luis's *pelotas* and though Luis is decidedly unsettled by the sensation, he decides that this one time he doesn't mind.

57

Jamie is home when the mail arrives, and when Michael tells him there is a letter addressed to him, he is excited.

"From who?" he asks. "From who?"

"Your mom," Michael tells him, having recognized both the stationery and the graceful handwriting.

Jamie stares at him a moment.

"Read."

"You can do it."

"No. You. Read."

Michael carefully opens the letter and takes out the single page. He studies it a moment, preparing, trying to find her voice inside himself.

" 'Jamie,' " Michael says. " 'Your mother loves you so very, very much. She will come back to you. But first she has to learn to love herself. She will. I promise. Take care of Bear-Bear. He's always yours. Love, Mom.' "

Michael studies his son's face, trying to decipher what he might be feeling, unable to. He wonders if he should show Jamie the other piece of mail that arrived, a bank statement in Jamie's name, a balance of almost fifty thousand dollars, Michael the custodian. No. He wouldn't understand. Save it for the future.

"My mother is off in the world of men."

"Yes. Yes, she is."

"She will be back."

"That's what she says."

"She loves me."

"We both do."

"I do too."

Later that day, Michael finds the letter taped to the bathroom wall, under the photographs.

Mom.

Dad.

58

They meet at Starbucks, which is silly because Tisha Beacham orders tea and Michael is ambivalent about three-dollar coffee. But Starbucks it is unless you're going to meet for a beer somewhere and Michael doubts his ex-mother-in-law has ever had a beer in her life.

"Neal tells me you turned down his job offer."

"You might say."

Tisha Beacham, Michael has always thought, is an unsettling woman. Like Anita, desirable and distant in equal measure but with none of her daughter's very human frailties showing.

"May I ask why?"

"His job didn't include the people I work with."

"Loyalty. No wonder he thinks you're a fool."

"I think he is. I don't know how you stay

with him."

"I have no choice really. He's been diagnosed with Parkinson's." Tisha sips her tea. She stares at Michael. Waiting.

"I'm sorry," he finally says.

"Why? What goes around comes around."

"No, I mean, I'm sorry for you."

"God doesn't give you more than you can handle, Michael."

"Nice of him."

She regards him a moment.

"There are two separate back-to-back cottages down on Ocean Avenue just off Mission Bay. Do you know the area?"

She's segued so quickly he feels like he's talking to his mother. "I do. Back to back?"

"Individual lots. They're owned by a family trust. The trust is interested in tearing them down and putting in a luxury apartment building, six to eight units."

"Who's the family?"

"That's not important. Would you like the job?"

"Are there strings attached?"

"No strings. Just a job. You'll have to find an architect. Someone young and smart that you can create an ongoing relationship with."

"I can do that."

"I'll tell the lawyer to call you then."

He sips the expensive coffee. The family, of course, is Tisha's. Michael knows all about the trust. He's often felt it was one of the things holding Anita back.

"You mind if I ask why you're doing this?"

The gaze is unwavering. "Jamie. I want to help him. I want to help you. You're a decent man and I like you. And I'm tired of arm's length."

"I can't promise anything on that front."

"I already told you. No strings." Pushing her cup aside and rising, Tisha gathers her things. "I've got to run. I have church." She hesitates. She decides. "If you hear from her, anything at all, you'll let me know?"

"Of course. You do the same."

Tisha nods. Turning, she moves away, looking straight ahead, her steps decisive and resolute.

If Anita has half her mother's strength . . .

Michael doesn't complete the thought. He looks at his watch, his father's watch, the one he is wearing full-time again. It wouldn't do to be late.

"Hey, Luis! How you doin', my man!" Robert Caulfield shouts out, shocking Luis completely. Busy applying drain wrap to a second-floor exterior wall, he didn't even hear the man's little *coche deportivo* pull up to the worksite. Why isn't he bothering somebody else?

"Lookin' good, dude!"

Increíble.

How a gringo in silly sports clothes should know his name is beyond Luis. And that anyone should think manufactured fiberglass sheeting looks good is equally *ridículo.* Or maybe the man's *un maricón* and his "lookin' good" was meant as a compliment. Luis has nothing against fairies. His cousin Emanuel wears his hair long and likes to paint his nails. *No gran cosa.* But if this pale, chubby *bastardo* so much as looks at him cross-eyed, Luis will make him eat his designer sunglasses.

The man takes a step closer and Luis prepares to deck him. "So listen," says Robert Caulfield. "Mike was telling me you got a nephew, bright kid, lookin' to get into Stanford. He says you need some recommendations."

¿Qué demonios? thinks Luis. What the hell? He shrugs, noncommittal. "Maybe we do." He has no idea where this is going. Obviously it's not about drain wrap.

"Well, it just so happens, Luis," says Robert Caulfield, "that *I* am a Cardinal."

"A bird?" says Luis, more confused than ever.

"No!" Caulfield laughs. "Stanford, my man! Undergrad and med school. So, look, I'd be happy to meet the kid, chat with him, see where he's at, see what I can do to help."

"You would do that?" Luis can't believe it. This has got to be a trick. The man must want something.

"Luis, look at me. Look at my car. Look at this house I'm building. I'm a lucky guy. God gave me a brain, but he also cut me a few breaks along the way. I know it and I'm grateful for it. If I can help a kid like your nephew, if I can give back a little, that's where I'm at. 'Cause what goes around, comes around, know what I mean?"

In Luis's experience what's usually going and coming is *mierda*. But not this time. No, not this time.

"Anything you need, anytime, you ask," says Luis. "We are friends now."

"Good," says Robert Caulfield, beaming. "Good."

59

Fari takes passport, ticket, and baggage claims from the airline counter attendant and, turning, sees Michael standing beyond the passenger rope, about ten yards away, waiting for her. Her astonishment is only matched by the delight she feels at the sight of him. She had given up on him calling back. She had convinced herself it was for the best. She approaches carefully, trying to hide her pleasure.

"What are you doing here?"

"Seeing you off. I wanted to introduce you to someone before you left," Michael says, and he steps aside. "This is Jamie."

The boy, Fari sees, looks like his mother. He stands, very still and unaffected, at Michael's side, his father's hand on his shoulder.

"Jamie, this is Dr. Akrepede."

The boy's gaze doesn't waver. He doesn't blink.

"Hello, Jamie," Fari says, hoping a smile will help.

"Do you give shots to people?" he says.

"I'm sorry?" Fari suddenly feeling on uncertain ground.

"He's talking about injections," says Michael.

"Oh." The ground feels solid again. "No. I'm not that kind of doctor." She hopes she hasn't disappointed him. "Why?"

"I said I didn't need one but the doctor said I had to."

"I'm sure he had a good reason."

"Yes. Are you going to see your mom?"

The boy is going too quickly for her. But at the same time she realizes this is coming from Michael. He has obviously been talking about her. "Yes, I am. In England."

"Is she nice?"

Fari glances at Michael, who seems amused and not obliged to help her. Is it a test? she wonders.

Be that way.

Fari kneels so that she and the boy are face-to-face. "She is. She's very nice."

"My mom is nice but she had to leave."

Again, Fari quickly looks at Michael. And sees from his face that it's true. She turns back to Jamie.

"I'm sorry. I'm sure she'll be back."

"I'm ready to go now," Jamie says.

"Little man, they're selling gum over there." Michael points to a kiosk just across from them. "Why don't you get Dr. Akrepede some for her plane ride."

It must be telepathy, Fari thinks gratefully. She'd love a moment alone with him. "Jamie, do you have money?"

"Yes, I do." And oblivious to the two sets of eyes following and protecting him, he moves away toward the counter.

"He's remarkable," says Fari.

"He's something," says Michael. Who will start? he thinks.

I will.

"What are your plans?"

"Six hours to New York. A change of planes. My sister will meet me at Heathrow."

"Round-trip?"

"I haven't booked the return yet."

"Soon I hope."

"I think it will be."

As one, they move the short distance into each other's arms. Holding a person for at least thirty seconds, Fari has read, lifts serotonin levels, elevates mood, and creates happiness. She feels this one lasts at least that long.

"I don't want to leave now," she says.

"I'm not going anywhere," he replies.

"I got you peppermint," says Jamie.

And *how* did you do it so fast? Fari wonders as she slips from Michael's embrace.

Children.

"Peppermint is my favorite. It was nice to meet you, Jamie."

"Yes, it was."

A last look at Michael. "Soon," he says again. Fari nods. She turns and starts down the concourse. Looking back, she waves. He raises a hand in return. "Hey," he calls. "Answer your phone!" Fari reaches into her pocket, pulls it out and holds it up. Feigning excitement, like a young girl with too much to say in one breath, she puts it to her ear. She turns away, already contemplating the time change.

60

It's as her mother said. There is nothing in the apartment that is meaningful to her. Not even a memory. Anita closes the door and doesn't look back. She gets in the car and drives. It is a direct route, Interstate 10, out through Palm Desert and Indio, continuing east to Phoenix and then south. About five hundred miles altogether. The Prius should make it on one tank.

She has found his number — in the book, as he said — but she hasn't called to say she is coming. She wants no obligations. She might not even call once she gets there. But she thinks she will. She has a sense there is healing there. Divine intervention, Anita thinks, places its angels in unexpected places and in unlikely packages.

61

The new puppy, Robin Williams, all stomach, huge feet, and ears, races across the back terrace to pounce on the resting Abigail.

"Oh, you are just the most abusive creature," says Penelope, looking up from her newly blooming roses. It has been three days since Michael brought the puppy home from the shelter — "for Jamie" — and despite her initial reserve, Penelope has quickly fallen in love. Abigail, who merely tolerates the new presence in the house, rises from the bricks, upending her attacker, and dignity intact, meanders back into the house.

"You are a beast," says Penelope. "A horrible, brutal little beast."

"Brrff," says Robin Williams, and he waddles back across the patio to reclaim the leather shoe he's been chewing on.

■ ■ ■ ■

Jamie, led to the garage by his father, has his eyes closed.

"Okay. Open'm."

Jamie does so. To see that Michael is holding . . . *something.* It is long and smooth and polished to a high gloss with three odd-looking fins on the bottom.

"What is it?"

"Dude. It's a surfboard."

"Oh."

"It's yours, little man. See?" There are large dark letters beneath the last coat of resin — *Jamie Hodge* — *8'6"* — *by Michael Hodge.* "You're the owner. This is the length of the board. This is the name of the shaper."

"You. You did it?"

"Yes. What do you think?" Michael suddenly has his doubts. The solemn expression on his son's face doesn't bode well. Jamie dislikes gifts, usually rejects anything he doesn't pick out himself. Still, Michael had hoped.

"I love it," says Jamie.

Giving has never felt like this before.

"You want to hold it?"

"Yes."

"Careful," says Michael, "it's a little heavy."

But not too. Michael is sure of that. The board, with its rounded nose and tail, is long and thick enough to be stable in the water but should still paddle and turn easily. It might hurt Jamie if it accidentally hits him but that's surfing. That's life.

"It's beautiful," says Jamie, cradling it to his chest.

"You want to try it out?"

"Today."

"I've got to put a leash on it first. And we need to get you a wet suit."

"Today."

"Yeah, okay. Today."

Michael is backing out of the drive, the board in the back of the pickup, jury-rigged with bungee cord, when Jamie leans out the passenger window and calls to Penelope, who stands in the driveway watching them depart.

"Nana? You will be here."

It is both a question and a statement.

"Well, of course, my darling," calls Penelope Hodge. "Where else would I be?"

This departure could suddenly take a while and Michael quickly shifts into drive, with the hopes it won't. He gets a good ten yards.

"Go back! Dad, go back, go back!"

Penelope, puzzled now, watches as the truck reverses back to the driveway. Jamie pops out the window again.

"Nana!"

"Yes, dove?"

"Even when we're not here, we love you!"

Stop it, Penelope says to herself. Only silly old women choke up and weep for no good reason. "Over the rainbow, darling. Over the rainbow you go."

"Back soon," calls Michael. And then they're off and running.

"It's going to be a splendid evening," Penelope whispers. What did an old teaching colleague of hers call it, the moment when the sun hits the horizon? Alchemy hour. A time to turn base metals to gold.

Phoo.

Who needs gold when we have each other?

The waves at Tourmaline are small but they're enough. Michael is out in the water with Jamie. They both wear new wet suits. Body Glove. They've been out for a while. Paddling, getting used to the board, getting up and falling down, Michael doing most of the work.

"Okay, now remember — push down with your arms, when the board drops, the feet jump up."

"Okay," says Jamie, determined. Michael, already knowing that the strength and balance aren't there. With time perhaps, but not today.

"You ready? Last wave of the day."

"O-*kay*!"

Michael turns. A small wave is forming, moving toward them. "Here it comes."

"I'm ready!"

Michael gently pushes the board and the wave takes it. "Okay," he calls out. "Now jump and stand! You can do it! Stand, Jamie! Stand up!"

Jamie struggles slowly to his feet, left foot toward the back — goofy foot. He wavers on the slow-moving board, struggling for balance. At any moment, Michael knows, he will bail and fall. But there is always next time.

"I'm surfing! Dad, I'm surfing!"

Jamie's voice is loud and clear like the call of a singularly beautiful bird. He stands, steady now, his arms out, his feet splayed widely. He's doing it, thinks Michael.

He's doing it.

"Good, Jamie, that's good! Just like that!"

He's doing it.

"Yes, Jamie! Yes!"

You're doing it.

"I'm surfing! Dad! I'm surfing, Dad!"

Michael whoops and screams and slaps the water. He watches his son ride toward the beach. The voice is getting fainter and farther away but is still clear.

"I'm surfing! I'm surfing, Dad! I'm surfing!"

As Michael starts in toward shore, behind him the horizon flashes green.

The employees of Thorndike Press hope you have enjoyed this Large Print book. All our Thorndike, Wheeler, and Kennebec Large Print titles are designed for easy reading, and all our books are made to last. Other Thorndike Press Large Print books are available at your library, through selected bookstores, or directly from us.

For information about titles, please call:
   (800) 223-1244

or visit our Web site at:
   http://gale.cengage.com/thorndike

To share your comments, please write:
   Publisher
   Thorndike Press
   10 Water St., Suite 310
   Waterville, ME 04901